S0-ARM-826

From: Delphi@oracle.org
To: C_Evans@athena.edu
Re: investigative reporter, Winter Archer

Christine,

I understand that the recent kidnappings at Athena Academy were just the first unraveling threads of a much larger web. Looking at the information you sent me, I have to agree with you. It seems Marion Gracelyn, Athena Academy's founder, may have had a formidable enemy, one who arranged for Marion's murder. One who is still plaguing Athena's students and graduates.

The incidents leading up to Marion's murder—and our current situation—are most likely buried in the past. Who better to deal with old secrets than Winter Archer? She's uncovered older lies than these. Give her a call. Maybe her research into Marion's life will lead us closer to our enemy.

D.

Dear Reader,

I've been a part of Athena Force since the beginning, so I felt really honored to write the story of Athena Academy's matriarch, Marion Gracelyn. As you'll discover, Marion's story is also the story of Athena Force's greatest enemy, a deadly female assassin who has plotted against Marion and her dreams since 1968.

To me, a veteran Athena Force author, Marion Gracelyn has always been a real person. It was like someone I'd heard a lot about and just happened to miss at critical junctures. Getting the chance to step back into 1968 and tell Marion's story has been a blast. And I have to tell you, I regretted not being able to incorporate one of the most important things that happened that year: The '68 Comeback Special of Elvis Presley. No one but no one wears black leather like the King of Rock and Roll!

Marion was a role model back then, one of the first female assistant district attorneys. And her love interest, Adam Gracelyn, was, as it turns out, anything but senatorial material back in his early days. They were a definite match, and I enjoyed watching them meet on opposite sides of the legal table, fall in love despite that, and take on the most dangerous killer either of them had ever faced.

Of course, we wouldn't know about Marion's story without the research of Athena grad Winter Archer, whose own love affair with David Gracelyn begged to be told. So there! You're getting two love stories for the price of one. Enjoy!

Meredith Fletcher

Meredith Fletcher

VENDETTA

Silhouette®

ATHENA FORCE

Published by Silhouette Books

America's Publisher of Contemporary Romance

If you purchased this book without a cover you should be aware
that this book is stolen property. It was reported as "unsold and
destroyed" to the publisher, and neither the author nor the
publisher has received any payment for this "stripped book."

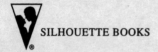

SILHOUETTE BOOKS

ISBN-13: 978-0-373-38975-9
ISBN-10:   0-373-38975-9

VENDETTA

Copyright © 2007 by Harlequin Books S.A.

All rights reserved. Except for use in any review, the reproduction
or utilization of this work in whole or in part in any form by any
electronic, mechanical or other means, now known or hereafter
invented, including xerography, photocopying and recording, or in
any information storage or retrieval system, is forbidden without
the written permission of the editorial office, Silhouette Books,
233 Broadway, New York, NY 10279 U.S.A.

This is a work of fiction. Names, characters, places and incidents are
either the product of the author's imagination or are used fictitiously, and
any resemblance to actual persons, living or dead, business establishments,
events or locales is entirely coincidental.

This edition published by arrangement with Harlequin Books S.A.

® and TM are trademarks of Harlequin Books S.A., used under license.
Trademarks indicated with ® are registered in the United States Patent
and Trademark Office, the Canadian Trade Marks Office and in other
countries.

Visit Athena Force at www.eHarlequin.com

Printed in U.S.A.

MEREDITH FLETCHER

maintains a healthy interest in travel and history. She's been to the top of Pike's Peak and to the bottom of Carlsbad Caverns. She's seen the Reversing Falls in St. John, New Brunswick (and eaten purple seaweed) and snorkeled plane crashes in Cozumel.

She comes from a large family and loves sitting at the table while everyone shares their stories. She's also an avid reader and movie enthusiast, enjoying every love story from *Casablanca* to *Spider Man 3,* which she firmly maintains is a love story in spite of all the trappings of superheroes.

To the intelligent and generous women
who make Athena Force fly:
Natashya Wilson, Tara Parsons and Stacy Boyd.
And to my fellow writers in suspense and thrills:
Rachel Caine and Nancy Holder.

Chapter 1

"You don't trust me, do you?" Winter Archer curbed the indignation she felt as she locked eyes with the tall, handsome man standing at the office window.

"It's not my place to trust you, Miss Archer," he replied coolly. The reply was tactful. Exactly the way Winter would expect a United States Attorney General to say it.

His name was David Gracelyn. Winter remembered him from the time she'd spent at Athena Academy. She'd been a student then, barely into her teens. He was a few years older than her, but that gap wasn't so pronounced these days as it had been back then. Back then, four years had separated them into different worlds.

In those days David Gracelyn had been a senior at Phoenix, attending a public school at his insistence so he could play competitive baseball. His parents hadn't been fully supportive of his decision because being in the public eye had been risky.

Marion and Adam Gracelyn had been deeply enmeshed in politics. Their work hit society pages as well as front pages of papers, and they were regularly mentioned on the nightly news. Marion had also been the driving force behind Athena Academy.

After high school, David had gone on to play baseball at college as well. Winter had read about him in the newspapers and seen occasional snippets of games on the local television news. He'd been a good player. Just not a great one.

He was lean and athletic even now. Winter was willing to bet that he worked to keep himself in shape, though not out of vanity. He'd always had that competitive edge. Although David didn't compete against the girls who had attended Athena, he had competed with his sister, Allison. But only because Allison had unmercifully taunted him. She'd also beaten him on several occasions.

He wore his dark brown hair short and neat, well clear of the shirt collar. His brown eyes held a sadness in them that Winter couldn't remember being there even after his mother's death a few years ago. Winter had returned for Marion Gracelyn's funeral, of course. Most Athena grads had, but it had been easy to get lost in the ocean of mourners that had shown up.

Now, Winter sat in one of the comfortable chairs in front of Christine Evans's desk. The woman was the principal of Athena Academy and had been all those years ago as well. Newspaper stories about past graduates of the academy covered the walls. Christine Evans had been part of a lot of successes. Winter took quiet pleasure in seeing that at least one of those articles concerned her career.

"If you trusted me," Winter said to David, "you wouldn't be here."

A trace of irritation tightened his eyes. He turned to face her more squarely, silhouetted against the window filled with bright March sunshine. He crossed his arms over his chest and forced a smile.

"I'd hardly call my presence a declaration of distrust," David said.

"That," Winter told him, "is because you're not sitting where I am."

The look of irritation tightened into a grimace. David took in a deep breath and let it out through his nose. "It's better if we wait to discuss this matter until Christine arrives."

"The matter that Christine called me out here for?" Winter asked. "Or the fact that you don't trust me to do whatever it is she's going to ask me to do?"

"All of it." David pushed back his shirtsleeve and compared the time on his watch with the wall clock. "She should have been here by now."

Winter surveyed David, reading him effortlessly. Years of experience with interviewing politicians, murderers, good cops and bad ones had honed her natural skills.

David Gracelyn was nervous, agitated and angry. He kept his jacket on, like a knight refusing to shed his armor in a room where he should have been totally comfortable.

It's not me that he's concerned with, Winter decided. That meant it had to be Christine Evans. She had been one of the best friends David's mother had ever known. She'd practically been a second mother to Allison, and Winter was certain she'd been around David a lot as well.

"Look," Winter said, "if it helps, I don't know why Christine called me out here. I heard about the kidnappings that took place on the campus a few weeks ago, but I'd heard that had all been resolved." She was fishing, of course, and she figured that he probably knew it. But there was also a chance that he would offer some clue.

The kidnapping story had been covered by a number of news services, mostly because of Athena Academy's reputation and partly because kidnappings of teenage girls generally did hit the news.

"No. It's not about the kidnappings." David took a breath. "Not exactly."

And what did that *mean?*

Winter waited, thinking maybe he would open up about whatever it was. But he didn't. Winter had been curious ever since she'd gotten Christine Evans's cryptic call yesterday. That was Winter's nature: always curious. That was part of the special skill set that made her an investigative journalist.

Christine's short conversation had drawn Winter back to Athena Academy. She couldn't help wondering if Christine had withheld information just to enhance Winter's curiosity. It was possible. During her stay at Athena, Christine had gotten to know Winter well.

After a moment, she reached down into her purse and took out her iPAQ Pocket PC. She turned on the PDA, then opened up a

Microsoft Word document she'd been working on during the plane trip into Phoenix.

"What are you doing?" David asked. Suspicion dripped in his words.

"Working." Winter didn't look up. She wrote with the stylus, watching as her script was transformed to type a heartbeat later.

"You shouldn't be writing any of this down."

"I'm not writing this down. I'm working on another project. I figured since the conversation wasn't exactly pleasant that I could get something worthwhile done."

A frown turned down David's full lips. Winter couldn't help noticing that they were very attractive lips.

"And what would I be writing down?" She couldn't help needling him. Pompousness of any sort always drew out her claws.

He didn't answer for a moment. Then he said, "In some circles you're known to be quite creative with your writing. You...*infer* a lot."

Winter bridled at that. "I *infer* a lot because there's a lot people try to hide from me. Generally they're not good enough at it. That's why my publishers allow me to *infer* as much as I do. Because I get it right."

"The school has had enough problems lately," David said. "They don't need old ones stirred up."

"What old ones?"

Again, he didn't answer. She didn't expect that he would, but she wanted him to know that he couldn't talk to her like she was brainless. Talking made him vulnerable. Not her.

The Athena Academy had been in the news lately. Before the kidnappings, Lorraine Miller—another Athena graduate—had been murdered. Her death had at first been ruled an accident, but subsequent investigation had revealed that as a lie.

Then there were the rumors about genetic testing, political coverups, and international incidents that had persisted. Pieces of a much larger story had surfaced from time to time in the news.

Winter had seen the stories and guessed at the overall larger picture, but she'd stayed away. Mostly out of respect, but she'd also been busy working on other projects. Her writing career occupied most of her time these days, and there was always something she needed to do.

She'd practically had to move heaven and earth to be here today. *Just so David Gracelyn could look down his nose at you and make you think that* maybe *you never did get over that crush you had on him.*

Winter let out a long, slow breath. She so didn't need this. She'd only come because Christine Evans had asked her to.

"I'm here as a favor to Christine," Winter told him, deciding to let him off the hook, "not to cause problems."

David shot her a look of disapproval. "That's not exactly what Henry Carlson would say, is it?"

Anger quivered through Winter then. It was one thing to question her motives, but attacking her work was another matter entirely. She was good at what she did. She enjoyed her work. Her writing *defined* her.

"What happened to Henry Carlson and his family is regrettable," she said softly. "But it wasn't my fault."

"A lot of other people don't see it that way."

"People have skeletons in their closets. I didn't put them there."

"Maybe not, but you sure as hell don't seem hesitant about trotting them out when you find them."

Winter thought about that. She'd had a choice about revealing everything she'd discovered in the Carlson matter, of course. Her publisher had even had a choice in deciding whether to go to press with the book. In the end, they both decided to go forward with what she'd found out. In their minds, revealing the truth served the greater good.

"What I relayed in my book had been whispered about in Hollywood for years," Winter told him. "Victoria Chase, Carlson's maternal grandmother, had been suspected of being a Nazi sympathizer."

"Those documents you found seriously hurt Carlson's international corporate image. Wall Street bailed on him as soon as word about your book hit the streets."

Winter knew that. She still felt badly about how it had gone. But Henry Carlson and BriteFutures Pharmaceuticals were rich enough to afford a fickle stock market for a time. In the end, Carlson was a success because he was a good businessman. His grandmother's twin careers of Hollywood diva and German spy wouldn't change that.

"I'm not here to defend that book, Counselor." Winter returned her attention to the iPAQ. To her way of thinking, revealing the fact that Victoria Chase had been a Nazi spy had shown again how strange Hollywood could be, and how disillusioned and vulnerable. In the book, Winter had used the example to address some of the other bizarre behavior exhibited by stars and the Hollywood crowd.

"You need to realize that some things are better left alone," David said.

Ah-ha! Winter squelched the sense of triumph that surged through her. Although Christine had told Winter on the phone that she preferred not to get into the matter until they could talk face-to-face, she'd given Winter the impression that the matter was of grave importance.

The whole "some things are better left alone" riff told Winter that what they were talking about was history. But whose?

"What things," Winter asked quietly, "need to be left alone?"

David's face reddened. Before he could respond, if he was going to, the door opened.

Christine Evans entered the room and closed the door behind her. For a moment Winter could hear the familiar noise of the outer office, computer keyboards clacking and students talking to office personnel. It took her back twenty years in a heartbeat, and she remembered how happy she'd been at Athena Academy.

And how incredibly young and naive.

"Hello, Winter," Christine said, then cut her eyes over to David Gracelyn. "David."

David nodded curtly.

"Hi," Winter said in greeting.

"I hope I haven't kept you waiting too long." Christine walked behind the desk but didn't sit as she checked through the memos on her computer screen.

The years had been good to her, Winter decided.

Almost sixty, Christine Evans still maintained the erect military posture she'd learned while serving in the United States Army. Short-cut gray hair that almost matched the color of her eyes—even the left one, which was artificial, the result of a military encounter that she'd never shared with anyone—looked immaculate. She wore a dark blue business suit.

The last time Winter had seen Christine had been at Marion's funeral nearly twelve years ago. Winter had almost returned a couple of years ago after Lorraine Miller had been killed. But she hadn't been part of Rainy's group. Winter had also been working undercover on a book about the Asian Triads in Seattle that had won her a Pulitzer Prize.

"You haven't kept us waiting too long at all," Winter replied. "David and I were just catching up on old times."

Christine raised an eyebrow at that, then returned her attention to the computer.

Behind Christine's back, David scowled. He didn't say anything.

"I hadn't expected you here, David." Christine made a couple of notes.

"I told you I might drop by."

"I thought we'd agreed to follow this course of action."

"You didn't mention who you were bringing in to handle this."

"No." Christine faced him. "I didn't. I only told you that I was bringing in the best that I could."

"What you're talking about doing is incredibly sensitive," David said.

"It's also incredibly important that it be done well," Christine countered. "You know that."

Winter's curiosity shot up immediately. She also felt vaguely flattered that Christine would hold her in such high regard. However, at the same time, she couldn't help thinking that the whole production might be an act designed solely to get her to lower her defenses. She was no longer the naive young woman she'd been when she'd left the academy.

"Athena Academy and secrets have always gone hand in glove," David said.

Winter knew that. When the decision had been made to build an all-girls school that would specialize in preparing young women for successful lives that included career paths for intelligence agents, military officers, investigative and forensics law enforcement personnel, a lot of government interest had been sparked. Winter had heard stories of agreements for funding from different government branches that Marion Gracelyn had considered and maybe accepted.

That would be a story, wouldn't it? Winter told herself. Over the years of her career, she had been tempted to tell the story of Athena Academy and the iron-willed woman who had envisioned it. But there had been a code of silence about the school that no one, not even television news reporters Tory Patton or Shannon Connor—also Athena grads—had broken.

"I know that," Christine said. "I've helped with some of those secrets myself." She paused. "Now, with all due respect, David, let me get on with what I need to do. This is the best course of action at this juncture."

David's eyes swiveled to Winter. "Perhaps. But you're extending a lot of trust."

"I am," Christine agreed. "But I would rather trust one of our own than someone from outside." She turned to Winter. "You just got in from a long drive. Maybe you'd like to stretch your legs and have a look at the improvements that have been made since you were last here."

"Sure." Winter stood, ignoring David and falling into step with Christine as they left the office. She felt his eyes on her until the door closed behind her.

Uneasy and angry, David Gracelyn glared through the window of Christine Evans's office. It was situated so that it faced the front of the school.

One of the short school buses was letting out a group of girls that had gone off on a field day. The academy believed in putting the students into real-life circumstances on a regular basis.

A moment later, Winter Archer and Christine Evans stepped into David's field of view. His eyes were drawn immediately to the writer's slender body. He could remember what she'd looked like when she'd gone to school with Allison, his sister.

Winter Archer was the only daughter of wealthy, career-driven parents who had been too glad to find a private school for their daughter. As a young girl, David remembered that Winter had always been an observer, never one for saying much. She'd struck him as pretty then, and that beauty had blossomed during the intervening years.

She had thick black hair, perfectly arched eyebrows, and plump lips. Her skin was pale, not unhealthy, just untanned. Like cream. The color made her hair and her light purplish hazel eyes stand out even more.

Winter's eyes were what David remembered most about her.

She'd always been watchful. But she'd been so quiet she'd been hard to get to know.

It was strange that he remembered her after all these years. He knew who she was, of course, because he'd read some of her books.

As an investigative reporter specializing in reconstruction of events and happenings that had complicated timetables, Winter Archer had few peers. Her books came out slowly, but they sold strongly. She worked on projects that covered the history of countries to the personal lives of media figures.

She had a reputation for telling the truth. But sometimes she told too much of the truth. The Carlson book was a perfect example.

A sour bubble of bile burst in the back of David's throat. Even though the kidnappings had been solved and the girls had been returned to their families, he'd known the situation wasn't over.

The letter from the mystery person had only confirmed that. The naked threat against anyone looking into the identity of "A" had remained in his mind.

And Christine's, he reminded himself. After having two of her students kidnapped, Christine felt especially vulnerable. She'd also made her case: for someone to have known so much about the inner workings of Athena Academy, about its very existence, that person would have had to know about the school from its founding. Whoever they were looking for must have some connection to Marion Gracelyn's past. Only an enemy with intimate knowledge of Marion's legacy—and a huge grudge—would have pursued vengeance this long and this hard.

David knew his mother, but he didn't know her as the woman she'd been before he'd been born. He didn't know her life as Marion Hart, before she'd gotten married to Adam Gracelyn. That was what Winter Archer was here to uncover: Marion Hart's life, from the time she was born until her murder.

The thing was, he and Christine both believed that "A," the person involved with the recent kidnappings, had also been involved with Marion Gracelyn's murder.

David knew he would never forget that day. A year ago, when part of the truth had come out about his mother's murder, he'd been shocked. Everyone had believed they'd finally gotten to the truth of the matter.

But they hadn't.

The kidnappings and the note had proven that.

Outside, Christine took Winter by the arm and pointed out some of the academy's newest features. Winter looked interested, but she also looked like her focus was elsewhere.

David reached inside his jacket and took out his cell phone. He touched a button and listened to the connection ring. Once.

"Yes." The voice was crisp and efficient, a perfect match for the man at the other end.

"She's here," David said.

"I know. We picked her up at her house in L.A. We've been with her ever since."

"Good." David felt a little better already. The man he'd contacted had come highly recommended in Washington political circles. He was a man that could be trusted to keep his mouth shut, do what was expected and never walk away from an assignment no matter how tough it got.

"Where's she going to be staying?" the man asked.

"Here." David knew that Christine had finalized arrangements on that end. Winter might not know where she was staying yet, but Christine wouldn't give her much choice.

"That will make things easier," the man said.

"It'll also make them more dangerous, if anything happens. I don't know that I'm comfortable with that."

The man said nothing. He was careful, but even he hadn't gone without losing people who had been in his charge.

"Keep a close watch on her," David said.

"Is there anything or anyone I should keep her away from?" the man asked.

"No," David said. "I just want to make sure she's safe for the moment."

"You've never said what she was here for."

"No, I didn't." David intended to keep that confidential for as long as possible. He knew his silence might interfere with how the man did his job, but that was how it had to be. He closed the phone, not feeling nearly as relieved as he'd hoped he would.

Athena Academy had been built on secrets. His mother, God bless her, had engineered most of them. And he was certain that one of those secrets had reached out of the past and killed her. Now Winter Archer was here to find out the truth.

Chapter 2

Athena Academy
Outside Phoenix, Arizona
Now

"As I recall, you loved horses when you were younger." Christine smiled from where she stood beside the paddock.

"I did," Winter agreed. She knew that she was wearing an unaccustomed goofy grin, but she couldn't help it. Horses had always brought out that side of her. Even when she'd gotten in trouble at the academy and had been assigned to mucking out the barn, it hadn't been a true hardship. She'd gotten to be around the horses. "I still do. I just don't have as much time for riding as I used to." She gazed across the paddocks where the horses were kept.

The big animals stamped and blew. The sounds echoed through the cavernous barn. Athena Academy kept several head of horses on hand. The stink of horse sweat, fresh hay and leather mixed made the air thick. But it smelled just right to Winter. Dozens of memories she'd thought lost and gone forever scampered through her brain like mice.

Before she realized what she was doing, Winter grabbed a handful of sweet feed from the bag hanging on a center post. She crossed to the nearest horse.

The young paint stallion rolled his eyes at first and trotted away from her. He snorted aggressively and laid his ears back against his head as if he was the fiercest thing on the planet. One sharp hoof stamped the ground in defiance.

Winter held the feed out and didn't move. Drawn by the smell of the grain, the colt approached skittishly and took the offering from her hand with his quivering, whiskered lips. His teeth *chomped* together hollowly.

"Maybe you'll find time to ride while you're here," Christine said.

"But I'm not here to ride, am I?" Winter ran a hand through the colt's wiry forelock as he ate. He threatened to shy away, but his greed to fill his belly outweighed his instinctive fear.

"No, you're not." Christine's smile slipped and faded.

"Maybe we could get to that then." Winter petted the colt. Amusement coursed through her when the young horse rolled his eyes wildly and trotted away after he'd eaten all the food. She let him go. She knew that she could get him back.

Christine hesitated.

Winter kept silent. She'd learned to be quiet during an interview while in classes at Athena. The person that wanted to talk—to confess or to simply tell something they no longer wanted to carry on their own—would talk to fill the void. Eventually the person would get around to whatever was on his or her mind. The trick was not to offer any deflection from whatever they wanted to talk about.

"There's no easy way to tell you this," Christine started.

The colt pranced on the other side of the fence as if taunting Winter to give chase. Despite the solemnity of the moment, she smiled at his antics.

"I need someone to investigate Marion's past," Christine stated. "Someone good. Someone thorough." She paused. "Someone I trust."

Even as open-minded about the meeting as she'd been, the announcement caught Winter by surprise. She forced herself not to look at Christine. She didn't want the woman to see the disbelief in her eyes.

"You don't have anything to say?" Christine asked after a moment.

Marion Gracelyn was the matriarch of this school! She was your best friend! Hell, yes, I have a lot to say! And a lot to ask!

But Winter held back. "Christine," she said softly, "you've already made up your mind to trust me or I wouldn't be here. You've already decided that I'm the one you want to investigate Marion Gracelyn." She turned to face the woman. "I'll do whatever you need me to do."

Christine's real eye grew moist. That was the only time any of the girls at school could tell which eye was a prosthetic. And Christine Evans didn't often let her emotions show.

"Thank you," Christine whispered. "I told David you'd understand."

The mention of David Gracelyn's name irritated Winter somewhat. *He* didn't trust her or want her there. He'd made that perfectly clear.

"Marion Gracelyn is dead," Winter said. "She's been dead a dozen years. Why would her past suddenly be of interest? You want someone to write her memoirs?"

"No. This is of a more serious nature."

Leaning against the paddock, Winter remained attentive. She was a good interviewer and she knew it, but that skill was sometimes complicated if she intimately knew the person she was interviewing. She not only knew Christine Evans, but she respected and liked the woman tremendously.

"Marion took a lot of secrets to her grave," Christine said. "I couldn't even imagine how many until these last few years. And those have been—" She stopped herself and shook her head. "Getting the academy funded and staffed was difficult."

Winter hadn't thought about that while she'd been attending the school, but after she'd gotten out in the world and started working as an investigative journalist she'd realized just how monumental the undertaking had been.

"You think Marion did something wrong?" The question didn't come out as smoothly as Winter had tried to make it.

Christine took in a quick defensive breath. "No. I don't. Not intentionally. But so many things had to happen simultaneously in order to make the academy a reality. Even Marion, as good as she was, wasn't able to be everywhere at once."

"She didn't have to be," Winter said. "You were there."

"Thank you for that." Christine relaxed a little. "But there were still a lot of problems."

"We're not talking about problems, though, are we?" Winter asked. "You mentioned secrets." She couldn't help pushing a little. It seemed like the time to do so. And even her patience wasn't inexhaustible.

"We're talking about secrets." Christine hesitated. "I think that one of those secrets has come back to haunt us."

"Which one?" For the life of her, Winter couldn't imagine what it might be. Marion Gracelyn had always seemed so open and aboveboard.

"Somewhere in Marion's life, she made a very powerful enemy." Christine pursed her lips. "Over the last few years, that enemy has made himself or herself known to us."

"Who's the enemy?"

"That's part of the problem, you see. We don't know."

Winter quivered inside. She loved mysteries. They were delectable little things that could encompass her every thought as she sorted them out. No matter what the secret was, it couldn't remain hidden. There was always a trail. Normally that trail was marked by money or sex.

"How did you find out about this enemy?" Winter asked.

"That's a long story."

Winter smiled at the older woman gently. "You brought me out here, to one of my favorite places, to tell me this much. Maybe we could go to your favorite place and you could tell me the rest of the story there."

Some of the sadness clinging to Christine lifted. She raised an eyebrow over her real eye. "Putting an interviewee at ease?"

A mischievous grin pulled at Winter's lips. "Perhaps. Is it working?"

"I started being more at ease the moment you agreed to come." Christine took a breath and nodded. "Let's go."

As they strolled through the gardens the horticulture and chemistry classes maintained, Winter listened to Christine talk about the investigation several former students had put together into the "accidental" death of Lorraine Miller. Walking amid the bright spring tulips, lilies, amaryllis, daffodils and irises and talking about murder and illegal genetic experiments seemed incongruous.

Hell, it *is* incongruous.

Astonished, Winter listened to the story of Lab 33 and the genetically enhanced young women that were—essentially—Rainy Miller's "children." Christine didn't reveal who those young women were, but she talked about the strange physical abilities they had.

Winter couldn't believe that only bits and pieces of the real story had ever surfaced in the media. There had been some flap over the story, but nothing had ever connected in the way Christine laid it out.

Then, seated on one of the small stone benches placed through the gardens, Christine started explaining about how Rainy's death might have been connected to Marion's and the recent kidnapping of the three young Athena Academy students. The story was long and Christine took pains to be thorough.

"You think the two girls that were taken were specifically chosen because they were created in Lab 33?" Winter asked.

Christine stood at the island in the kitchen and prepared chicken breasts. After talking for hours, she'd suggested they get something to eat, then offered to make dinner.

"Not *in* Lab 33. In a medical facility in Zuni." Christine rolled a chicken breast in a liquid mixture and set it aside.

"How do you know that?" Winter wielded a chopping knife on salad ingredients with a dexterity she'd learned at the academy. When she'd first realized she was going to have to take culinary classes as part of her curriculum, she had demanded to know why. Her steadfast refusal to participate in class had prompted a visit to Christine Evans's office. Christine had explained in no uncertain terms that learning to cook for oneself was just as important as any of the other skills she would be learning at the academy. She still didn't necessarily enjoy the process, but she knew how to do it.

"We've managed to reconstruct some of Aldrich Peters's notes from Lab 33," Christine replied. "We're still working on other pieces, but it's getting harder."

"But the girls were egg babies?" The term was foreign to Winter, but she'd picked it up because Christine had used it. She'd often unconsciously picked up sentence structure and vocabulary from people she interviewed.

"Yes. We knew they had special powers, but the method of their conception was a surprise."

"Whoever took them knew more about the students here than you did."

"We realized that later." Christine cubed the chicken and scattered it across a hot pan. The meat sizzled and started browning at once.

Winter pushed the chopped vegetables into a salad bowl and shook them. She washed her hands in the sink and gazed around the kitchen.

Christine lived on-site at the school. Most of the faculty did. Of course there were a few teachers and specialists who were transitory and taught only as specific coursework was offered.

The house showed military order and precision. Winter would have expected nothing less. But there was also a softness and a personality that she hadn't been prepared for. When Winter was in attendance, every student at the academy knew Christine Evans as firm but fair and as an ex-military officer. They even knew a little bit about her family, but none of them had ever been invited to her home.

"It's good, in a way, that whoever was behind the kidnappings knows more than we do," Christine said. "I feel more certain that it's not someone here."

Retreating to the island, Winter rested a hip against it and picked up a carrot stick. Her mind spun and clicked through the variables.

"Not necessarily," Winter said.

Christine looked at her.

Winter counted off points on her fingers with her carrot stick. "Someone here could have decoded more of the DNA fragments you're working with than anyone else has. Someone could have found more of the fragments than you know about. Or someone here might be working with this mysterious A person."

"I truly hope not. We've already had one betrayal. A recent hire helped lure the girls away from the school. With everything that's gone on, I don't know how another betrayal in our midst would affect us."

Winter quietly agreed. She crunched the carrot stick and thought some more. "What do you hope I can do?"

"Find Marion's enemy."

Oh? Is that all? Winter barely kept her sarcastic comment to herself. She pushed her breath out and tried to relax.

"How am I supposed to do that?" Winter asked.

"We've decided to give you free rein at the school. Through the records. Through Marion's notes. Everything."

Winter choked down the carrot and couldn't believe what she was being offered. "There are a lot of people connected to the Athena Academy. Important people. Politicians. Military leaders. Philanthropists."

"We know that."

"Big philanthropists. People who don't like their names in the news."

"That's right."

"Information like that isn't just handed out to anyone."

"No," Christine said, "it isn't. That's why I insisted on getting you." She turned the chicken on the stove.

"Why did you insist on me?" Winter sat at the round table in the breakfast nook a few minutes later. The view outside the French doors looked out over a small, elegant English garden.

Christine offered chicken cubes to Winter. "Because you're good at what you do."

Winter put the chicken over her salad. "How do you know?"

"Because I've read your books." Christine fixed her own salad. She'd also prepared baby corn and placed it over the greens as well.

"Read them before or after you decided to call me?"

"I've always read them." Christine poured sparkling white wine into two glasses.

"Always?" Winter couldn't help prodding a little. She was shamelessly seeking out ego pampering, but she couldn't help herself. Her parents, affluent and as distant as ever, couldn't be bothered. Every day she seemed to have less and less in common with them.

"Yes. I read. I listen to music. I follow sports. And I appreciate artwork. Our young women have been successful in all those fields."

Winter knew that. She'd recognized names in the media from her days at Athena Academy.

"Athena graduates have also become spies, forensics experts, military officers, attorneys and taken their places in careers that aren't so easy to track."

"I make an effort to follow them whenever I can." Christine took a bite of salad. "You'd be surprised at how many of them actually stay in touch and let me know what they're doing."

Ouch. Guilt much? Winter knew she hadn't been in touch often. There had been occasional Christmas cards, though Christine hadn't missed a single one.

"If you've read my books and followed my career," Winter warned, "you know that once I start following a story I don't back off and I don't take direction well."

"I know. That's why David isn't happy about your involvement."

Gracelyn Ranch
Outside Phoenix, Arizona
Now

Winter parked her black Lexus SC 430 in front of a large family home that sat off by itself just west of Phoenix proper.

The grounds had been heavily landscaped. Gardeners walked through the immense area with wheelbarrows and other supplies. The grass looked like regulation green on a golf course. A tall security wall ran around the perimeter. Closed-circuit cameras had overlapping fields of vision.

During her career as an investigative journalist who specialized in reconstructing the lives of famous people, Winter had sometimes been around those who lived extravagant lifestyles. She hadn't been impressed. Her parents owned larger houses than most of those she'd seen.

The Gracelyn family didn't look as though they lived extravagantly, though. The house and grounds were large, that was true, but they also looked lived in. They weren't just as showcases.

A young, impeccably dressed houseman came out to the car. Winter remained where she was and allowed him to get the door.

"Ms. Archer?" he asked. There was something about the way that he carried himself that suggested exposure to the military. His blond hair was cut high and tight. "I'm Gary. Mr. Gracelyn is waiting inside for you."

"Thank you." Winter stepped from the car. She wore black Capri pants and a burgundy blouse under a thigh-length jacket. She reached back into the car for her computer bag.

"I can get that for you," Gary offered.

"No, thank you. I can manage."

"If you'll leave me your key, I'll arrange to have the car garaged while you're here."

Winter dropped the rental's keys into Gary's hand. He pocketed them and took the lead.

"Mr. Gracelyn has arranged for you to use Senator Gracelyn's home office." Gary threw open the double doors and revealed the spacious office where Marion Gracelyn had spent a large chunk of her life.

Drawn by her curiosity, Winter stepped into the room and gazed at the walls. Two of them held shelves of books from floor to ceiling. The books didn't look like they were there for show.

The other two walls held photographs of Marion Gracelyn at various stages of her career. Many of them showed her shaking hands with powerful men and women in political and financial circles. They ran the gamut of her career, from her early days as an assistant district attorney in Phoenix back in the 1960s to her final days as a state senator.

The years were kind to you, Winter thought as she looked at the pictures. In the early pictures, Marion had light brown hair that swept down to her shoulders. It was shorter than most women had worn their hair in those days because Jackie Kennedy's trend-setting hadn't spread to everyone yet, and most women hadn't been in jobs where the upkeep of long hair would have been almost impossible.

She'd had deep brown eyes. Intense eyes, Winter realized, that reminded her immediately of David Gracelyn's. Marion had been slim in those pictures and the outfits she'd worn made her look beautiful.

Even thirty-odd years later, Marion had been a beautiful woman. She didn't look like she'd gained an ounce, and even looked fitter than ever in one of the photographs in tennis whites. Her hair was shorter, of course, because the style had changed.

"Ms. Archer," Gary called from behind her.

Winter turned and found David standing beside the houseman. She hadn't heard him come up. Then she got irritated because he'd stood there and watched her without saying a word.

David frowned at the houseman as if he resented being ratted out.

"Good morning, Mr. Gracelyn," Winter said smoothly.

David nodded. "Ms. Archer." He looked around. "I trust the office will suit?"

"Yes. Thank you." Winter decided she would only reply to the social amenities and not give him one damn thing more. He could get over whatever was bothering him on his own. He was a big boy.

The problem was, she was aware that he was, too.

He was dressed more casually than she would have expected. He wore only jeans and a casual knit shirt that revealed his broad shoulders and chest and emphasized his narrow waist. He wore sandals instead of shoes. His hair even looked tousled like he'd just rolled out of bed.

And that started thoughts that Winter didn't even want to entertain.

"If you need anything, Gary can see to it." David started to leave, then hesitated.

Winter arched her brows at him.

"If there's anything I can help with," David said, "just let me know."

It'll be a cold day in hell before I ask for your help. But she said, "Sure."

He left. Was he making a feeble attempt to play host or marking territory?

"Is he always so cheerful?" Winter placed her computer bag on the large desk and opened it.

Gary paused for a moment before speaking. "It isn't you, Ms. Archer. I think that everything going on has just brought Senator Gracelyn's absence more sharply into focus for everyone. We still miss her very much."

Keen observation there, Winter chided herself. *You should have seen from the way Christine reacted how hard this was going to be on everyone.*

"Duly noted," Winter responded. "Sometimes I think I take people's reactions too personally." In truth, that rarely happened. There was just something about David Gracelyn that set her off.

"That's all right, Ms. Archer. As I understand it, you've a most arduous task ahead of you."

Winter gazed around at the file boxes against the wall. According to Christine, David would provide Winter with all of Marion

Gracelyn's journals, notes, press clippings, and whatever other records she'd kept.

"I've been instructed to help you," Gary went on.

As she surveyed the boxes, Winter felt that old familiar tingle of excitement thrill through her. She loved what she did. Absolutely freaking loved it. There was nothing like trolling through someone's life, secrets and accomplishments.

There always seemed to be two people involved: the person that everyone saw, and the person that person could be when no one was around. Expectations—whether from self or from others—shaped so many people. Some rose to meet them in glorious ways. Others shattered or crumbled in failure. Most usually survived in the gulf or narrow crack that existed between the two.

So who was Marion Gracelyn really?

"Ms. Archer," Gary prompted.

She looked back at the man and tried to regain control over her distraction. "Yes?"

"Would you like anything? Or for me to help?" Gary asked.

"Do you have Diet Coke?"

Gary looked surprised. It was understandable. It was only a little after eight o'clock. Most people probably drank coffee.

"I never acquired the coffee habit," Winter admitted, "but I'm still a caffeine junkie." She and Christine had stayed up into the small hours of the night talking. The early morning hadn't come easily.

"Of course. I'll see to it immediately." Gary excused himself and vanished.

Winter sat in the chair behind the desk and started rifling through the boxes. The first thing she needed to do was familiarize herself with everything and get it organized in her mind.

Three days later, still working in the borrowed office and aware that David Gracelyn and Christine Evans were getting a little impatient despite their best efforts, Winter was starting to think that she was on a snipe hunt. Marion Gracelyn had angered a lot of politicians over the years, and one of them had finally killed her in a fit of pique. He'd been the only real enemy Winter had turned up.

Her inability to find anything was wearing at her confidence. Maybe she wasn't the person for the job. Maybe David Gracelyn didn't have anything to worry about.

Then the word *Murder* on a news clipping caught Winter's eye. She reached down into the box where a notebook had fallen open to reveal a news story.

The notebook wasn't actually one of Marion's. It belonged to Adam Gracelyn, her husband. Some of his things had evidently gotten mixed up with his wife's over the years.

Winter placed the notebook on the desk and leafed through the pages till she came to the news story she'd spotted. It was dated Thursday, May 16, 1968. The headline screamed:

Vietnam War Hero Found Murdered

Early this morning Thomas Jefferson Marker, a decorated ex-Army colonel in the Vietnam War, was shot to death by an un-identified woman in the Kellogg Motel near Laveen.

The Maricopa County Sheriff's Office responded to calls reporting gunfire at the motel but officers arrived too late to save Marker's life. Deputies took the unidentified young woman into custody at the scene.

Many people across the United States know of Colonel Marker's heroic efforts in Vietnam to bring back American soldiers held in prisoner-of-war camps.

"He was a great man," Beverly Sorensen, a Cincinnati mother, said when interviewed this morning. "He brought our son home to us when we thought he was lost to us forever. He brought a lot of sons and daddies home from that awful place."

In their war on crime, the district attorney's office had their newest recruit, Miss Marion Hart, in the field last night. Ms. Hart, a life-long resident of Phoenix, arrived shortly after the murder.

"We're working leads now," Ms. Hart said at the scene. "The district attorney's office will get to the bottom of it."

A picture accompanied the story. It showed Marion Hart standing in front of a low-rent motel. Behind her, two men rolled a sheet-covered body out on a gurney. Deputy sheriffs holding shotguns flanked her.

According to Winter's timeline, Marion had been twenty-eight years old. She hadn't yet married Adam Gracelyn. But the two had known each other. According to the news story, Adam Gracelyn had become the woman's defense attorney.

That must have been some meeting.

Intrigued, Winter kept reading.

Chapter 3

The ringing blasted Marion Hart into wakefulness. She groaned and rolled over in bed, then reached for the phone on the nightstand. As she pulled the receiver to her ear, her brain kicked to life.

The soft green glow of the uranium-tipped hands of the alarm clock showed the time was 3:41 a.m.

She'd gotten two hours of sleep. She sat up with her back against the headboard and said, "Marion Hart."

"Marion, did I wake you?"

She recognized District Attorney Geoffrey Turnbull's gravelly voice immediately. Adrenaline thudded through her body. During the seven weeks she'd been with the district attorney's office, Turnbull had never called her in the middle of the night.

They'd attended one of the mayor's political campaign functions earlier. *No,* she told herself. *That was yesterday.*

But God help her, that didn't feel like yesterday. It felt like minutes ago.

"Yes, sir," she replied.

"Sorry," Turnbull said. He was in his fifties and had held the office of district attorney for seven years. He'd been an A.D.A. before that and was a fishing buddy of Marion's father. According to the local gossip, that was one of the main reasons Turnbull had hired her into the D.A.'s office.

"It's all right," Marion said. "I was only…sleeping."

Turnbull chuckled. "I was, too, when I got the call."

"What call, sir?"

"Stop calling me 'sir.'"

"Yes, sir." Marion had tried. She didn't automatically give a lot of men respect, and she didn't give many offices immediate respect, either. Turnbull was a lot like her dad, though, and she gave men like that respect.

Turnbull sighed. "I hate to ask this, Marion, but I need you to handle something. I hadn't planned on a murder taking place when I spent last night drinking. Driving over to cover this is out of the question. I'm still half in the bag."

Marion wanted to say, *Only half?* But she didn't. Turnbull was well-known for his drinking proclivity, though he'd never let it interfere with his job. A lot of deals were made over drinks and cigars. Marion knew that from waiting tables to put herself through law school.

"And I damn sure didn't think a celebrity would go and get himself killed," Turnbull added.

"'Celebrity'?" Marion repeated. The part about the killing didn't surprise her. A phone call late at night had already brought that possibility to mind. No one called the D.A.'s office at night to ask legal questions.

"An honest-to-God war hero." Papers rustled. "His name's— *was*—Tom Marker. He was a colonel in the army. Have you heard of him?"

"Yes." It would have been hard not to have heard of the man. Marker had brought back Brian Ellis, the scion of the Ellis airline empire, only a year or so ago. The story of the father and son's reunion after nearly eighteen months in a Vietcong war prison had been in all the papers and on television. "Who killed him?"

"A woman. The sheriff's office caught her at the scene."

Marion switched on the lamp next to her bed. The bright light hurt her eyes. She opened the nightstand drawer and took out a notebook and pen.

The notebook was a five-by-seven bound edition. All the pages were numbered. That had been one of the things Turnbull had insisted on when she accepted the job. Everything was written in bound notebooks and with a pen. The notebooks were part of the evidence chain the prosecutor's office might have to provide.

Marion turned to a clean page and made a notation of the day and time. She wrote Tom Marker's name, then Death Investigation.

"Do we know who the woman is?" Marion asked.

"Not yet, A.D.A. Hart," Turnbull replied. She heard the grin in his words. "That's going to be one of the first things you need to let me know. In the morning. I'm going back to bed. From what Fred Keller says, this thing should be a slam-dunk. If you need anything, try to wait till morning. I'm going to be hungover as hell and I have to be in front of Judge Ferguson at ten o'clock for an arraignment."

"All right. But what am I supposed to—"

"Just get to the Kellogg Motel, Counselor. Talk to Fred. He'll walk you through the crime scene. Oh, and take your camera. The sheriff's office will have a photographer there taking pictures, but I always like to have our own photos in a murder investigation. Especially if it involves celebrities. I'll see you in the morning."

Turnbull hung up before Marion could say anything. She took the phone from her ear and stared at it for a moment.

Then the shock wore off and excitement flared again. *A murder.* And Turnbull was letting her handle it. Grinning, she cradled the phone and climbed out of bed. She grabbed a suit from the closet on her way to the apartment's tiny bathroom.

It was her *first* murder case. And she'd take a slam-dunk any day. Court cases were all about the win.

Thirty-seven minutes later, freshly showered and feeling more awake, Marion pulled her 1965 Mustang Fastback off the highway and into the Kellogg Motel parking lot. The pavement glistened like black ice from a recent light rain.

The motel was laid out in a large U so that the two legs encompassed the parking area. The manager's office was in the right leg at the front. Red neon tubing marked the office and gleamed from the front of the Pepsi machine.

A tall deputy in a yellow slicker waved her down with a flashlight.

Marion pulled up next to him and rolled down her window. She hated letting the rain into the car. Although it wasn't new, it was new to her. The old Rambler her dad had helped her buy and repair had finally given out a week after she'd gotten the job in the D.A.'s office. The payments came dearly and she still occasionally winced over the doubt she'd seen in her dad's eyes. Both her parents were schoolteachers. Money had never been plentiful in their household.

"I'm sorry, ma'am," the grizzled deputy said. "I'm afraid you're gonna have to move along. This here motel is closed."

"I'm with the district attorney's office." Marion switched on her interior light and showed him her identification.

The man read the identification, then scrunched down and took a better look at her. "But…you're a *woman*."

I am, Marion thought fiercely. *And you'd better get used to it. There's a new world coming.*

"Gee," Marion said, "you stay sharp like that and I'll bet you make detective someday." The words were out of her mouth before she knew it. She regretted them at once. Creating ill will with the sheriff's office wouldn't endear her to anyone. A fast-talking, sarcastic woman definitely wouldn't be appreciated.

But she hated the condescending attitude men had toward women. She'd faced it the whole time she'd put herself through law school. Most of the men there had waited for her to fail out or break down from all the pressure. Instead she'd graduated near the top of her class.

But the deputy wasn't angry; he grinned. "Well I'll be. A woman. And you're young, too. This should be interesting." He stood up and backed away. "You go on ahead, ma'am. Sheriff Keller will meet you at the room."

"Thank you." Marion put her identification back into her purse. "Which room?"

"I expect it'll be the one with the dead body in it, ma'am."

Okay, you had that one coming, Marion thought sourly. She gazed through the rain-dappled windshield at the motel rooms.

Sheriff's cars and an ambulance sat in front of only one of them. The red and white lights cut swaths through the neon-spattered darkness. The mercury vapor lights made the blue cars look purple.

Marion eased ahead and parked well short of the traffic congestion. She didn't want to chance any door dings. She got out of the Mustang, slung her purse over her shoulder, skidded for a moment on her pumps and crossed to the motel room.

Sheriff Fred Keller of Maricopa County was a no-nonsense kind of guy. Even though Marion knew Turnbull had told Keller she was coming, it was obvious that the sheriff didn't approve of her presence.

She tried to ignore that, but it was a fierce struggle. He was the kind of aloof male that drew fire with just a glance.

He stood almost six feet tall and was solid and muscular. From the look of his craggy face and iron-gray hair, Marion guessed he was in his late fifties. His dark skin offered mute testimony that he spent a lot of the day under the hot Arizona sun. The pistol on his hip looked massive.

"You mind if I smoke, ma'am?" Keller asked. Before Marion even had time to reply, he reached into his shirt pocket and took out a pack of cigarettes. He lipped one and lit up with a Zippo lighter. The wavering flame drew his features briefly out of the shadows. He blew a plume of gray smoke out into the rainy night.

Marion knew she could be no-nonsense herself and decided to show the man. She stepped under the eave out of the rain and opened her notebook.

"What happened?" Marion asked.

Keller looked at her over the hot orange coal of his cigarette and then lowered his hand. "An unidentified woman came to this motel room—" he pointed with his cigarette to indicate the unit Marion stood next to "—that would be unit thirty-seven—and used a .357 Magnum to nearly blow off Colonel Tom Marker's head, ma'am. That's what happened."

Marion took quick notes in shorthand. She'd learned that while still in high school when her parents thought she was going to be a teacher like them. At the time, she hadn't known how helpful it would be in her job as an attorney.

"Were there any witnesses?" Marion asked.

"Yes, ma'am. The night manager's name is Bud Overton. I've got a man down to his office who's taking a statement."

"I'll want to talk to Mr. Overton."

"We're getting a statement. You can just read what he tells us. I'll have the report right out to you."

Marion met the man's eyes. "Will you be putting Mr. Overton on the stand and questioning him about what he saw tonight during the murder trial, Sheriff Keller?"

Keller took a hit off his cigarette. "No, ma'am."

"Well, I will be." *If this turns out right,* Marion told herself. "I'll need to speak to Mr. Overton tonight."

"Yes, ma'am." Keller frowned in distaste and rubbed his stubbled jaw. "I think it would have been better if Turnbull had sent someone else down here."

"If D.A. Turnbull had felt that way," Marion said evenly, "I expect he would have done just that. Don't you?"

Keller grimaced. "Yes, ma'am."

"Walk me through the murder."

Marion took notes as Keller talked. She was attentive and spoke only when she needed clarification. Evidently that impressed him because some of his surliness went away. But maybe that was because he was a total professional when it came to his job. His pride and thoroughness were evident.

According to Overton's story, the woman had walked into the motel parking lot wearing a thigh-length jacket. Overton had noticed her because she was "a good-lookin' woman" and he didn't see many of those at the motel. Except for the ones who were trying to drum up a little business.

Keller said that before he thought about it. He paused, colored briefly and apologized. Marion quietly accepted the apology, not because she'd been embarrassed—because she wasn't—but because she knew that the discomfort Keller felt gave her a slight edge over the man.

The woman had gone to the unit and—

"She came directly to this unit?" Marion interrupted. She glanced at the door. The unit was neatly marked with brass numbers on the door. It was room number 37.

"Yes, ma'am. Overton says there was no hesitation."

Marion thought about that. "Marker could have called her here."

Keller shrugged and nodded. "I thought of that. Don't know how we'd prove it."

"We could subpoena phone records," Marion supplied. That course of action was relatively new.

"I suppose so," Keller replied, looking a little impressed. Then he continued with his account.

The woman had paused at the door for a moment, then took her pistol out and walked into the room.

"Marker let her in?" Marion asked.

"We don't believe so, ma'am," Keller said. "There are fresh scratches on the lock. We found lockpicks on the woman. And Overton says there weren't any lights on in the room. We believe Colonel Marker was asleep when she entered."

Once inside the room, the woman had switched on a small flashlight and opened fire almost immediately.

"Overton says the muzzleflashes lit up the room just seconds after she entered," Keller told Marion. "Says it was like a lightning storm started up in there."

"Are flashes like that normal?" Marion hadn't seen gunfire at night.

"Yes, ma'am. Muzzleflashes can be awfully bright in the dark."

The sound of the shots had rolled out over the motel parking area. At that point Overton had dived behind the counter and dragged the phone down with him.

"The woman was still here when you arrived?" Marion asked when the sheriff finished his summation.

"Yes, ma'am."

"Why?"

"You'd have to ask her that."

"Are you ready to do this?" Keller asked.

Marion stood at the door's threshold. So far she hadn't ventured inside the room. But the thought of the corpse lying in wait hadn't been far from her mind.

Until this moment, the only dead bodies she'd seen had been in funeral homes. She'd still felt uncomfortable around them. There was something about the emptiness of the body and knowing that the eyes would never open that scratched at her nerves.

"Yes," Marion whispered.

Keller looked at her. "You don't have to do this," he said gently.

"Are you trying to protect me, Sheriff Keller?" Marion appreciated that from him at the same time that she resented it. She'd fought hard to earn the respect of the men she'd worked with and she wasn't going to lose the foundation of that respect by allowing them to be nice to her.

Needing protection wouldn't further the recognition that a woman could do the same job as a man.

"Yes, ma'am," Keller answered without hesitation.

"Don't do me any favors," Marion told him.

"No, ma'am. If you don't mind me asking, Counselor, have you seen a murder victim before?"

Marion hesitated. "Only in photographs."

Keller nodded grimly. "Well this here's a lot worse than any photographs would be. You can't smell the blood and stuff through a picture. You might want to rethink going into that room."

I can't, Marion thought. *If I back down now, if I don't face this, it's going to haunt me.*

"Let's go," she said.

"The reason I'm telling you this," Keller said, "is that we've got news reporters on the scene now."

Looking over the sheriff's shoulder, Marion saw a loose semicircle of people standing out beyond the striped sawhorses the deputies had put up. As she looked, a man lifted a large camera and took her picture. The bright light from the flashbulb temporarily caused black spots to whirl in her vision.

She hadn't noticed the presence of the reporters.

"They're always circling," Keller said. "Like vultures. Somebody else's bad news is their good news." He frowned like he'd bitten into something sour.

Marion knew from her studies and her exposure in the D.A.'s office that she would have, at best, an adversarial relationship with the press. Anything less would amount to all-out war.

"What I'm saying," Keller went on, "is that those vultures would

love to hang a picture on the morning's paper of Phoenix's newest
A.D.A. throwing up."

"Nice thought," Marion said.

"I'm just saying," Keller protested, "that you don't want it to
happen to you."

Marion thought about that for a moment. "You're right. But I'm
still going into that room."

Keller eyed her levelly for a moment, nodded. "Yes, ma'am.
Whenever you're ready."

Facing the door, Marion took a deep breath and let it out.

"When you get inside," Keller said, "try breathing through your
mouth. Not your nose. It helps cut down on the smell."

"Thank you." Marion steeled herself and walked into the motel
unit.

Chapter 4

Kellogg Motel
Off I-17
Outside Phoenix, Arizona
Thursday, May 16, 1968
The Past

The smell of death slammed into Marion as soon as she crossed the threshold. She opened her mouth and started breathing that way. It helped—a little. The nauseating odor still hung in the air.

Marion froze as her stomach tried to rebel. In front of her, a powerfully built man with coal-black hair lay sprawled on the dark green carpet. Blood threaded the man's hair and pooled out around him. The bullets had nearly destroyed his face.

Without warning, Marion's legs turned rubbery. Her stomach lurched and the sour taste of bile filled the back of her throat. She swallowed and forced herself to remain standing.

Three other men stood in the room. Two of them were deputies. Another wore a plain black suit and a white beard. All of them watched Marion with bright interest.

Since she'd been with the D.A.'s office, Marion had seen the violence people could do to each other. She'd taken statements from families who had lost loved ones in an altercation and from rape victims and domestic abuse victims in the local E.R.s. The hardest investigations had been those involving children. Those still haunted Marion.

"Are you all right, ma'am?" Keller's voice was quiet and controlled.

Marion started to reply, then thought maybe her voice wasn't up to the task. She nodded contritely. Even that made her head swim.

The bearded man in the suit studied Marion. He took a cigar from inside his jacket and lit up. He waved the smoke out of his face.

"You runnin' sightseein' tours now, Frank?" the man asked.

"Not hardly, Doc. This is Assistant District Attorney Marion Hart. Turnbull sent her over to cover tonight's festivities."

"Oh." The man's eyebrows rose in surprise. "He sent a woman to something like this?"

Resenting the man's question and his attitude, Marion took a breath to keep herself in check.

Be calm, Marion told herself. "Who are you?" she asked the man pointedly.

The man smiled. "Takes her job seriously, doesn't she?"

Marion waited but made no comment.

"I'm Dr. Benjamin Shetterly. I serve as medical examiner for the state of Arizona. I'm here to assume custody of the body."

Marion wrote the information down. "You were called out to the murder scene?"

"I don't rely on a crystal ball, if that's what you mean."

The two deputies in the background laughed out loud.

Ignoring the sarcasm, Marion asked, "Who called you?"

"Sheriff Keller. He usually does for one of these. And sometimes he calls me for poker night if he's got an empty chair."

"You've worked murders before?"

"Of course. I've logged plenty of court hours on the witness stand."

Marion wrote that down. Turnbull would probably already be familiar with Doc Shetterly.

"Dr. Shetterly," Marion said.

"Call me Doc," the man requested. "Everybody does."

"Thank you. What can you tell me about the victim?"

Doc flicked ash from his cigarette into a plastic bag in his pocket. "He was shot to death. Close range."

"How do you know that?"

Shetterly regarded her thoughtfully. "How strong is your stomach?"

"Strong enough."

A smile thinned Shetterly's lips. "I guess we could test it then. If you really want to know the answer to that question, come here."

That's a challenge. Marion knew the invitation for what it was. Swallowing the lump in her throat, she tried to ignore the stench of fresh death in the room and crossed over to Shetterly's side. *This is what you signed on to do. Get it done.*

The coroner took an ink pen from his pocket. Leaning over the dead body, he pointed toward black spots on what was left of the dead man's face.

"Do you see this?" Shetterly asked.

Marion had a hard time discerning the black spots at first. All she could see was the gory ruin of Marker's face. Broken ivory bone showed through the crimson pulp. Blood covered the bed sheets.

Not trusting her voice, Marion nodded.

"Those are tiny burns from the muzzleflashes of the murder weapon. When you hold a firearm close enough, when you shoot, it'll cause those."

"I've seen them before," Marion said hoarsely.

"Really? Where?" Shetterly seemed immediately interested.

"In classes on physical evidence. Never—" Marion's voice broke. She sipped a quick breath. "Never in person before."

Shetterly nodded. "Burns like these generally mean the murder was personal."

Marion seized on that. "You think Marker knew his killer?"

"I've got near a lifetime spent working things like this," Shetterly said. "Somebody kills this close up, it's because there's a lot of emotion involved."

"It also means the killer wanted to make sure the job was done," Keller added.

"Was Marker awake when she killed him?" Marion asked.

"That's hard to answer." Shetterly moved his face within inches of the dead man's. He used a stainless steel forceps to sift through the wreckage. The physician breathed out smoke and the gray vapor flushed across the torn and broken flesh. "If he was awake, she didn't allow him to sit up."

"How do you know?"

Shetterly slid the dead man's head over to reveal the ragged mattress below. "I expect we'll find the bullets in the floor below."

Marion's stomach flipped a little. "How many times did she shoot him?"

Keller answered that. "When we took the .357 Magnum off her, all the rounds had been fired."

Grateful for the chance to turn away from the corpse, Marion looked at the sheriff. "How many rounds does the pistol hold?" She thought she knew, but she wasn't certain. She didn't like to assume.

"Six."

She fired six rounds into a man's face at point-blank range. Marion tried to imagine what would drive someone to do something like that. She had no idea.

"I think he was awake for a moment," Shetterly said. "But only just."

Marion swiveled back to the physician. "Why?"

Lifting the dead man's left arm, Shetterly indicated the torn flesh across the knuckles. "Those tears are fresh. I think he managed to hit his killer before she killed him."

Leaning down, Marion took pictures of the damage that showed on the knuckles. Light glinted from the military ring the dead man wore. "You're sure this is recent?"

"Yeah. There's no sign of clotting or scabs. He hit her, then she killed him. There was no time for the healing to begin."

Marion shifted her attention back to Keller. "Does the woman have any marks to corroborate this?"

Keller touched his left temple. "Here. You can see the bruising and scratches. Probably from the ring."

"There's something else," Shetterly said.

"What?"

Shetterly pointed to the dead man's chest. Marker had gone to bed shirtless. The physician traced a muddy print on the lifeless flesh with his forefinger. "It was raining when the woman arrived."

"What is that?" Marion asked. Then, just before Shetterly answered, she recognized it.

"That," Shetterly said, "is a muddy footprint." He looked up at Keller, who had come over to join them. "I spotted this after you went outside. Thought you'd like to see it."

"Can we get a print off it?" Keller asked.

"Take pictures of this," Shetterly said. "Then take pictures of the bottom of the shoes that woman has on. It's almost as good as fingerprints."

"She put her foot on him?" Marion asked.

Shetterly nodded. "I think so."

"Why?"

The medical examiner took glasses from a shirt pocket, slipped them on and examined the muddy print. "Looks like she used her foot to hold Marker down while she shot him. He knew it was coming. She made sure of that."

"Do we know what Marker was doing here?" Marion stood outside the motel room while Shetterly and his assistant took care of the body.

"No." Keller smoked and watched the rain pouring from the eave.

Marion glanced at her wristwatch. Almost an hour had passed since her arrival. It had only seemed like minutes. The death smell clung to her and she couldn't wait to get home to shampoo the stench out of her hair.

"There is the connection to the Ellis family," she said. "We could follow up on that."

Keller nodded. "Got that penciled in. But folks like the Ellises don't live the same lives you and I do, Counselor. The air's a mite more rarified where they are."

Marion knew that. Phoenix tended toward a city of absolutes. Rich and poor families lived there, but they seldom interacted.

"Even if we do get a chance to interview them, they're not going to tell us any more than they want us to know."

"Personal experience, Sheriff?" Marion asked.

"Yes, ma'am." Keller hesitated a moment. "Brian Ellis may have come home from Vietnam as a returning prisoner of war and a military hero of sorts, but he didn't leave here that way."

"What do you mean?"

Keller shook his head. "I already said too much. I shouldn't have said what I did."

Marion decided to let the comment pass but she made a mental note to have a look at whatever the D.A.'s office had on Brian Ellis. "Where's the woman?"

Keller nodded toward the sheriff's office cars. "I've got her in one of the cars. Maybe Marker got lucky with that punch before she blasted him. She was out on her feet, more or less. She was walking back along the parking lot when the first cars arrived. If we'd been another couple minutes later—" He lifted his shoulders and dropped them. "We might have missed her."

"I want to see her."

Marion followed Keller's broad back to one of the nearest sheriff's cruisers. Rain pelted her in fat drops. The rainfall was abnormal for the time of year, but the weather sometimes did strange things due to the White Tank mountain range.

They stopped at the car and Keller nodded to the deputies standing guard. The man put his hand on his sidearm and gingerly opened the door.

"You'll want to be careful, Cap'n," the young deputy said. "She fights something fierce. Jonesy is at the hospital getting his ear stitched up where she bit him. Got to wonder if he needs his rabies vaccination, too."

They're afraid of her, Marion realized. That surprised her. She hadn't seen men afraid of women very often. Or if they were, they'd given no indication of it.

The woman sat in the backseat with her hands cuffed behind her back. Her dark chestnut hair cascaded across her shoulders. Her profile was strong. Pale skin picked up the lights from the motel parking lot. Even seated she looked taller than average and extremely athletic.

She ignored them as they stared at her. The effort reminded Marion of the wild animals that had gotten trapped in the attic of her family home. She and her dad had once had to relocate a whole family of raccoons. They'd used live cages to capture them. While caged, the raccoons had pointedly ignored them in the same manner as this woman. But when the cage was rattled, they attacked immediately. Marion suspected the same would hold true of the woman in the back of the sheriff's car.

"I'm Marion Hart," Marion said. She felt guilty simply

staring at the woman. Despite what she'd done, she wasn't a zoo animal.

The woman ignored Marion and kept her gaze locked on the front windshield.

"I'm with the district attorney's office," Marion said.

Slowly the woman turned her head and looked at Marion. Deep blue eyes gleamed like daggers in the pale light waxing over the motel parking lot. They were cold and devoid of emotion.

"Prove it," the woman challenged. Her voice was flat and harsh. There was a nasal quality that made Marion immediately think she was from somewhere back East.

Taken aback by the woman's decision to speak and the unflinching challenge that had rung out in her voice, Marion opened her purse and removed her identification. She started to lean in with it but Keller intercepted her hand.

"She's who she says she is," Keller said.

Resentment flashed over Marion. "I'm quite capable of—"

"Capable of getting yourself killed," Keller growled. "This woman does things with her fists and feet that I haven't ever seen done before." He handed Marion her identification back.

"A woman," the woman mused. "Interesting."

"I have some questions," Marion said.

"I don't care." The woman turned and went back to staring through the windshield.

Despite repeated attempts to get the woman to talk, Marion finally gave up in disgust. The newspaper people were pressing forward as well. Keller shut the door on the cruiser and ordered the driver to take the prisoner to jail.

"We're not going to get anything out of her," Keller said as the departing car's taillights flared red.

"She has to talk," Marion said. "What kind of woman would walk into a man's motel room, shoot him dead and then show no emotion?"

"She's already shown emotion," Keller commented. "That was the part where she put all six rounds through Marker's head."

They watched in silence as Doc Shetterly and his team brought the body from the motel room on a gurney. White sheets covered the dead man, but blood soaked through and turned the material dark.

Bulbs from the reporters' cameras flashed. Marion was also

certain she heard someone cheering. She tried not to think about how quickly a person went from living to being a temporary news sensation.

Life had to be worth more than that.

Back at the Maricopa County Jail, Marion watched as the jailer matron, a hefty dishwater blonde named Whitten, forced the woman to strip and subject herself to the obligatory shower to kill possible lice infestation. The prisoner stood arrogant and proud before the stares of the other women.

Her body was a work of art. Hard, lean muscle created dynamic curves. She was a woman, Marion realized, that would turn men's heads no matter where she was or what she wore.

But the beauty was marred. Several scars—bullet, knife and burns—marked the prisoner. Miraculously nothing had touched that gorgeous face.

However, the bruising from the blow they suspected Marker had delivered before he'd died was starting to darken. The prisoner's left cheek was puffy from it. A long scratch held blood crust. Due to the darkness in the cruiser, Marion hadn't noticed the damage.

Marion made a note to have a medical doctor take a look at the woman. She didn't want charges of law enforcement abuse or coercion to taint the case.

Staring at the signs of present and past violence, Marion couldn't help wondering what kind of life the woman had lived. If she was a product of abuse, how accountable could she be held for her actions?

Domestic abuse had always been something practiced behind closed doors, but cases were being brought out of the homes into the courts these days. When she'd grown up, Marion had lived next door to a family where a woman had been abused.

Marion's father had intervened on more than on occasion. He'd grown more and more frustrated with his helplessness. The neighbor had been a long-haul trucker and the beatings had been as regular as the work that had taken the man out of town.

Marion's mother had advised the woman to leave her husband one night while tending the bruises and cuts the man's fists had left. The whole time, the women's two young children had clung to

Marion and quivered. In the end, the woman had cried pathetically and told them that she couldn't leave her husband because she wouldn't be able to care for her children.

Immediately following one late-night episode, Marion's father had called the police. Marion had been frightened for her father because the trucker's rage had been dark and out of control. He had threatened to kill Marion's father.

In the end, though, the police had done nothing. The woman had sworn she'd fallen down the stairs. One of the policemen stated that she must have fallen *up* the stairs as well to do all the damage they'd seen. She'd refused their offer to take her to the hospital and asked them to leave. Without testimony, the officers hadn't been able to act.

That experience remained within Marion's mind. Women sometimes ended up helpless not because they lacked the will or ambition to take care of themselves. Many of them ended up victimized by men and life simply because they lacked options.

Marion hadn't wanted to be that helpless. But there were several women who still were. Someday, somehow, she wished she could help them realize their potential instead of accepting a secondary citizenship role. She also wanted to change the law so police officers could act to protect the welfare of a family without testimony.

Marion had taken the job as an assistant district attorney not just because she loved the work, but because she'd wanted to show other women that they could succeed outside the home, too.

That hadn't worked out as well as Marion had hoped. Most of the wives of the men in the D.A.'s office resented her because they viewed her as a threat, not a role model. Some disliked her because she spent more time with their husbands than they did.

Marion had always heard that nothing worth having ever came easily. She tried to remember that to convince herself she had made the right choices, but it was hard.

Once the shower was over, the woman stepped into a pair of white cotton panties, a bra and pulled on the jumpsuit Whitten issued her. She pulled her wet hair back into a ponytail and secured it with a rubber band. During the whole process, she never once acknowledged anyone else in the room.

Marion felt sorry for the woman. During her time with the D.A.'s office, Marion had never watched anyone processed through an arrest. The whole experience seemed demeaning.

Like dealing with cattle, Marion couldn't help thinking. But then she focused on what the corpse had looked like in the motel room. Whatever family Colonel Thomas Marker had left behind couldn't even have an open casket service. No one would be able to replace what the woman's bullets had taken away.

But thinking like that only raised the question of the woman's motivation in Marion's mind again. She really wanted to know what had happened in that motel room.

They stood the prisoner against one wall and took pictures of her right profile and full face. She was booked under the name Jane Doe.

A few moments later, Whitten looked at Marion curiously. "Where do you want her?" the matron asked.

"Put her in interview room D," Marion responded. "I'll be along shortly."

The jailer nodded. She took the woman by the arm and guided her through the door. Before they'd gone three steps, the woman slid into sudden movement as graceful as a dancer's choreography.

The woman lifted her captured arm, folded it, then rammed it into the matron's face. The meaty impact filled Marion's ears. Blood gushed from the matron's mouth, but she was a big woman and used to dealing with violent prisoners. The matron reached for the woman.

The prisoner ducked beneath Whitten's arms. She turned and spun on one foot. The other leg folded then snapped forward like a coiled spring. The prisoner's bare foot caught Whitten in the throat with enough force to lift her from her feet.

The matron stumbled backward and crashed to the floor. The other two female jailers rushed forward and tried to grab the prisoner.

The prisoner grabbed the outstretched arm of one jailer as she sidestepped. She whirled and maintained her grip on the jailer's arm. Something snapped with a sickening crunch. The jailer flipped and landed flat on her back. Her breath left her lungs in a rush.

The other jailer slid her nightstick from her belt and swung at the prisoner's head. In a blur of movement, the prisoner lifted her left arm, trapped the jailer's arm under it, then spun back outside of the jailer's reach. The prisoner delivered two punishing elbows to the jailer's temple. The jailer crumpled but the prisoner stripped the nightstick from her hand before the woman collapsed.

Marion stepped forward but wasn't certain what she was going to do. Before she reached the prisoner, the woman whirled and smashed the nightstick across Marion's forearm.

Pain ignited in Marion's head. Her senses screamed. Driven more by instinct than any planning, she tried to step back. But it was too late. The prisoner circled behind her and slid the nightstick across her throat.

"Okay, muffin," the prisoner said in that nasal accent. "It's just you and me now."

Chapter 5

Panic swelled through Marion as the prisoner held her. The crushing pressure against her windpipe was merciless. She knew she was only inches from death.

"How do you feel now, muffin?" the prisoner whispered in her ear. "Are you afraid? Fear isn't going to get you out of a situation like this. You've got to control your fear. Use it. When you can work with it, fear makes you faster, stronger. You're never more alive than when you're at the edge of death. Don't you feel it?"

Marion didn't answer. She reached for the nightstick.

The prisoner pulled the nightstick tighter. "Don't. Get your hand down or I'll snap your pretty little neck."

With effort, Marion got control of her fear and dropped her hand. She swallowed hard and hoped she didn't throw up. Her senses swam, but she was certain that was more from the blood flow getting cut off to her brain than anything else. She almost fell.

The pressure from the nightstick lessened.

"Don't pass out on me, muffin," the prisoner commanded. "We've got places to go. Things to do. We're going to start with getting out of here."

Across the room, Whitten got to her feet. The big woman gasped and wheezed. She helped one of the other jailers to her feet. The jailer cradled her broken arm.

The third jailer lay on her back. Blood pooled beneath her from the laceration on her face. Whitten touched the woman's neck. Marion's stomach gave another sickening lurch when she realized Whitten was checking to make certain the woman was still alive.

"I didn't kill her," the prisoner snarled. "I could have if I'd wanted to." Savage joy resonated in her words. Marion heard it. But desperation was there as well. "I could have killed you too, piggy."

"You're not getting out of here," Whitten croaked.

"I think I will." The prisoner shook Marion. "I'll bet nobody around here wants their token women's libber in the D.A.'s office to end up dead this morning."

Whitten beat on the door without taking her eyes from the prisoner. Marion saw anger on the big woman's face, but she saw fear as well.

The door opened and a deputy shoved his head inside. He took in the scene at a glance, drew his weapon and started to come into the room.

"Stay out," the prisoner ordered. "Or I'll kill her."

The deputy froze.

"Get the sheriff," the prisoner said. "Get Keller."

The deputy stepped back outside. Whitten started to step through the door, too.

"Not you, piggy," the prisoner said.

Whitten pointed at the unconscious woman lying on the floor. "She needs a doctor."

"She can wait."

Marion felt the prisoner's breath hot against her neck and ear.

"Are you still with me, muffin?" the prisoner asked.

Speaking past the nightstick pulled tight against her throat was hard, but Marion managed. "I'm still here." She was surprised at the defiance in her voice.

"You sound spunky. Good. I don't need you passing out on me when we walk out of here."

"I'm not going to pass out." Marion held on to her anger and used it to bolster her strength.

"I hope not. But just so you know, if you do pass out I'm going to drag you out of here anyway."

Marion forced herself to focus through the panic that threatened to paralyze her. Her heart hammered inside her chest. *You can get out of this.* Even as she told herself that, though, she realized she had no doubt that the prisoner would kill her.

She couldn't help thinking how her parents would react if something happened to her. Three weeks ago at an accidental death, she'd seen parents devastated by their son's overdose on heroin. She didn't want to put her parents through that.

"Let's go, muffin," the prisoner grated. She pushed Marion toward the door. "Stay back, piggy."

Whitten glared at the prisoner but lifted her hands in the air and stepped back from the door.

Out in the hallway under the bright fluorescent lighting, Marion felt light-headed. Panic ripped at her with sharp claws. Her legs trembled with the desire to run.

The prisoner stayed close behind Marion. She felt the woman's body pressed against hers. The warmth took away some of the chill of her damp clothing.

Six deputies stood in the hallway with drawn weapons. Sickness swirled in Marion's stomach. She forced herself to sip air.

"Keep moving, muffin," the prisoner ordered.

"Y-you're not h-helping your case," Marion said. Embarrassment flooded her as she heard her stuttered words.

The prisoner laughed. The sound was totally without mirth. "You sound like you're still going to try me."

"I am. Y-you're not going to g-get out of here." Marion wished she could keep from stuttering. That would have helped her sound more convincing.

"I'm going to get out of here," the prisoner replied. "I don't have a choice about staying here. If I stay here, I'm dead. There are people who'll kill me long before you ever get me to trial."

Marion seized on those words and wondered what the woman meant by them.

"If you play your cards right," the prisoner went on, "you'll get out of here, too."

"H-how do I know you w-won't kill me like you did Marker?"

"I don't have a reason to kill you."

"What reason did you have to kill Marker?" Marion couldn't believe she was asking questions with her life on the line. But she couldn't be quiet and there were so many questions swimming in her mind.

"That's my business and none of yours."

"H-how did you f-find him?"

The woman sounded irritated. "You talk way too much, muffin. This isn't part of a guided tour. Keep your trap shut."

Sheriff Frank Keller stepped into view at the end of the hallway. He had a two-handed grip on his revolver and stood with his left foot forward.

Marion closed her eyes for just a moment and resisted the urge to be sick. *You're going to lose that battle one of these times,* she told herself.

"Hold it right there," Keller thundered. His pistol never wavered.

Marion tried to stop, but the prisoner kept pushing her from behind.

"Move," the prisoner commanded.

"You're not leaving this building," Keller declared. "If you don't cease and desist this instant, I'm going to shoot you."

Disbelief swept over Marion. She stared at the cavernous mouth of Keller's big pistol. Surely he was kidding.

"Are you that good a shot?" the prisoner taunted.

Marion knew the woman was crouched tightly behind her. She stared at the unwavering muzzle of the pistol Keller held. Bare inches of the woman had to be exposed.

Keller's face was cold stone. "I think I am." He thumbed the hammer back on the pistol. "I'm not going to tell you again."

"I guess we're going to find out how good you are," the prisoner said, "because I can't be here long. I've already over-stayed my welcome."

Knowing that she was trapped, Marion chose to take command of her fate. She rammed her head back into the prisoner's face. Something crunched. The prisoner's breath gushed out against the back of Marion's neck.

Reaching up, Marion caught her captor's forearm and the loose folds of the jumpsuit just as the nightstick tightened and shut off her wind. She held on tight as she bent forward suddenly.

The prisoner flipped over Marion's back and slammed against the tiled floor. Blood streamed over the woman's face as she gazed up at Marion in shock. The prisoner's recovery was inhumanly quick, though. She pressed her hands against the floor, vaulted to her feet lithe as a cat and crouched.

Marion backed away before the woman could come after her. She didn't stop until she reached the wall behind her.

"Down on your face," Keller commanded.

For a moment, the prisoner hesitated. Marion's breath caught in the back of her throat as certainty that she was about to see the woman executed in front of her eyes surged within her.

Then, with a wry smile through the blood, the prisoner dropped to her knees and put her hands on top of her head. She bent forward till she lay prone on the ground. The movement was fluid and effortless. Blood dripped from her nose to the floor.

Deputies rushed forward and cuffed her as she lay on the ground.

Marion stood on trembling knees, but she stood. She took pride in that. She also took pride in the fact that she'd saved herself in spite of everything.

The prisoner gazed up at Marion in open appraisal. "Not bad, muffin. I didn't expect that out of you."

"Get her to lockup," Keller growled.

The deputies hustled the prisoner away.

Keller surveyed Marion. "Are you all right?" he asked.

Marion nodded. "I think so." Her stomach churned.

"That was a nice move. Slick." New appreciation showed in Keller's hard eyes.

"I took a class in jujitsu while I was in college."

"Jujitsu? I think they're teaching that stuff to the federal agents."

Marion couldn't help talking. She couldn't keep quiet, but she didn't want to talk about what nearly happened. Any topic was better. "Bruce Lee's role on *The Green Hornet* got everybody interested in self-defense. I took it to fulfill a phys ed requirement. It was interesting. I was good at it."

"You were good at it today," Keller said.

Marion looked at the sheriff. "Would you have shot her?"

The big man hesitated for just a moment. "Yes, ma'am. I've never had a prisoner escape. I wasn't about to start this morning."

"And if you'd missed?"

Keller smiled and shook his head. "I don't miss. Truth to tell, Counselor, you just saved her life. Might have been easier all the way around if you'd have let me shoot her."

Marion couldn't believe Keller was so casually discussing taking the life of another person. "Killing her isn't an answer."

Surprise pulled at Keller's features. "What do you think you're going to be doing when you put that woman on trial, Counselor?"

In the bathroom, Marion pulled a paper towel from the dispenser and patted her face dry. She looked at her reflection in the mirror.

The nausea, thankfully, had subsided. She hadn't thrown up even though she'd felt she would have once she'd reached the privacy of the bathroom.

You're okay, she reminded herself. *Everything's going to be all right.*

But Keller's words haunted Marion. She knew she wasn't going to be directly responsible for the woman's death. Her actions, the physical evidence at the scene and the testimony of the witness were going to do that.

She was just going to try the case.

Not try it, she amended. *Hopefully you'll get to be part of it.* She opened her blouse front and looked at the bruising across her neck and collarbone. *After this, Turnbull had better let me on as co-counsel.*

She placed her purse on the sink and took out her emergency makeup. Her hands grew steadier as she fixed the damage done by the struggle. While her hands and eyes worked automatically, her mind concentrated on her questions.

When she got out of the bathroom, a deputy directed Marion to Keller. She found the big man standing at the observation window looking into one of the interview rooms.

The female prisoner sat at the small rectangular table inside the featureless room. Her hands were cuffed behind her back and manacles secured her ankles. Cotton balls filled her nostrils.

Keller looked up as Marion entered the room. "How do you take your coffee, Counselor?"

The question took Marion aback. Then she noted the percolator on a small hot plate on the table in the corner. The aroma of the coffee made her hungry.

"It's fresh perked," Keller said. "But that's about the only thing it has going for it. I'd advise disguising the taste a little."

"Cream. Two sugars." Marion felt odd watching Keller get her a cup of coffee. "I can get that."

"I know you can." Keller poured coffee into a ceramic cup, then poured in cream and dropped in two sugar cubes. He looked around and finally found a saucer to serve it on.

Marion took the coffee gingerly. She'd hoped her hands would be steady, but they weren't. They shook and the cup and saucer clattered just a little.

"That was pretty scary back there." Keller didn't look at Marion when he spoke. His attention was riveted on the woman.

"Yes." Marion sipped the coffee. It was still so hot she barely tasted it.

"I talked to Whitten before she went to the hospital."

"How is she?"

Keller nodded. "She's gonna be fine. Whitten's one of the toughest women I've ever met."

"What about the other jailer?"

A frown tightened Keller's face. "Ambulance guys said she probably had a concussion. Maybe a cracked skull and a dislocated jaw. They also said she was lucky she wasn't dead."

Marion remembered how smoothly the woman had moved during the fight. "If she'd wanted anyone dead, she would have done it."

"Maybe you're right."

There was no maybe to it. Marion knew she was right. "She chose not to kill them."

"The same way she chose to kill Marker?" Keller looked at Marion. "Don't go getting soft on her, Counselor. Whatever else that woman is, she's a cold-blooded killer."

On the other side of the one-way glass, the woman sat unmoving. Blood dripped down her face to the jumpsuit. Except for the steady drip of blood, she might have been carved of stone.

"Did Whitten tell you about the fight?" Marion asked.

Keller nodded. "Said she used some kind of karate or something."

"It wasn't jujitsu." Marion sipped her coffee and found it a little cooler. "But it was something organized. Something dangerous."

"Something like Bruce Lee in *The Green Hornet?*" Keller smiled mirthlessly.

"Yes. Where would she get specialized training like that?"

"Who said she was trained?"

"Do you think she wasn't?"

Keller's eyes narrowed as he regarded the woman. "Oh, I think she was trained. I've been contemplating the possibility that the Russians trained her."

The Russians? Then Marion grasped the meaning behind the suggestion. "You think she's a spy?"

"The kind of training that woman has? The cold-blooded way she killed Marker?" Keller nodded. "I bet when we figure out who she really is, we'll find out she's a Communist spy."

Although the newspapers and television media kept the threat of a nuclear war in the public eye, Marion didn't buy into the thinking as much as many others did. She chose to believe the Cold War would defuse itself before international.annihilation manifested.

"You think she killed Marker as part of her assignment?" she asked

"Don't know yet. But I know she intended to leave a message for somebody."

"Why?"

Keller slipped two fingers into his shirt pocket and took out a thin rectangle covered in clear plastic wrap. "Because she left this at the murder scene." He held the object out. "Careful when you handle it."

The evidence was a playing card. Specifically, it was the Queen of Hearts. Dark smudges of fingerprint powder marred the card's surface and gave the queen a dirty face.

"These are her fingerprints?" Marion asked.

"And Marker's."

"That doesn't mean that she brought the card to the murder

scene. Since Marker's prints are on it, he could have just as easily brought the card."

"So while she's pointing a gun at him, with her foot in the middle of his chest, he asks her to take a look at a playing card? Or let's say Marker did that. Why would she take the card while she's holding a gun on him?"

Marion handed the card back. "I don't know."

Keller tucked the card back into this shirt pocket and buttoned the flap. "I think she used the card because it meant something to Marker. It was something he'd recognize. Since they've got a history—"

"You can't prove that."

"You don't just break into a stranger's motel room, put your foot on his chest and shoot his face off," Keller said gruffly.

Marion winced.

Keller sighed. "Sorry about that. Sometimes I'm a little too plainspoken."

"That's all right."

"But the fact of the matter, Counselor, is that those two people—Marker and that woman—knew each other before they came here. We've just got to figure out how."

"What do we do now?"

"We talk to her," Keller said. "See if she's ready to tell us why she killed Marker."

Looking at the woman, Marion sincerely doubted that was going to happen.

Someone knocked at the open door. A deputy leaned into the room. "Sheriff Keller? There's a man in the lobby who says he's that woman's attorney. He's demanding to see her."

That surprised Marion. She looked at Keller. "Has she called anyone?"

Keller shook his head. "Did the attorney give you a name?"

"Yes, sir. Even gave me a card." The deputy entered the room and handed it over.

Keller took the card. Marion looked over his shoulder.

Adam D. Gracelyn
Attorney-At-Law

A mild expletive escaped Keller's lips. He looked at the deputy and nodded. "Bring Gracelyn to me."

Marion knew the name. The Gracelyns were part of the old money families in Phoenix. She'd never met any of them, but she'd read about them in the *Phoenix Sun* society pages. There had been something about Adam Gracelyn passing the bar exam a few years ago.

The deputy left.

"This isn't good," Keller said quietly.

"Why?"

"Adam Gracelyn's a real firebrand when you get him riled. With all his daddy's money, you'd think he'd just settle down to a nice long stay as one of daddy's corporate lawyers. Instead he signed on with the public defender's office. He specializes in representing minorities and the disenfranchised. He's going to be trouble."

Chapter 6

Gracelyn Ranch
Outside Phoenix, Arizona
Now

David stared at the picture in his sister's Athena Academy yearbook. His younger sister Allison lived in Washington, D.C., these days, but she kept most of her personal things at the family home.

Besides, knowing Allison, she probably had another yearbook with her. She had two copies of everything. She was the most thoroughly organized person David had ever seen. She currently worked for the National Security Agency in a job so secret she never talked to anyone about it.

Allison had been best friends with Lorraine "Rainy" Miller. But that relationship had been troubled. Even though Allison wouldn't have admitted it then—and might not even admit it now—she'd been somewhat jealous of Rainy's successes at the academy. Allison's own student group, the Graces, had constantly vied with

Rainy's team, the Cassandras, for top honors but had often come out second-best.

The competition had been fierce, and it had also been good for both groups. But the competitive edge had never truly gone away.

Later, when circumstances required Rainy to live with Allison at the Gracelyn home for a while, David had fallen in love with Rainy like he'd never fallen for a woman before.

But that didn't work out, did it? David chided himself. *And you've certainly got more to do than spend your morning moping over old yearbooks and wondering what might have been.*

Still, he stared at the picture of Rainy and the group of girls she'd mentored through the academy. All of them were there: Kayla Ryan, Tory Patton, Alexandra Forsythe, Josephine Lockworth, Samantha St. John, Darcy Steele and Rainy at their center.

The picture had been taken somewhere in the hinterlands of the White Tank Mountains where the academy was located. The Cassandras had to have been on a team-based excursion. All of them wore climbing gear.

David thought he could remember the story. Allison had told him one version of it, and Rainy had given him another.

In the picture, Rainy was young. She had to have been seventeen, maybe eighteen. She'd only gotten more beautiful and more defined as she'd gotten older.

For a while, David and Rainy had been close. Then something happened. He still hadn't been sure what. But while he'd been away at college, Rainy had grown distrustful of him. Then she'd left the Gracelyn home.

The next time he'd heard about her had been when she'd enrolled at Harvard as he was graduating. They'd just never connected again. Then she'd gotten married.

Now she was dead.

Silently David cursed Winter Archer's presence at the house for bringing up all the old memories and pain. He cursed Christine Evans as well, but he was equally certain that Christine was right. The answers to the puzzle of Rainy's death, the genetically mutated children and the kidnappings lay in his mother's past.

He just didn't know how he was going to handle Winter Archer's investigation without going crazy thinking about what could have been.

* * *

Winter walked through the big, silent house to David's office. During the last three days, they'd seen each other very little. She had the distinct impression that had been because David wanted it that way.

If she hadn't reached an impasse in her research, or if the story about the woman who had murdered Colonel Thomas Marker hadn't been so compelling, Winter knew she wouldn't have sought David out now.

The sooner you get out of here, the better off you're going to be. You need to be back home in L.A. working on another book. You're at your best when you're working.

If it hadn't been for Christine—and now her own curiosity—Winter knew she'd have been gone in a heartbeat. But Christine was involved, *and* she couldn't walk away from that story without knowing the rest of it.

News about Marker's murder had gradually subsided. In the end, it had disappeared. There were only a couple of footnotes that let her know Marker's body had been shipped back to distant family members.

Of course, given what had happened in 1968 at about the same time, losing sight of one unexplained murder wasn't a big thing. The assassination that had taken place at around the same time had shaken the world.

David's study door was open. Winter crossed to it and lifted a hand to rap against the door frame. The sight of him sitting so grim and silent at the desk gave her pause. He was a beautiful man. He sat with his shirtsleeves rolled nearly to his elbows and his tie at half-mast. He had one hand against his head with his fingers threaded through his hair.

There was something wounded and innocent in his posture. All those feelings she'd felt back when she was a girl echoed within her.

You're still crushing after all these years? Winter couldn't believe it. *Get over it. You don't have time for this. And if he wasn't interested back then, he's definitely not going to be interested now.*

Then she saw he was staring at a book lying open on his desk. As she watched, he carefully thumbed through pages filled with pictures.

A photo album? Winter wasn't sure. But the possibility made her feel badly. Her presence there, in the house where he'd known his mother, had to have made that absence even sharper and more empty. *Oh, Christine, you can't have known what you were going to trigger.*

Winter knocked.

David looked up immediately. Guilt made his movements jerky as he closed the book and slid it to one side.

"Yes?" he said.

"I need more information."

David leaned back in the chair. "You have everything."

Slightly irritated that he didn't ask her in, Winter crossed the threshold and entered the room anyway. She wasn't a vampire. Withholding an invitation wasn't going to keep her out.

"I have *most* of everything," she said. "I've noticed an obvious discrepancy but have been too tactful to mention it." She folded her arms over her breasts, then noticed she was in a defensive posture and grew angry with herself. David Gracelyn wasn't going to make her feel threatened.

He held her gaze for a moment. "What do you think you're missing?"

"Your mother journaled extensively. Some of her work is used in Athena Academy curriculum. I've read it. A few of her books, mainly collections of essays and speeches, are in the library. In all of those books, she referred to journal entries—sometimes even printing them in their entirety—that dealt with those writings."

David didn't say anything.

"Therefore, I submit that those journals she referenced have to exist somewhere," Winter said.

Clasping his hands before him, elbows on the desk, David settled his chin on his thumbs. "My mother's personal writings are—well, they're personal."

"I'll keep them that way. No matter what they are, I need to take a look at them. Some of them."

Frowning, David leaned back in his chair and crossed his own arms. Then he noticed the unconscious behavior and gripped the chair arms.

"You've found something," he said.

Winter hated revealing anything before she was certain of its validity. Unfortunately she was certain David was resolved not to let her have anything unless he knew what she was looking for.

"Possibly," she answered.

"What?"

For a moment Winter considered holding her ground and refusing to answer. She knew that David would fight, though, and she didn't have the energy to argue. Besides that, she was eager to know if she truly had something or if she was following a false lead.

"Did your mother ever tell you how she met your father?" Winter countered.

"During the course of their work."

"She never mentioned any mitigating circumstances?"

"Were there any?"

Winter drew a breath. She hated when interviewees tried playing cagey with their answers. Things usually got much harder than they had to be. "Yes."

"What?"

Taking out her iPAQ/phone, Winter checked the time. It was 12:43 p.m. "Have you had lunch?"

David frowned again.

Even his frowns are sexy. Winter gave herself a mental shake. *Do not get derailed. Focus on getting the journals.*

"What difference would my having lunch make?" David asked.

"If you hadn't eaten, I thought I could tell you the story over lunch."

"I've got too much to do to leave here." David gestured at the desk.

"Surely this big house has a kitchen. If you don't know the way, maybe we could ask Gary." Winter resented the sarcasm at once, but it was far too late. The genie was out of the bottle. She scrambled for something to say that would take the sting out of her words.

David pushed up from the desk. "I know the way to the kitchen. But you're going to have to produce a strong argument to get at my mother's journals." He strode through the door without a backward glance.

Curbing a response, Winter silently watched him walk away. The khaki pants fit him well, and it was obvious he kept himself in great shape. After a moment, she followed.

"You know how to cook?"

David resented the question. He pulled his head out of the

massive refrigerator and glared at Winter. She sat demurely at the island and looked as if the question was more casual curiosity than a thinly veiled insult.

"Yes, I know how to cook. My mother taught me. So did my father." David took a deep breath as he looked around the spacious kitchen. "This is one of the places where I miss her most. When she was at home, she often spent part of the day in here. On good days, Allison and I got to prepare a meal with her."

Winter had the decency to look contrite. "I apologize. I didn't mean—"

"I know you didn't mean to hurt me, and you didn't. But you did intend to be crass, and you were."

Winter looked as though she were going to say something, then thought better of it. She broke their gaze and looked down at her P.D.A.

And you're not exactly the charming host, either, are you? David could hear his mother remonstrating him over his manners.

Marion Gracelyn had always believed the kitchen was a safe haven for everyone. He'd seen her entertain belligerent dinner guests over steaming pots and pans. Most of the time she'd managed to reach some accord right there in the kitchen.

"Look," he said finally, "maybe we're both getting on each other's nerves a little."

"You think?"

The reply was smart-ass, but David sensed there was no malice attached. "Yeah. So what are you in the mood for?"

Her hesitation surprised him. As he recalled, Winter Archer had always had an answer for everything.

"Surprise me," she replied finally.

"I missed breakfast this morning, too. Maybe we could have a really late brunch."

"All right."

"While I cook, maybe you could talk."

By the time Winter finished reiterating what she'd learned about Colonel Thomas Marker's murder and the strange woman who had briefly taken Marion Hart prisoner in the county jail, David had prepared blueberry waffles from scratch, omelets, spicy diced potatoes and onions and bacon and link sausage. He'd even prepared the link sausages by boiling them in water in a covered frying pan instead of frying them.

"Not exactly what my nutritionist would have recommended," Winter commented as she finally surrendered and pushed her plate away.

"Maybe next time you could cook," David growled.

For a moment Winter was so lost in the idea of a next time and the possibility of cooking breakfast she forgot to be slightly insulted. That had been the intention, though.

"I can cook," Winter replied.

David glowered at her doubtfully.

"I didn't mean that as an insult. I enjoyed breakfast. It was good."

Slightly mollified, David nodded. He finished the last bite of blueberry waffle and pushed his plate away.

Without a word, Winter got up and started clearing the dishes.

"What are you doing?" David asked.

"You cooked. The least I can do is clean up the mess." Winter opened the taps at the sink and looked around for dishwashing liquid.

"You don't have to do that."

"I don't want to leave it. Gary probably has enough to do." Winter looked under the sink.

"There's a dishwasher."

"There aren't that many dishes." After finding the dishwashing liquid under the sink, Winter squeezed some into the sink and turned the water on.

"Are you always this pigheaded?" David growled. His chair scraped as he got up.

"No," Winter shot back. "Sometimes I'm obstinate."

"I can believe that." David reached her side.

Winter looked up at him. Though it was insane, she had every intention of fighting him for the dishes. Asking him for his mother's journals hadn't been as easy for her as he'd acted like it was. She knew the kind of pain she was digging into.

"I'm doing these dishes," she declared.

David looked at her for a moment, then nodded. "It'll take both of us half the time. Do you want to wash or dry?"

"Wash. You know where everything goes." Winter did, too, because she'd watched him take everything down. She had a good memory. She plunged her hands into the hot, soapy water and started scrubbing.

Without another word, David started drying the dishes after she rinsed them. "Mom and Dad met during that murder investigation."

"They told you that?"

David shook his head and put a plate in the cupboard. "No. Not exactly. They talked about how they'd met as opposing counsel. Mom was trying to prosecute Dad's client."

"Did they talk about it much?"

"No. To be honest, I never thought much about it. Parents tell you stories all the time."

"Not all parents," Winter replied.

David looked at her but was too polite to ask the question that was obviously on his mind.

"My parents were more hands-off than yours." Winter tried to keep the bitterness out of her voice and hoped she succeeded. She hated whining. Especially her own. "I was raised by live-in nannies. None of them stayed too long. I was something of a brat."

"I can see that."

Winter turned to him and started to say something.

David waved the dish towel in surrender. "Hey. No foul intended. I meant that I can see you're strong-willed. I seem to remember that from when you were at the academy."

"I was." Winter took pride in that. No one had ever gotten her to back down.

"Christine told me a story about you that I didn't know. It was when she was broaching the subject of bringing you in to investigate this. She said Allison dared you to discover the name of one of the teachers' boyfriends."

"Ms. Clemens. The French teacher."

"Christine didn't mention who it was. But she did say that you didn't back down from dares. She said you were always trying to prove yourself."

Because my parents were too busy chasing their private agenda to pay attention to their daughter, Winter thought.

"It took me nine days to find out Ms. Clemens's boyfriend's name," Winter said. "I ended up having to borrow a car—"

"Before you had a driver's license, I was told."

"I had a permit. I knew how to drive."

"So you tailed that poor teacher."

"That poor teacher had us all wondering about her. For six weeks a dozen roses arrived every Friday morning. She could have kept those out of the classroom. She chose not to. She placed them on her desk and told everyone they were from her *secret admirer.* Of course we were curious. We were teenage girls."

David grinned at that. "So did you find out who it was?"

"Of course. But I got busted by the local P.D. for driving without an adult in the car. Luckily Christine was able to intervene so none of the reports reached my parents. They would have taken me out of school and had me institutionalized for emotional issues."

David looked appalled.

"Not really," Winter said. "That was pure drama. But they would *not* have been happy."

"Who was the boyfriend?"

Winter grinned at him. "Maybe one of these days I'll tell you."

They worked in silence for a time after that. Winter was surprised how quickly and smoothly they worked together. They finished the dishes and the kitchen cleanup.

"You haven't found any other leads in my mother's press releases? Other than this murder?" David handed her a bottle of water and took one out of the fridge for himself.

"Not yet. I haven't finished, though. It's possible that the answer lies somewhere else."

David was quiet for a moment. His face didn't show any emotion, but he was evidently contemplating his decision. He sipped the water as he thought.

"Let's follow this story," David said finally. "So far there doesn't appear to be anything else."

"I could keep looking, but this...*feels* right."

"'Feels' right?"

"That's how I work."

"Not very scientific."

"People aren't very scientific when you get down to it," Winter pointed out. "There are many fields of study regarding people and society, and no one has it all figured out yet. I've found that trying to quantify people and reduce them to a string of mathematical equations doesn't work. They're unique and different. And just when you think you have them figured out, they'll do something that will surprise you."

Like make you breakfast, Winter thought.

"My mother's journals are kept here in a vault," David said after a moment. "They're all neatly labeled. But they're also full of talks and encounters that I'm sure she and the people involved wouldn't have wanted aired."

"I don't want to read them all." Now that was a lie and Winter knew it. She loved getting her hands on diaries and journals. There was no better way, outside of an actual interview, to get to know someone. People often revealed more about how they thought and felt in journals—if they kept them in detail—than during even casual conversation.

"You just want the 1968 journals."

"Particularly the months of May, June and July."

David hesitated a moment longer, then nodded. "All right."

Marion Gracelyn—then Hart, her maiden name—had written in her journals every day. Judging from the content in the three slim hardbound volumes David gave her, Winter guessed there was a library somewhere in the house that contained hundreds of journals.

In a way, it was no surprise. Marion Gracelyn had been a dynamo and a visionary. Winter flipped through the books and briefly studied the elegant handwriting. The books weren't quite as neat as she'd envisioned. Marion had written in the margins and the ink wasn't uniform.

"Some of it may be hard to read," David said. "Mom was more interested in getting the words on paper than in getting them down neatly. When Allison and I were kids, we used to tease her about it."

"I've seen worse." Winter was already distracted and she knew it. Halfway through the first volume, she found the entry that related Marion's arrival at the Kellogg Motel. "I appreciate you letting me borrow these."

"The books aren't to leave the premises."

Surprised by the undercurrent of anger in David's voice, Winter looked up at him. All she saw was his back as he strode from the room. Then she realized how dismissive she must have sounded.

Winter cursed, thought about going after him, then thought better of that. She had the books now. Whatever the source of this animosity between them, trying to mollify his feelings might only make it worse.

For now she had the books and she could pick up the story once again. She focused on that and resumed her seat at Marion Gracelyn's desk.

In a matter of minutes, Winter was gone from the sunlit office and back in the Maricopa County Jail during the night of Colonel Thomas Marker's murder in 1968.

Chapter 7

Maricopa County Jail
Phoenix, Arizona
Thursday, May 16, 1968
The Past

"I'm Adam Gracelyn."

Although Marion had seen his picture in the newspaper and occasionally on local television bits, she hadn't known what to expect from the man. She briefly took the hand he offered while she stood with Sheriff Keller in the hallway outside the interview room where the woman from the motel was being held.

Adam's hand was warm and strong, but he didn't try to intimidate her with his grip. He had warm, attentive brown eyes that looked into hers with an open honesty that she hadn't expected.

He wasn't drop-dead handsome, but he was browned by the sun and had chiseled features that promised quiet strength. He was dressed casually in jeans and a chambray work shirt. His brown hair was long by current standards. Marion knew her father would have approved. Beard stubble lined his strong jaw.

He had the same generous smile that seemed to be the trademark of the Kennedys.

"Marion Hart," Marion said.

Adam dropped his canvas backpack—*A backpack! Not a briefcase!*—on the floor at his feet and took out a small spiral-bound notebook.

"You're with the district attorney's office, Ms. Hart?" Adam asked.

"A.D.A. Hart. And yes, I am."

A smile quirked Adam's lips and revealed dimples in his cheeks. He was a guy who liked to smile a lot. Marion figured he probably told jokes around the water cooler in the courthouse and got by on his father's influence.

"I figured a murder would have brought Turnbull out," Adam said. His manner suggested that he knew exactly what had kept the district attorney home.

"This one is such a slam-dunk that the district attorney didn't see any reason to get out of bed," Marion replied coolly.

Adam smiled bigger and his eyes glinted mischievously. "I meant no offense, A.D.A. Hart."

"None taken."

"Maybe you can point me in the direction of my client."

"Your client," Keller stated evenly, "just put two jailers and a deputy in the hospital. She also attacked A.D.A. Hart."

Some of the humor left Gracelyn's face. "When did this happen?"

"Just a few minutes ago."

Adam glanced at Marion. "Are you all right? Were you hurt?"

"I'm fine." Marion was aware of the swelling at her throat. She was also aware that such a direct question in front of Keller served to discover whether she and the sheriff stood apart or together. Maybe his interest was about her health, but maybe it was to check the solidarity he faced.

"Good. I'm glad to hear it."

Marion noted that Adam didn't try to excuse his client's behavior.

"If you'll allow me." Keller touched Marion's chin and tilted her head up. "You can already see the bruising, Mr. Gracelyn."

Adam peered closely. Marion felt slightly flustered at the intensity of his gaze.

Keller took his hand back from Marion's face. "Your client's already killed one man tonight."

Adam regarded Keller. "That's how you tell it, Sheriff Keller."

"It's what happened."

"I need to talk to my client."

"Sure. I can put an officer—"

"Alone," Adam interrupted. "And in a private room. Not one of those with one-way glass and a speaker system."

Keller hesitated for just a moment, but Marion knew in the end they didn't have any choice.

"All right," the sheriff agreed.

"What name is she booked under?" Adam asked.

"We'll get you the paperwork, Counselor," Keller said as he led the way down the hall. "You enjoy your visit."

Adam stood in front of the door and buzzed with excitement. During the last three years, he'd defended a handful of killers. Three of them had been jilted spouses; two wives and one husband. One had been a father who had fought his teenage son over a pistol while the son was strung out on drugs. The fourth had been a biker in from L.A. who had gotten into a fight with a local at a bar.

Guns had been used in four of the homicides. One of the wives had used a knife. Adam had only been able to get two of the wives off on self-defense due to the injuries they'd received while fighting with their spouses. In each case Adam had been able to substantiate a history of physical abuse on the part of the deceased.

He hadn't been able to get the knife-wielder off. She'd lain in wait for her husband, jumped him at the door and stabbed him thirty-seven times. The only reason she hadn't gotten the death penalty was that no one on the jury could believe the crime was premeditated.

Murder trials were hard.

While Adam waited for Keller to get him inside the room, he casually glanced at Marion Hart. The woman was good-looking. Her face was pretty and…interesting was the only word Adam could come up with. She wore slacks and a good jacket.

She gazed at him with open interest. Adam knew it was because of the case, though. Growing up with his father's money, he knew when women were infatuated with him primarily because of the family estate. Gracelyn money was generations old. It had arrived in the state with the trains and transportation companies. The wealth had stayed on and grew in mining and other local business.

He'd known the district attorney's office had acquired a new recruit, but he hadn't kept track of who it was.

"You sure you want to do this, Counselor?" Keller asked.

Shifting his attention to the sheriff, Adam nodded. Keller pushed the door open and ushered Adam inside.

The room offered featureless four walls covered in white paint. None of them held a window or mirror filled with one-way glass. A small rectangular table sat in the center of the room. Two metal chairs sat on either side.

The woman sat at the table with her head resting on her arms. The ill-fitting jumpsuit couldn't quite disguise her slender curves. The handcuffs and leg irons looked ugly and crude on her wrists and ankles.

"I can put an officer inside here with you," Keller offered.

"No." Adam remained adamant. "Are the restraints—"

"Enough?" Keller looked guileless. "God, I hope so."

"—necessary?" Adam finished.

"They are," Keller said. "I've got one murder on my hands tonight already. I don't intend to add you to the list."

Adam frowned, but he couldn't help being a little concerned. He hadn't often had dealings with hardened criminals, and he didn't much care for the vibe he was getting off the woman at the table.

"Some well-meaning counselor from the public defender's office might drop down and turn an open-and-shut murder investigation into a locked room mystery." Keller smiled. "I'll post an officer at the door. When you're ready to leave, just knock."

So he was going to be locked in. The feeling of unease circulating through Adam's stomach turned cold and cutting.

But he nodded affably. "I'll let you know." Taking command of his own fate, he closed the door and turned back to his client.

After the door closed, Marion looked at Keller. "What do we do now?" she asked.

"We do what ninety percent of this job entails," Keller replied. "We wait." He took in a deep breath of air and let it out. He clearly didn't look happy. "But we'll wait in the all-night diner across the street."

"You're not worried about Gracelyn?" Marion couldn't help thinking how easily the woman had taken the jailers off guard. Adam Gracelyn might be bigger than the woman, but Marion didn't think he'd be prepared for the kind of violence the woman was obviously capable of dealing out.

"I'm not his mom." Keller took the lead.

Marion hesitated just a moment, then hurried to catch up. "I found it interesting that he didn't know the woman's name."

"Me, too," Keller agreed.

"You have to wonder who knew she was here that would know to call Gracelyn."

"Or the public defender's office."

"This late at night? I'll bet you a dinner that the call went straight through to Gracelyn."

Keller grinned at her crookedly. "You're a mighty interesting woman, A.D.A. Hart."

Marion flushed a little at that. "Thank you. I think."

"I meant that as a compliment. But I'll do you one better. The most interesting question in the mix is why anyone would call Gracelyn down here."

Marion thought about that. "On the surface, you'd think that she has a friend in the area who's looking out for her."

"Yeah."

"But there's a possibility that one of Colonel Marker's friends is hoping to even the score for Marker's death."

"I like the way you think, A.D.A. Hart. Twisted. With a touch of mean and conniving. You may have a long career in law enforcement ahead of you."

"So what do we do while we're waiting?"

"We see if we can learn anything more about the woman. We've still got her personal effects. Maybe we'll find something there."

"Miss?" Adam sat his backpack beside the chair on the other side of the table. Deputies had already gone through it looking for weapons or anything that could be used as a weapon.

The woman ignored him.

Adam thought maybe she was asleep, though how anyone could

sleep while chained up was beyond him. He reached across the table.

"Don't touch me." The woman's voice was cold and hard, as if it had been squeezed out between two flat rocks.

Adam withdrew his hand and wondered how she'd known he'd reached for her. She'd never once looked up. "I'm Adam Gracelyn," he told her. "Your attorney. I'm here to help you."

The woman lifted her head and fixed him with a glare. "You're not my attorney."

Adam surveyed the damage done to the woman's face. "Are you all right?"

"I'm fine."

"Did the jailers do this to you?"

She looked at him and lifted an eyebrow. A smile curved her lips. "Yes. But I did it to them first."

The calm in the woman's voice confused Adam. None of the people he'd defended who had been charged with killing someone else had been this quietly controlled so soon after the event.

"You attacked the jailers?" Adam asked. He struggled to keep disbelief from his voice.

"Yes."

"Why?"

The woman held up her hands to show off the handcuffs. "I wanted out of here."

Adam couldn't argue that. "Have you seen a doctor?"

"Tonight?"

"Yes."

The woman smiled. "That was a joke. No, I haven't seen a doctor. The sheriff's people seem to think I'll live."

"That's not their decision. You could be seriously injured." Adam started to get to his feet. "We need to—"

"Stop."

The woman's voice froze Adam in place. Astonishment flooded him as he tried to figure out what she was doing.

"I want to help you," he said.

"Then help me. Get me out of here."

"That may not be possible. They're saying you killed a man."

"I did." The woman's voice held no regret or any other kind of emotion.

Adam glanced at the hurried notes he'd taken about the case. There hadn't been many. The man who had called him at home had talked quickly and kept the conversation short.

"You killed Colonel Marker?" Adam asked.

The woman feigned a look of innocence. "Was that the man in the motel?"

Adam thought about not replying so he wouldn't fall into whatever game she had going on. "It was."

"Then yes, I did kill the man in the motel."

"Why?"

The woman wiped blood from the corner of her mouth with a knuckle. She wiped the knuckle on the jumpsuit. "Does it make a difference?"

"If you were fighting for your life—"

"If I'd let him know I was coming," the woman said, "he'd have killed me without breaking a sweat." She paused and wiped the blood from her mouth again. "Maybe. I'm a lot better than he remembers me being."

"Better at what?"

The woman grinned. "You were a Boy Scout, weren't you?"

Adam's cheeks flamed briefly, but he pushed the discomfort away. "Miss—" He waited for her to supply a name.

She didn't.

"You're in here on serious charges," Adam said.

She lifted her manacled hands and dropped them to the tabletop. "I figured that out when they equipped me with all the accessories."

For a moment, Adam just studied her. He'd seen men who'd come back from the Vietnam War who acted as cold and callous as the woman in front of him. The L.A. biker had been like that, but he was still using drugs. After he'd started detoxing in jail the man's composure had changed drastically, for the worse.

"I don't know your name," Adam admitted.

"Do you have a favorite?" She looked at him with sweet innocence, but the expression played falsely due to the blood on her face and the swollen jaw.

"I want to help you," Adam said.

"You'd help a murderer? A woman who shot a man in cold blood while he was asleep in his rented bed?" The woman shook her head. "You *are* a Boy Scout."

"You're going to be charged and arraigned," Adam said. "I need to prepare—"

"How did you get here, Boy Scout?" the woman asked.

Adam paused. He wasn't certain how much he should reveal.

"A man called you, didn't he?" the woman asked. "A man whose voice you didn't recognize and probably won't hear again in your lifetime."

The caller had possessed a strange voice that Adam hadn't known. The message had been brief and to the point. A woman accused of murder was locked down at the Maricopa County Jail and he should check it out. There had been enough mystery to get Adam up from bed to make a phone call.

"Do you get many calls like that, Boy Scout?" the woman asked.

"No," Adam replied. "And I think it would be better if you wouldn't call me—"

"What I call you isn't going to matter. Neither are your intentions. No matter how good or noble." The woman regarded him with those beautiful eyes. "If I don't get out of here—soon—I'm going to be dead. If you stand too close to me, you'll be dead, too. Someone calling you tells me that they know where I am."

"Who's 'they'?" Adam asked.

The woman shook her head. "Believe me. It's better if you don't know."

Marion stared at the small pile of personal effects on the diner table. They were all the woman had possessed when she'd been taken into custody.

There wasn't much: change, a Zippo lighter—but no cigarettes, a lipstick that matched the color the woman was wearing, a small bottle of perfume, a box of tissues, two ink pens—neither with names of businesses on them, two thousand three hundred eighty-seven dollars in cash, and a ring with two keys that didn't have any markings.

"I can't believe she didn't have any identification," Marion said as she sorted through the items one last time.

"I can." Keller ran a weather-roughened hand over his stubbled jaw. "She deliberately left out anything we could use to identify her. Driver's license. Receipts. Anything that might tie her to anyplace other than the Kellogg Motel."

The casual conversation of a half-dozen diner guests, a radio in the corner playing country and western songs, the sizzle of the flat grill and passing traffic threaded through the diner. A slight chill clung to the window beside Marion. The clock behind the counter clicked over to 4:38 a.m. The city was already starting to rouse to start another day.

After a moment, Marion said, "She did leave us with one thing that ties her to a past."

"What?"

"Colonel Thomas Marker. She hated him enough to kill him like that. If we look through his past long enough, I'll bet the woman turns up somewhere."

Keller smiled. "You're a smart cookie, aren't you?"

"I read a lot of Nancy Drew mysteries growing up," Marion said. She'd always liked the independence Nancy Drew had exhibited. No one had thought of the books as being so feminist until Nancy and her friends had influenced generations.

"Just remember one thing, Counselor," Keller said.

"What?"

"Nancy didn't get her pretty little nose blown off while snooping around in places she didn't belong. Those books had neat, tidy and happy endings. Real life tends to be messier."

"I'll keep that in mind." Movement out in the parking lot in front of the diner caught Marion's attention. She recognized some of the people in the small group headed for the diner.

Keller cursed and drained his coffee. "Okay, that's the press. Evidently they've finished up with the latest reports at the emergency room. They're coming for fresh blood now. Somebody ratted us out."

Marion got up and left money on the table before Keller could get his hand out of his pocket. "My treat," she said.

Keller seemed caught off guard. "I'm not in the habit of having women pay for my coffee."

"It won't be a habit. Now do you want to go or do you want to hang around and answer questions?"

"Well, since you put it that way." Keller hitched up his gunbelt and led the way out the diner's back entry as the first of the reporters reached the front door.

* * *

Marion was working on her notes when Adam Gracelyn knocked on Sheriff Keller's borrowed office. She looked up and automatically closed her notebook.

"Sheriff?" Adam said.

Keller waved Adam in as he folded the newspaper. The headline screamed information about Robert F. Kennedy's bid for presidential nomination. "Something I can do for you?" Keller asked.

"I want my client taken to the hospital for treatment," Adam said.

Keller's swivel chair squeaked in protest as he leaned back. "Why?"

Adam grimaced in disbelief. "Because she's injured."

"She's well enough to stay here."

"Are you an authority on internal injuries?" Adam demanded.

"I know a life-threatening injury when I see one," Keller countered.

"She needs medical attention." Adam spoke calmly, but there was a definite note of authority.

From the set of Keller's jaw, Marion knew the sheriff was going to fight the request. She spoke quickly before the argument could start.

"I think getting medical treatment is a good idea," Marion said.

Both men looked at her in surprise.

"The D.A.'s office doesn't want to face culpability in a wrongful death suit," Marion said. "She's in our care. Let's make certain that she's taken care of." She faced Adam. "Mr. Gracelyn, tell your client that we'll be transporting her in—" She looked at Keller.

"Fifteen minutes," Keller grudgingly allowed.

Adam nodded. "Fifteen minutes then." He looked at Marion and smiled, but this time it wasn't in triumph. The expression offered genuine thanks. He turned and left.

After Adam had gone, Keller turned to Marion. "Do you want to tell me what that was about?"

"That," Marion said, "was about getting more information about our suspect."

Keller cocked an eyebrow.

"We get to be privy to her treatment," Marion explained. "Whatever Adam Gracelyn finds out, we get to find out, too."

Understanding dawned on Keller's hard face. "You're thinking a doctor is going to be able to tell us more about her."

"If we get an experienced doctor," Marion said, "maybe we can get a better idea of where all those scars came from. I'm hoping there may be other factors I haven't thought of that may give us more clues about her past."

"You've got a real devious streak, you know that?"

Marion smiled. "Not yet. But I'm working on one."

Chapter 8

Southern Oaks Medical Center
Downtown Phoenix, Arizona
Thursday, May 16, 1968
The Past

Adam glanced at his watch. It was almost 7:00 a.m. Sheriff Keller had been as good as his word. The woman had been escorted out of the Maricopa County Jail fifteen minutes after Keller had told Adam she would be. She'd been placed in the back of a cruiser, still manacled at wrists and ankles and driven to the hospital.

As they sat in the waiting room, drawing curious stares from the other people there, Adam was beginning to think Marion Hart had pulled a fast one on him. The A.D.A. had agreed to the hospital visit far too easily. He sat across from his client, who was seated between two burly deputies who looked nervous about the job they'd been assigned.

The woman sat in a corner of the waiting room. Her manacled wrists sat in her lap, but she self-consciously clung to the coat she'd been given to hide the handcuffs. She had her head leaned back against the wall and seemed to be asleep.

Adam couldn't believe she was taking everything so calmly. *She must have ice water in her veins.* He was tense and nervous himself. The gravelly voice on the phone kept haunting him.

As he sat in the waiting room, he realized how open the area was and how unprotected they were. Then he realized he was talking about *they.*

If you stand too close to me, you'll be dead, too. The woman's words kept cycling through his thoughts. Sheriff Keller had stepped outside, probably to smoke, but Adam wished the sheriff had stayed nearby. Somewhere in the E.R., the men and women injured by his new and mysterious client were undergoing treatment. It was a sobering realization.

Nervous energy thrummed through Adam. He glanced across the room and saw Marion Hart working diligently with a legal pad resting on her crossed thighs. Curiosity dawned in Adam. He wondered what she was working on, and he wondered what she knew that he didn't know. Because he had a hunch that she was already preparing her offense.

He studied the way her hair fell across her shoulders and framed her face. She was pretty. He knew that, but he wondered if she knew that.

She's standing too close, too. The thought nudged Adam's casual thoughts aside. He also got the distinct feeling he was being watched. He turned back to his client. The woman watched him through slitted eyes.

When they made eye contact, she turned away from him. A half smile curved her lips.

Feeling awkward, Adam shook his foam cup and found only the dregs of his coffee remained. He didn't particularly care for coffee, but it helped keep him awake. He'd stayed up far too late last night, and had attended the same public event that District Attorney Turnbull had attended.

Although he didn't really want it, Adam decided he needed more coffee. Last night's event had lasted until the small hours, and he never quit on the night life early. He stood and slung his backpack over one shoulder.

The two deputies Keller had stationed in the room watched him. The female jailer escorting his client watched Adam as well.

Adam approached the nurses' station.

The young, petite nurse working the desk looked up at him. She was in her early twenties, all big blond hair and blue eyes. Her white nurse's uniform fit her like a glove and emphasized her feminine curves.

"Mr. Gracelyn," she greeted.

The fact that she knew him didn't surprise Adam. He and his family had received a lot of attention from the press over the years. He was something of a celebrity in the Phoenix area.

Then why call me? Adam couldn't help wondering. But he wasn't thinking about the nurse. He was thinking about the man who'd called him and told him about the woman being held in the county jail. For the first time he realized the unknown man had chosen him for a reason. But what was that reason?

"Is there something I can do for you?" the nurse asked. Her name tag read Becky Elliott, R.N.

Adam held up the cup. "Coffee, if I could."

"Of course. How would you like it, Mr. Gracelyn?" The demure question was loaded with double entendre.

A grin spread across Adam's face. He liked the attention from young women. Being something of a celebrity had its perks.

"Call me Adam." The correction was immediate. He'd been doing it all his adult life. "Mr. Gracelyn is my father."

"Sure, Adam. How do you take your coffee?" The nurse had an inviting smile filled with promise.

"Three creams, three sugars."

"Do you take a little coffee in your cream and sugar? Is that how it is?"

Adam smiled back. "I do."

"I prefer hot chocolate with whipped cream when I can get it." The nurse plucked the cup from his hand and walked to the rear of the nurses' station. Her skirt swished from side to side.

Adam couldn't help watching, but he wasn't as distracted or as interested as he might have been at another time. He turned and looked around the room. A.D.A. Marion Hart was watching him.

Now that was interesting. And it was also irritating. Was he going to get caught by every woman in the room while he was looking at other women?

He expected Marion to glance away. She didn't. Her eyes remained focused on him. She put her legal pad back into her brief-case and stood. Picking up her briefcase, she approached the nurses' station with her cup in hand.

Adam moved aside. He detected a green apple-scented herbal shampoo on her hair.

"How are you doing?" Adam asked.

Marion turned to face him. "I'm fine. How are you doing, Mr. Gracelyn?"

"Call me—"

Marion cut him off. "Mr. Gracelyn will do. Unless you'd prefer to be called Counselor Gracelyn."

Wryly Adam shook his head. "Mr. will do. And I'm fine."

He thought about what his client had told him about the pos-sibility of people coming after her, leaving no doubt about what kind of people she meant. Marion Hart was in harm's way. By not telling her about the possibility of danger, was he responsible if anything happened?

Of course, he owed his client some reticence, and there was the chance that the woman was lying. She wouldn't have been the first client to lie to him since he'd started working in the public defender's office.

"Do you have any other deputies around the hospital?" Adam asked.

Interest flickered in those intelligent brown eyes. "That's an interesting question, Mr. Gracelyn. Why would you ask?"

Adam shrugged. "Colonel Thomas Marker was a popular guy. The men he hung around with are out of Vietnam. Some people say the guys fresh out of the bush aren't exactly civilized."

"Do you think Colonel Marker's friends might try to kill your client?"

"Given the severity of the crime she's been accused of, I think I'd have to entertain that notion."

"You would?" Marion arched one slim brow.

"I would."

Becky Elliott returned with Adam's coffee. The nurse wasn't quite as friendly about getting Marion a refill.

"Why would you do that, Mr. Gracelyn?" Marion asked.

"To be prepared."

"I see." Marion accepted the cup from the nurse. "How did you find out she had been taken into custody?"

"I was called."

"By whom?"

"I didn't take down the caller's name." Adam sipped his coffee and met Marion's gaze. As he looked at her, he realized that a lot of men would underestimate how intelligent she was. It was a factor that would stand her in good stead. *And she could trip you up with it.*

"Interesting," Marion replied.

"I was told there were a number of journalists out at the motel."

"There were. Was your caller one of them?"

"I don't know."

Marion sipped the coffee and looked at him over the cup. "You were called at home?"

Adam saw no reason not to give the answer. "Yes. I'd attended the party last night, the one Geoffrey Turnbull was at."

"I was there, too. I didn't see you."

"You could ask around. A number of people saw me."

"I will."

Irritated, Adam stared at her. Surely Marion didn't think he was part of whatever was going on. Then again, he'd appeared at the county jail as mysteriously as the woman had. A warning tingle thrummed through his body as he gave brief consideration to the possibility he'd been set up.

"Is your home phone number listed?" Marion asked.

Adam grinned in surprise. But he also immediately felt on safer ground. "Why no, A.D.A. Hart. It isn't. Would you like that number?"

"If I need it," Marion stated quietly, "I'm sure I can get it. However, I have to admit I'm puzzled."

Adam was, too. He'd had so many women ask after his number, in canny ways, that he'd felt certain that was what Marion was after.

"If the person who called you was one of the journalists at the Kellogg Motel," Marion continued, "I'd have to wonder how he got your home number."

Adam didn't say anything. But he'd wondered the same thing.

"I have a few friends who work for the newspapers and local television news stations."

"Then the list of names for the one you…*forgot* should be a short one."

"If it becomes important, I might be able to remember it."

"If it becomes important, Mr. Gracelyn, I'll let you know." Without another word, Marion left him there and returned to her seat.

Adam watched her walk away. He appreciated the tight roll of her hips beneath the slacks. Most men he knew didn't care for pants on a woman, but he did. He'd found any number of women looked more seductive in them.

He got the feeling that he was being watched again. Glancing back at his client, he saw that she had caught him staring at Marion, again. She smiled knowingly, then leaned her head back and closed her eyes again. To look at her, anyone would have thought she was totally relaxed and in control. It was almost unnerving.

"You're infatuated with her."

Adam frowned. He was uncomfortable in the examination room to begin with. His client sat on the table barely clad in a gown that failed to cover one smoothly rounded hip. She didn't have a tan line, and that brought up images of the rest of her body that Adam wasn't comfortable with, either.

"No, I'm not," Adam said.

"I saw you watching her. I saw the look in your eyes. You're infatuated."

"Who's he infatuated with?" Dr. Alan Bernhardt asked. He stood in front of the woman and ran his fingers over her head under her hair. Bernhardt was in his late forties, a thin man with salt-and-pepper hair, black horn-rimmed glasses and a starched white lab coat.

A doughty Hispanic nurse stood at the doctor's side.

The proximity of the doctor to the woman bothered Adam. If she was as skilled at physical encounters as Marion and Keller had intimated, Bernhardt was in danger throughout the whole examination. The large female jailer lounged against the room's only door, though, and three uniformed deputies waited in the hallway outside.

Keller had been adamant in his orders to use whatever force

was necessary to subdue the woman if it came to an altercation. The sheriff had warned the woman as well, but she hadn't looked impressed.

"He's interested in the assistant district attorney that wants to put me on trial for murder," the woman said.

"Murder?" Bernhardt gripped the woman's chin and explored her abrasions and bruises.

The woman looked at the doctor with wide-eyed innocence. "Can you believe it?"

"Of you?" Bernhardt shook his head. "Of course not. So your young lawyer is attracted to the assistant district attorney?"

"Yes. You should see him watch her." Even facing murder charges, the woman seemed to enjoy Adam's discomfort. "It's shameful."

"Sounds like something out of *Peyton Place,*" Bernhardt said.

"What's that?"

"An evening soap opera. It's filled with all kinds of stories like this. People having affairs. Secret babies. All of that. The missus loves it. The show just went to color a couple years ago. She loves it even more now. Personally I prefer stories about nubile young—"

"*Doctor!*" the nurse admonished.

"My tastes are different from the missus," Bernhardt said. "I like science fiction. Those short skirts and scanty outfits on the women in *Star Trek* really—"

"*Doctor!*" the nurse interrupted in a more strident voice.

The woman spoke in rapid-fire Spanish. The nurse responded, then broke out into raucous laughter. The prisoner joined her.

Adam didn't understand a word of the exchange. He'd always meant to take a course in Spanish.

Bernhardt took a tongue depressor from a jar on the nearby shelf. "Open your mouth, dear."

The woman did.

Stooping, once more within reach, Bernhardt peered into the woman's mouth. "I see signs of lingual gum bruising on the upper and lower right quadrant."

"I got hit," the woman said.

"Yes, you did. Quite hard, in fact. There's nothing here that requires any treatment on my part, but I would recommend a salt-water rinse three or four times a day. To promote healing." Bernhardt glanced at Adam.

Adam nodded.

The physician continued his examination. Severe bruising along the right side of the woman's face made his list, along with several other bumps and abrasions. In the end, Bernhardt gave her a clean bill of health and asked for blood and urine samples.

"Why do you want those?" Adam asked.

"I want to make certain there aren't any internal injuries," Bernhardt said.

"You could X-ray her."

"I don't see anything here that would necessitate X-rays. The blood is to make sure she's not carrying a disease that we should know about. She did put a handful of people in the emergency room tonight." Bernhardt toyed with his stethoscope. "Furthermore, X-rays won't tell us much about soft tissue. The blood and the urine analysis should take care of that."

"So we don't know who called Gracelyn?"

"He won't say," Marion replied. She stood out in the hallway where the uniformed deputies stood guard over the examination room that contained the prisoner.

"Interesting." District Attorney Geoffrey Turnbull looked thoughtful. He usually did. The fact that it was 7:30 a.m. and he had a hangover from the night before didn't blunt that. He had one of the keenest, most insightful minds Marion had ever seen.

At fifty-three, he was five feet ten inches tall and looked great in a suit up in front of a jury. He carried just enough extra weight to look down home to rural residents summoned to jury duty. His brown hair was cut short and neat but was going gray at the temples. He held a pair of reading glasses in one hand and his ever-present "warbook," as he called it, in his other. He wore a gray suit today. He saved his black ones for court.

"The woman isn't local?" Turnbull asked.

"We don't think so."

"But we don't know."

"No, sir."

"Not 'sir,' dammit," Turnbull instructed. "You're a member of this office. Not an employee. Act like that and people are going to walk all over you."

Marion nodded. Turnbull had known the risks he was incurring by hiring a female assistant district attorney. He'd told her from the beginning that she couldn't act like a second-class citizen. She wasn't a woman in a man's world. She was an equal player. And, he'd pointed out, she was the first one who was going to have to believe that.

Turnbull was a good man. Marion's father had told her that. Michael Hart and Geoffrey Turnbull had gone to school together, then—for a time—college. They still maintained a friendship, and Marion knew that had a little to do with her appointment.

"We need to find out," Turnbull said.

"Because knowing if the woman's known around here will tell us who might have called Adam. Gracelyn." Marion made the quick correction, but she was certain that Turnbull—even though he was nursing a hangover—hadn't missed the slip.

"'Adam' is it?" Turnbull looked at Marion suspiciously.

"Calling him Mr. Gracelyn makes me think of his father." The excuse sounded weak even in Marion's ears.

After a moment, Turnbull nodded. "See if you can call in favors from the press. God knows they owe us a few after the stories I've given them since I've been in office."

Marion nodded. "You think a reporter phoned the public defender's office?"

"No, I don't. And whoever it was didn't call the public defender's office. He—or she—called *Adam*."

Marion ignored the jibe.

"If it was a reporter who made that call, they'd have filed a story on it first."

That was probably true.

"Do you really expect the press to figure out who made the call?" Marion asked.

"No. But they can distract *Adam* with their questions and put pressure on whoever did make that call." Turnbull opened his journal and consulted notes he'd made. "And if the call was made from someone from out of town, journalists might have a better chance than the sheriff's office. God knows the D.A.'s office doesn't have the manpower to go chasing after him. Or them."

"'Them?'"

"We live in an age of conspiracies. Something like this?" Turnbull shook his head. "I'd definitely look past the surface and dig a little deeper. Besides that, *I* got a call."

Marion waited.

"Agent Tarlton of the Federal Bureau of Investigation called me to request an interview with our suspect."

"Why?"

"He wasn't forthcoming."

"It might not be about the woman," Marion said.

Turnbull looked at her.

"Suppose it's about Marker," Marion said.

"Marker's dead."

"But what if he was holding something that the FBI finds interesting?"

Turnbull sipped a breath. "Have we released that motel room?"

"No."

"Don't. Have Blake get an investigative team in to toss the place. Somebody that knows what they're doing."

Marion took out a notepad and jotted that down. Blake Anderson was the D.A.'s chief investigator. If there was anything in that room worth finding, he or his people would find it.

"The sooner the better," Turnbull said.

"I'll make the call." Marion looked up as Turnbull started to walk away. "There's one other thing."

Turnbull stopped and sipped his coffee.

"Where did the FBI call you?" Marion asked.

"At home."

"You're not listed." Marion knew Turnbull zealously guarded his private number. Only his immediate staff had it. "How did the FBI get your number?"

Turnbull raised his eyebrows. "You know J. Edgar Hoover's boys. They investigate everybody. They know everything. Tread carefully, Marion. Call me if you need me." He tossed her a wave and departed.

Questions flooded Marion's mind. She'd been suspicious before of the woman's confidence. The interest being shown by the FBI was even more intriguing. What the hell was going on?

Chapter 9

Southern Oaks Medical Center
Downtown Phoenix, Arizona
Thursday, May 16, 1968
The Past

A few minutes later, the door opened down the hall and Marion watched as the female jailer led the handcuffed woman out. Adam Gracelyn fell in beside her. Even dressed in the jail jumper, the woman looked like a sinuous and sexual creature. It was a heady mixture of danger and eroticism.

The woman locked eyes with Marion for a moment, then stumbled as if she'd tripped over the leg chains. Adam reached out at once and caught her by the elbow to steady her. A mocking grin spread across the woman's face as she thanked Adam.

Adam talked to the woman soothingly. He continued to hold on to her elbow to aid her.

You're an idiot, Marion thought at Adam. She stepped aside and let them pass.

"Aren't you coming back to the jail?" Adam asked.

"I'll be there in a little while," Marion said. Her voice came out harder than she'd intended. As she watched, the woman leaned more heavily into Adam. He responded by taking more of her weight. They continued on.

Keller passed them in the hallway and joined Marion. "Full service attorney," the sheriff commented as the entourage disappeared around the corner.

"Looks like," Marion responded more sharply than she'd intended.

Keller glanced at her with a puzzled look. Marion guessed that he was puzzled by the venom in her tone. She hadn't been able to completely mask that.

"He's a fool," she said. "Falling for that helpless act."

"Well," Keller said, "he didn't see that woman in action. She looks different handcuffed."

"Oh, I'm sure he's imagined her in action." The thought left Marion feeling more unsettled than she had any right to feel. She didn't know where her irritation was coming from. She tried to push it from her mind. "At least he has deputies there to protect him."

"Yeah," Keller agreed. But his answer was short and direct, as if he were hesitant about saying anything that might be misconstrued.

"Turnbull said the FBI wants to talk to our suspect."

"That's what I heard. I got called by a guy named Tarlton. He called the nurses' station and had me paged. Same guy?"

"Yes."

Keller grunted and ran a hand through his hair. "Makes me curious."

"Me, too."

"Let's go see what Doc Bernhardt had to say."

Bernhardt conducted Marion and Keller to his private office at the hospital. He motioned them to chairs in front of the immaculate desk and slipped out of his lab coat.

"That woman is an interesting mix," Bernhardt said. "I'd say she hasn't been in the United States lately, and maybe not for a long time." He sat on the other side of the desk.

His nurse took at seat at the side of the desk.

"Why do you think that?" Marion asked.

"Well, she didn't know what *Peyton Place* is for one." Bernhardt slipped on a pair of reading glasses as he wrote in a file.

"That's not very conclusive," Marion said.

Bernhardt looked at Marion over his glasses. A faint smile pulled at his lips.

"Young lady—"

"A.D.A. Hart," Keller interrupted.

Bernhardt nodded in acquiescence. "A.D.A. Hart, nobody who lives in the United States these days doesn't know what *Peyton Place* is."

"The show's only a few years old—"

"It started in 1964. The novel came out in 1957. And it was hard not to know about the book. It was mentioned everywhere."

"—so she could have been away for a while," Marion finished.

"She's also had extensive dental work done. All of it appears to be Eastern European," Bernhardt said. "They still use a lot more gold than we do over here."

"How do you know that?"

"Doc Bernhardt was a medical corpsman in World War II," Keller said. "He also worked with the OSS in the same capacity."

It took Marion a moment to remember that the OSS was actually the Office of Strategic Services. After the war, the agency underwent a few permutations and became the Central Intelligence Agency in 1947.

"Point of fact," Keller continued, "Doc Bernhardt was with the X-2 branch of the OSS. That bunch hunted Axis agents. They got to know a lot about German and Eastern European work, dental and medical. He continued in the same capacity for the CIA for a while after getting his medical degree."

Marion was impressed. Keller had called in a favor to get Bernhardt to the hospital.

"Counselor Gracelyn doesn't know about your history, does he?" Marion asked the physician.

"Few people do," Bernhardt answered.

"Doctor enjoys acting like a schmuck in front of people," the nurse said. "He outdid himself this morning. He did his Andy Griffith shtick today."

From his chair, Bernhardt executed a half bow. "Thank you."

Keller grinned a little and winked at Marion. "You had a good idea. I just went you one better." He turned back to Bernhardt. "Okay, so she's had Eastern dental work. What else do you have?"

"Judging from the dental work that was done, I'd say your mystery lady has led a rather eventful life. Even without the bullet and knife scars. Her teeth were broken, not decayed. The work that was done is first-rate. Not cheap."

Keller was taking notes, which jump-started Marion to do the same.

"So she has money," Keller said.

"Has had. At least enough to fix her teeth. And she cares about how she looks. That's always good to know about someone with whom you may have to deal harshly." Bernhardt kept writing in his book.

Marion suddenly realized the physician was writing down his notes as he spoke. "You didn't keep notes while you were conducting the examination?" she asked.

"That, A.D.A. Hart, would have tipped off your suspect, would it not?"

Marion conceded the point.

"I've been around an interrogation or two."

"But if I had to put you on the stand as a witness—"

"I'd still be able to identify the scars and dental work if you showed me pictures of them. More than that, I've got a very good memory. The OSS trained us for the field. We often didn't have the luxury of field case reports."

"All right."

Bernhardt returned his attention to his notes. "Her hands display an inordinate amount of calluses. I'd say she's trained in martial arts for several years, based on the observations I've made of Japanese soldiers I interviewed during and after the war. Some of the Navy demolitions teams attached to the OSS had similar training for close-quarter killing."

Marion's curiosity grew geometrically as she wrote.

"This woman has been wounded on several occasions," Bernhardt continued. "She's been stabbed at least four different times, based on the age of the scars I observed, and shot twice. She also speaks Spanish fluently."

"You speak Spanish?" Marion asked.

"Francisca does." Bernhardt leveled a finger at the nurse.

"Very good," Francisca said. "Almost like a native."

"You suspected she spoke Spanish?" Marion was even more impressed.

"No." Bernhardt frowned. "We got lucky on that. Your suspect was showing off for Francisca."

"She was not very complimentary to Doctor," Francisca agreed. "In her place, I wouldn't have been, either. He didn't seem very professional."

"Thanks for the vote of confidence." Bernhardt looked at Marion and Keller. "I trust that helps."

"Yeah." Keller wiped his face with a big hand. "She's just gotten more mysterious."

Marion silently agreed.

"I still have a few other tests I can run here based on her blood and urine samples," Bernhardt offered. "I assume you'll want to know whatever I can find out?"

"Yeah." Keller got to his feet.

"About this conversation," Marion said.

Glancing at her, Bernhardt smiled. "What conversation?"

"Exactly." Marion offered her hand.

Bernhardt stood and took it. "Keller told me it was your idea to bring that woman here."

"It was."

"Bright girl," Bernhardt said.

Marion bridled a little at the word "girl," but she was certain Bernhardt didn't mean any offense.

"Thank you," she said.

"I want to talk to the sheriff and the assistant district attorney."

Seated once more across the table from his client, Adam couldn't believe what he was hearing. "We need to think about this."

The woman looked bored.

"As your attorney, I don't think talking to them is in your best interests," Adam said.

"If I choose not to talk to them, what will happen to me?"

"They'll get upset."

The woman leaned across the desk and stared intently into Adam's eyes. Her gaze was deep and thrilling, almost like staring into an abyss. He was at once reminded of the Friedrich Nietzsche quote: *If you stare into the Abyss long enough the Abyss stares back at you.*

Adam had always thought the German philosopher was talking about the dark side of life. There was plenty of human misery in the world. The current war in Vietnam was just another example of that.

Wherever the woman had been in her life, she'd seen a lot of darkness and death. Adam was convinced of that. *If you had any sense, you'd hand this off to someone else.*

But he knew he wouldn't do that. He'd never been one to walk away from anything.

"And when they get upset," the woman said in an eerily calm voice, "what will they do then?"

"Probably put you in jail."

"Can you keep me from jail?"

Adam shook his head. "No. When they're ready to put you into a cell, they're going to put you there."

The woman leaned back in her chair. "I don't care to be locked up in one of those small rooms. I've had enough of places like that."

"You've been incarcerated before?" Somehow it was more surprising that she would tell him something about herself than the fact that she had been locked up.

"I don't want to talk about that."

"The question may come up if you talk to Keller and Marion."

The woman cocked an eyebrow. "'Marion?'"

"A.D.A. Hart," Adam said. He regretted the slip immediately and blamed it on lack of sleep.

"So," the woman said, "did you call her 'Marion' because you see her as a beautiful woman? Or because you want to strip her position from her?"

"I called her Marion because it's her name. I tend to think of most women by their first names. If I knew yours, I'd use it to address you."

"Somehow, I don't think so. I don't think you feel toward me what you feel about…A.D.A. Hart."

"I don't know you."

"You," the woman said deliberately, "don't know A.D.A. Hart, either. She'll play you if she gets the chance."

Anger rose inside Adam. He wondered how the hell the conversation had suddenly become about him. "Talking with them is a mistake."

The woman didn't say anything for a moment. "If you ignore what I ask, I'm going to change attorneys."

For a moment, Adam almost told her to go ahead and get it done. But he didn't. Instead he nodded.

"She's interested in talking to us?" Marion sat at a desk in the office Keller had borrowed.

Keller stood at the window. He rested a haunch on the sill. Both of them were awaiting the arrival of the FBI agent, Tarlton.

"Yes." In the cold, thin light that blared through the window, Adam looked worn and haggard.

"Why?" Keller asked.

"You wanted to interview her."

Marion swapped looks with Keller. Neither of them had expected this.

"You authorized this?" Marion asked.

"I—" Adam hesitated. "I don't have a choice."

"What do you mean?"

"If I don't tell you this, she's going to ask that another attorney be provided for her."

"That might not be such a bad deal for you, Counselor," Keller said. "We've got your client dead to right with, literally, a smoking gun in her hand."

"There may be extenuating circumstances."

"None that will condone cold-blooded murder," Marion stated.

"Perhaps we'll let a jury think about that."

Keller shook his head. "You're a smart attorney, Gracelyn. You know you're not going to walk away from this thing clean."

Adam was quiet for a moment. Marion almost felt sorry for him, then. She saw that Adam recognized the truth of Keller's words. But she also saw a grim resolve inside the man that surprised and intrigued her.

"I can't leave her," Adam said.

"Because she played the wounded dove for you?" Marion couldn't resist asking. Although she respected Adam, part of her—a part she didn't quite understand—was still angry with him.

"Because I'm the best she's going to get when it comes to a defense attorney." Adam faced Marion squarely. "No matter what you do, A.D.A. Hart, I'm going to save that woman's life. I don't believe in capital punishment." He gazed at Keller. "Whenever you'd like to talk to her, she'll be ready.". He turned and strode from the room.

Marion leaned back in her chair. "He's right, you know."

"About what?" Keller asked.

"He's the best attorney she's going to get. The rest of the people in the public defender's office would put up a good fight, but they won't push a court case to the same limits that Adam Gracelyn will."

Keller folded his arms over his chest. "Maybe so. Do we need to talk to her?"

"I don't think she's going to tell us anything. On the other hand, since she's able to subvert her attorney's wishes, it might be interesting to see what she has up her sleeve."

"I'm game," Keller agreed.

In the end, the woman wasted two hours of Marion's morning. She felt certain she'd have been better served returning to her apartment and getting a couple hours of sleep before she filed all the motions to get the case before a judge.

The woman maintained that she went to the motel at Colonel Marker's request. She maintained that she had, upon occasion, worked for the colonel, though she declined to comment on what capacity. She couldn't tell them anything about her work for Colonel Marker without a clearance on the national level.

She didn't explain that, either, but it triggered thoughts of the FBI agent coming to see her.

According to the woman, Colonel Marker had been drunk. That had been borne out by the number of liquor bottles in the colonel's room. During their meeting, Marker had tried to pull her into his bed. She had resisted. Marker had gotten more forceful. In the end, certain she was fighting for her life against the man, she'd grabbed his pistol and shot him with it.

The story, Marion knew, was good enough to fit all the facts. She also didn't believe a single word of it. But it was possible that a jury would. Juries were strange animals that often acted in ways an attorney didn't anticipate. That was why no one at the district attorney's office or the public defender's office relished the idea of going to trial.

"You'd think that Colonel Marker would have released you after the first time you shot him in the face," Marion said.

The woman shrugged. "Perhaps he did." She touched the side of her face where the bruising was more pronounced now that additional time had passed. Her eye was partially swollen shut and her face was puffy. "I was pretty much out on my feet. I don't remember."

That part of the story held up, too. The officer who had arrived on the scene had stated in his report that the woman had appeared under the influence of drugs or alcohol. Since neither of those were likely to show up in her blood, that left only disorientation from the blow she'd suffered. And they all agreed that Marker had hit her.

"You emptied that pistol into a man's face," Marion said.

"I don't remember doing that." The woman looked guileless.

Marion looked at her notes. She hadn't gotten the answers to most of the questions she'd asked. The problem was that she couldn't break the story the woman was telling.

"What's your name?" Marion asked again. She kept returning to that one.

"I can't tell you."

"Why?"

"It's a matter of national security."

The first time Marion had heard that, she'd experienced a small tingle. The FBI agent's interest underscored that.

"Asked and answered," Adam pointed out from across the room. He stood next to the wall. It was telling that he didn't feel comfortable sitting next to his client.

"Asked but not answered," Marion rebutted. "Your client is being deliberately evasive, Counselor."

"She's bound by national security."

Marion rolled her eyes in exasperation. "Do you really believe that?"

"That's not relevant."

"Of course it isn't." Frustration chafed at Marion. She pinned the woman with a steely gaze. "I don't believe a word you've told me. Except about shooting Colonel Marker. I believe that just fine."

The woman didn't say anything. She picked up the foam water cup in front of her with both hands. The handcuff links rattled against the tabletop. She took a long sip.

Marion was getting tired of the woman's cool demeanor, too. No one should be that calm under the circumstances.

Someone knocked on the door. Keller answered it, spoke briefly, then turned back to Marion. "The FBI agent is here."

"Whoa!" Adam said, coming off the back wall and holding up his arms. "Time out. Nobody said anything about the FBI being involved in this."

"It's not our choice, Counselor," Marion said.

"What's he doing here?"

"I intend to ask him that. Maybe you'd like to help."

Adam nodded.

"When you two decide that you're going to stop playing games," the woman said, "tell the…*FBI* agent I'll be happy to speak to him."

Marion didn't say anything, but she was thinking this case was getting more unpredictable by the second.

Chapter 10

Maricopa County Jail
Phoenix, Arizona
Thursday, May 16, 1968
The Past

Marion examined Federal Bureau of Investigation Special Agent Bruce Tarlton's identification one last time, then handed it back to the man. Everything checked out. At least, it checked out as far as she knew. She'd never seen an FBI agent's identification before. She took her lead from Keller, who seemed satisfied.

Tarlton was six-one, slim and powerfully built. He was in his early thirties. His blond hair was cut short and so pale it stood out sharply against his tanned skin. He was darker than Marion would have guessed a desk type to be. His prominent cleft chin looked like something out of the Sunday *Dick Tracy* strip. His suit was immaculate.

"May I see her?" Tarlton asked as he accepted his identification back.

"Why is the Bureau interested in her?" Marion asked.

Tarlton's voice never changed inflection. He spoke in a monotone. "That's our business, Ms. Hart. I'm afraid I'm not at liberty to go into that."

Nobody's at liberty, Marion thought angrily. "We're conducting a murder investigation here, Special Agent Tarlton. If that somehow falls under the Bureau's purview, I need to know how."

Keller had a hip lodged against the desk in their borrowed office. He didn't look happy, either.

"I'm here to see your prisoner on a matter of national security," Tarlton said.

"Seems to me that's a blanket that the federal government likes to trot out a lot these days," Keller said.

"We live in dangerous times, Sheriff Keller. The Communists are getting stronger. Fidel Castro's just a few hours away from our coastline. Space is getting cluttered with potential atomic weapons. The power of the federal government needs to expand to cover all of these exigencies."

"And this is one of those?" Marion asked.

"I didn't say that." Tarlton's voice remained steadfast and resolute.

"Then what are you saying?"

"That I need to see your prisoner."

"And if I choose not to allow it?"

"If you interfere with my presence here, A.D.A. Hart, you could bring a world of hurt down on yourself." The thinly veiled threat in Tarlton's voice was immediately apparent. It was a definite change from the monotone.

Even Adam seemed surprised by the threat. "I'm her attorney," he said. "Maybe we could talk."

"I'm here to talk to the woman."

"You can't talk to her without talking to me."

The man's lips lifted in a cold smile. "Perhaps we could ask her that. I feel certain she'll want to talk to me."

"Who's your supervisor?" Adam said.

Tarlton reached inside his jacket and took out a letter in an official envelope. He extended it. "A.D.A. Hart."

Marion took the letter and opened it. The note inside was short and to the point.

To Whom It May Concern:
Please afford this person every consideration and assistance.
Don't attempt to ask questions. He's pursuing a matter that
impacts national security.

It was signed by the president of the United States. An official
presidential seal was under the signature.

Marion was impressed. She'd never seen a presidential letter
before.

"I'd hate to call the man who wrote that letter and tell him the
local law enforcement teams—and a public defender—were being
resistant," Tarlton said.

"How do I know the president wrote that letter?" Marion asked.

"You could call."

"I will."

Tarlton nodded. "While you're making that call, I want to see
your prisoner."

"No," Marion and Adam replied at the same time.

Amusement lit in Tarlton's eyes. "All right."

Marion made the long-distance call. It took a while to get through
the White House channels. Evidently the president wasn't an easy
man to connect with.

He was also short and to the point. The bearer of the letter,
whatever his name truly was because Marion got the impression
that the president didn't truly know, was given a blank check for
whatever he needed.

Tarlton sat in the outer office and looked as though he didn't have
a care in the world. He thumbed through an issue of *Field & Stream.*
When they entered the room, he put the magazine away.

"Well?" Tarlton stood.

"You get to talk to her," Marion said. Irritation thrummed
within her. While she'd been waiting on the White House connec-
tions, she'd also called Turnbull. The district attorney hadn't been
happy about the outside interference.

"If you'll show me the way," Tarlton said. "This shouldn't
take long."

* * *

Tarlton entered the room where the woman was being held. He was surprised at how small she was. Of course, she was tall for a woman, but from the stories he'd heard about her he'd expected her to be seven feet tall.

She appraised him at a glance. Despite her current incarcerated state, she appeared confident and relaxed. "Who are you?"

"Tarlton." Tarlton paused. "I'm with the FBI."

They both smiled at that.

"How did you find me?" she asked.

Tarlton crossed the room and sat in one of the wooden chairs across the table from her. "We were keeping a loose tail on Marker. Evidently it was a little too loose."

"If the two men who'd been watching Marker hadn't been lax in their assignment, I'd have killed them, too."

Tarlton believed her. He reached under his jacket and took out a pack of cigarettes. "Smoke?"

The woman cocked an eyebrow at him. "Doesn't the good cop/bad cop routine work better with a partner?"

"I can make the spread." Tarlton tapped on the bottom of the pack and knocked a cigarette out.

"How do I know it's not poisoned? After all, your agency trained me to use poisons."

Tarlton put the cigarette between his lips and lit it with a Zippo. When he had it going, he took a couple deep puffs and didn't die.

"All right." The woman reached for the cigarette with both manacled hands.

Tarlton put the lit cigarette on the table and took his hand back. He didn't want to take the chance that the woman could grab hold of him.

The woman took the cigarette and drew deeply on it. She released the pent-up smoke and watched it drift to the ceiling.

"I don't think you're supposed to smoke in these rooms," she said.

"I don't think either one of us care." Tarlton lit another cigarette for himself.

"You're sure we're not being observed?"

"I checked the exterior of the room. Still, it wouldn't be a bad idea to be circumspect."

"You and your government still have secrets to protect."

"It's your government, too." Tarlton watched her. He couldn't help wondering if she was truly as dangerous as everyone had told him. Then he thought about Colonel Thomas Marker. He'd stopped by the city morgue to make a positive identification. She'd shot Marker to hell and gone, and Marker was one scary guy.

"Your government stopped being my government a long time ago," the woman said.

"What am I supposed to call you?"

The woman just smiled mockingly at him.

"The Agency has at least two different names for you. None of them have ever checked out as your real identity."

"I stopped being real years ago," the woman said.

"I've come to see you," Tarlton pointed out. "The local deputies are going to press me for identification."

"And it would be better for your agency for you to identify me."

Tarlton decided not to play cagey with that one. "Yes."

The woman locked gazes with him. "Even if I gave you a name, you'd identify me as whoever your agency has set up for me to become."

That was true. Tarlton took another draw on the cigarette. The Agency already had an identity he was supposed to submit to the local P.D. and D.A.'s office.

"Because if you didn't identify me for them," the woman continued, "they could check around enough to find something embarrassing. Something that couldn't be just swept under the carpet."

"You're awfully sure of yourself." Tarlton studied the woman through the smoky haze of his cigarette.

"You should actually give me a bonus for killing Marker. He's never quit running his own games, you know."

Tarlton knew that. He'd also been briefed on Colonel Marker. "That's what you say."

For the first time, anger showed on the woman's face. "Marker set me up in Vietnam. He nearly got me killed."

"The Agency looked into that. No charges were brought against Marker."

"That's because he was one of the CIA's Phoenix Program assets."

A cold knife stabbed through Tarlton's stomach. They definitely weren't supposed to be talking about the Phoenix Program. That had been a joint venture between the CIA and the South Vietnamese intelligence community. Those efforts specialized in torture, intimidation and execution of enemy forces and anyone suspected of working with them.

"Circumspect," he suggested.

She smiled at him. "The locals have me up on murder charges. I think they mean to make them stick."

"You shouldn't have killed Marker."

"Marker should have made certain I died in Vietnam."

Tarlton found he couldn't argue that point. "How did you find Marker?"

"I was here on business," she answered.

Tarlton didn't ask what that business was. Both of them knew. The woman had been killing professionally for almost ten years.

"I spotted Marker close to my target," the woman said. "I decided to go for revenge rather than the payoff."

"I'd heard you were more professional than that."

"I am." She smiled. "There was every reason to believe that I could still go after my primary target here."

"Except that Marker almost managed to save himself."

"He managed to delay my escape," she said. "He was a dead man from the time I entered that room."

Tarlton crushed out his cigarette against his shoe sole, then dropped the butt to the ground. The woman flicked hers over to him and he stomped it out as well.

"We're still left with a problem," he explained.

"What to do with me?"

Tarlton nodded.

"I'd suggest you find a way to get me out of here," she told him. "The sooner the better. I don't especially care for the accommodations, and I think the little assistant district attorney is jealous of me and her lawyer boyfriend."

As he leaned back in the chair, Tarlton studied the woman. "I could kill you."

"And face murder charges yourself?"

"I've got a Get-Out-of-Jail-Free card in my pocket," Tarlton said. "Signed by the president himself."

"That still makes you a government assassin." She smirked at him. "If that was what you were ordered to do, or what you wanted to do, you'd have already done it."

Tarlton didn't say anything.

"You're carrying a pistol at your right hip," the woman said. "I'd guess it's a .45 semi automatic pistol in a pancake holster."

That was exactly right. The sidearm was the one Tarlton had carried over in Vietnam before he'd made it back a couple years ago.

"The Agency's worried that it might not be able to handle the backlash," the woman continued. "And there will be one."

"If you're wrongly identified, maybe no one will look."

She smiled at him. "The Agency's obviously worried about something. Or they want something."

Tarlton sucked on his teeth for a moment. "They want Evaristo."

Dark anger pulsed through the woman's face. "What do you know about Evaristo?"

"He's your lover. Before that, he was your mentor. You worked with him in East Germany and Russia."

Evaristo Melendez was every bit as dangerous as the woman in front of Tarlton. He'd been a highly paid hit man in Cuba, working for the Mafia as well as the Agency as they'd tried to make a stand against Fidel Castro's rise to power.

Even then, the man had been a ghost. After Castro had risen to power in Cuba, Evaristo had been driven from the country. He'd worked around the globe until his path at some point intersected that of the woman. He still wanted his country freed from Communist rule.

"The Agency wants Evaristo," Tarlton said.

"So if I give up my lover, you'll get me out of this jam."

Tarlton didn't hesitate. "Yes. The Agency sent me here to make that offer."

The woman laughed. It was a harsh bark of amusement. "Have you ever been in love?"

"I'm married."

"Are you in love?"

Tarlton thought about that. He was gone so much of the time because of his job, and there were the children now. He hadn't known children could change things so drastically.

"Yes." He knew he was lying as soon as he uttered the response.

The woman smiled. "And how many women have you bedded since you took your marriage vows?"

Tarlton scowled and shifted uneasily. He didn't bother to keep count.

"There's a difference between you and me," the woman said. "I love Evaristo. With all my heart."

"That's too bad. Because we're going to kill him."

"You're not that good."

"We have you," Tarlton said. "Here. You're not going anywhere soon."

"You're going to use me as bait?"

Tarlton grinned mirthlessly.

The woman leaned across the table. "If I get killed before I get out of here, there's a safe-deposit box in Havana that will be opened. I've got an attorney there who will forward those papers to various newspaper editors and television news directors who will have a field day with the information that'll be released. Those documents name names, the people I killed as well as the Agency handlers that hired me to get the job done."

The announcement dried Tarlton's throat. "I don't believe you."

"Maybe you should ask your supervisor if he does."

"It sounds like the plot of a bad spy novel."

The woman smiled. "I was a bad spy. That's what the Agency paid me to be. And where do you think I got the idea of putting together that little insurance policy?"

Tarlton didn't reply.

"I want out of this place," the woman said. "Take me to Mexico and turn me loose. I'll make my way from there. Otherwise if I don't make phone calls on a regular basis, my attorney will mail those documents out."

For a moment Tarlton contemplated taking out his service weapon and putting a bullet through her brain. He'd handled other occasions in exactly the same way. The letter in his jacket would get him a free pass out of town, then FBI Special Agent Bruce Tarlton would disappear, never to be found again.

"Do you feel lucky?" the woman asked. "If you do, then go ahead."

Without a word, Tarlton took the .45 from his hip and took aim dead center between the woman's deep blue eyes. He rolled the hammer back with his thumb.

She never flinched, never looked away and never even blinked.

"You don't have the authority to make that call," she stated quietly. "Talk to whoever does. Lay the deal out for him and tell him the clock is ticking." Then she closed her eyes and laid her head on her arms.

After a moment, knowing he couldn't pull the trigger, Tarlton felt stupid. He released the hammer, flipped the safety back on and holstered the weapon again. Reluctantly he stood.

"I'll be in touch," Tarlton said without looking back.

"Don't wait too long," the woman warned. "If they try me and convict me, it's going to be harder to get me out of a prison cell."

When Tarlton looked back from the door, he saw that the woman hadn't lifted her head from her arms. He'd never met anyone that cool and controlled. He had a very clear idea of what she would be like looking at him through the sights of a sniper rifle. In some ways, he supposed, Colonel Thomas Marker hadn't stood a chance.

The Agency security that had been watching Marker had screwed up, but in some ways that was going to work out for them. Marker was dead and soon to be buried. They had the woman where they could take her any time they wanted.

And Evaristo Melendez would come running to save his lover.

"We're going to need you to hang on to her a little while longer."

Seated at the desk with her journal and the files she was putting together in front of her, Marion looked at the FBI agent framed in the doorway. Tarlton's face remained impassive.

"Why?" she asked.

"There are a few other things we have to investigate before we can take any kind of position on this problem," Tarlton said.

"What problem?" Adam asked. He sat in the corner and had been working on a legal pad atop his backpack over his knees.

"I can't answer that," Tarlton replied.

"National security," Keller said. He stood by the window.

"That's right," Tarlton responded.

"Awfully big blanket you Hoover boys can throw out when you choose to." Keller's tone wasn't friendly.

"Sometimes it has to be. I'll be in touch."

"Wait," Marion said.

Tarlton looked at her.

"What's her name?" Marion asked.

After a moment, Tarlton said, "Amanda. Amanda Weaver." He reached into his briefcase and took out a file. He dropped the file on the desk, then he left.

Marion opened the file and saw a color eight-by-ten glossy with the woman's face peering up at her. She—*Weaver,* Marion reminded herself—truly was a beautiful woman. But merciless glints showed in the deep blue eyes.

She rifled through the papers. There wasn't much, but it looked roughly complete.

"May I?"

Looking up, Marion found that Adam had walked close to the desk. She liked that he asked when he could have demanded. Under the rules of discovery, she had to share everything she learned so he had a chance to provide an adequate defense.

"Of course," Marion replied. She turned the file so they could both leaf through it.

"I don't like the idea of Hoover's boys walking into town and spiriting away my client," Adam said.

Marion didn't, either. This was going to be her first big case. She didn't relish the idea of watching it walk away with the FBI.

Adam traced the name on the folder with a forefinger. "Amanda Weaver. Do you think that's really her name?"

"Probably not any more than you do," Marion replied. But, like she was certain Adam Gracelyn was doing, she tried to read between the lines. "Either the truth is going to be in here—"

"Or its absence is going to be so telling that we might be able to at least form the blanks even if we can't fill them in," Adam said.

Marion bent to the task. She was acutely aware of Adam's aftershave and natural musk. *Pay attention to your work,* she chided herself.

Chapter 11

"Quitting for the day?"

Winter paused in the doorway as Gary the houseman held the door open. Bright afternoon sunlight blazed outside. David stood on the stairway that circled the big room and led up to the other floors.

"No," Winter replied. "I'm not quitting for the day."

"Then where are you going?"

"Out," Winter replied pointedly.

David looked confused. "You've been working till midnight or later every day."

So he *had* been keeping up with her hours. Winter had thought so, but she hadn't been certain. *Maybe Gary had been telling him.*

Evidently Gary caught the meaning of the look she gave him. The houseman shook his head imperceptibly. "I wouldn't rat you out," he whispered.

Winter almost smiled.

"The only reason you'd quit is that you found something." The accusation in David's voice was raw and naked.

"I haven't found anything concrete," Winter replied. And that was almost the truth. "I wanted to get out of the house for a bit. Sometimes when I stay too close to source material, I develop tunnel vision. It's probably the same way when you're working on a legal case."

David hesitated. It was obvious that he didn't know what to do next. He was dressed casually, in olive Dockers and a tan golf shirt.

"Care to get out of the house, Counselor?" Winter asked. The question was out of her mouth before she knew it. She silently damned herself for asking. *All you had to do was just walk out of the house.*

Gary grinned slightly.

At least, Winter thought the houseman had. When she looked at him to make certain, his face was impassive.

"Where are you going?" David asked.

"Out." Winter went without another word. He wasn't her father. She didn't have to play Q&A with him. And she wasn't going to stick around while he made everything complicated. She felt a little miffed that he didn't just agree to accompany her if he was so interested. She slipped her Oakley Behave sunglasses from her purse and put them on.

"Wait."

Winter didn't. She was just as mad at herself as she was at David Gracelyn. When she was on the job, she didn't allow herself to be distracted.

David Gracelyn was getting to be a big distraction. Winter was starting to realize the problems Marion Hart had experienced in dealing with David's father while working on the Amanda Weaver investigation.

It felt odd calling the woman Amanda Weaver. Winter knew that wasn't the woman's name just as Marion and Adam Gracelyn had known that back in 1968. But it was the only name she had for her.

So far, Winter reminded herself.

David caught Winter by the elbow and stopped her. She whirled back to face him. Even on heels she was able to set herself and yank her arm free.

"What do you think you're doing?" she demanded.

"Didn't you hear me tell you to wait?" he countered.

"I don't work for you. I'm here doing a favor for Christine."

David looked irritated and confused at the same time. "I asked you to wait."

"You *told* me to wait. If I wanted to be *told* what to do, I'd work for someone other than myself. Maybe in some cushy political office."

"I want to know where you're going."

"That's too bad. I asked you if you wanted to go along. You declined."

"I didn't decline."

"You didn't say yes." Winter only realized then that his hesitation had stung more than she'd been prepared to handle. It had taken her back to all those years ago when she'd been an underclassman at Athena Academy.

"I've got a full schedule today."

"So do I, and you're wrecking it." Winter turned on her heel and walked toward the garage.

The chauffeur, probably alerted by Gary from inside the house, was backing Winter's Lexus out of the massive garage.

"Henry will bring your car," David said. "You don't have to walk to it."

"I like walking. It helps me think, and it puts distance between me and rude people I encounter."

David paced her. "I didn't mean to be rude."

"Unwanted physical contact, such as grabbing a woman's arm, is assault, Counselor. At the very least it's harassment. I would think you knew that."

"I do. I just wasn't thinking."

"You're a politician. You get paid to think." Winter didn't look at him. She wished it wasn't so far to the garage from the main house, but it was and she was already on her way. She wasn't going to stop.

"Winter," David said in a softer voice. "I apologize."

Winter didn't respond. She didn't know how she was supposed to react. She certainly deserved an apology, but now that she had one she didn't know what to do with it.

"This whole thing," David said. "The kidnappings. That threat that was sent. My mother's murder. Rainy's murder."

Winter recalled the Athena Academy yearbooks David had been

looking at and realized then what—no, *who*—David had been looking at.

"All of it just keeps falling all over the place," David went on in a half-whisper that was tight with pain. "It just won't quit. Whatever's going on was—is—a lot bigger than anyone imagined. It's infuriating and unsettling. And all of it keeps coming back to my mother."

Winter continued walking in silence for a moment. "Marion Hart was a *good* woman," she said finally. "She was a strong woman."

"I know. She used to drive Dad crazy."

"I see that in her journals."

"They were two different people," David said. "Mom came from a modest background, raised by schoolteachers and stepped into the legal arena. Dad was born with the silver spoon in his mouth but turned against a lot of what his father did because he believed in the environment and in changing the social consciousness."

"It's a wonder they ended up together."

"Definitely against the odds. Granddad had a number of stories that he used to tell about Dad. There was fire between them till the very end, old arguments as well as new ones, but you could tell they loved each other."

"People don't have to agree on everything to love each other. That can exist as something apart."

"I know. But it's hard these days making room for everything."

"Is that why you've never married?" Winter mentally shook her head. God, and why did she have to ask *that* question? It came from that same love-struck high school teenager that had fallen for the college baseball jock. The one who'd gotten hurt when he hadn't immediately jumped at the chance to come with her.

"Partly." David answered without looking at her. "And partly because I've been kind of hung up."

"Over Rainy Miller?"

David looked at her then. Winter returned his gaze but was grateful to the Oakley sunglasses for easing the glare. Okay, so she had that one coming.

"Rainy *Carrington*," David said.

Right, Winter remembered. Rainy had been married at the end. "I thought the two of you had a thing going for a while."

"I don't want to talk about that." David sounded tired and worn.

They'd reached Winter's sports car. She took the keys from Henry and thanked him.

"My pleasure, miss." The old chauffeur touched his hat bill and walked away.

Winter stood by the door. David was on the other side of the car. She knew neither one of them were through talking.

"The invitation is still there," Winter said.

"Where are you going?"

"To Southwest Hospital."

"Downtown?"

Winter nodded.

"Why?" David asked.

"Forty years ago, it was named Handley Hospital. Marion took a woman supposedly named Amanda Weaver there for an examination. I want to look at the files."

"Forty years ago?" David shook his head. "They won't still have those files."

"As it turns out, they do. Dr. Alan Bernhardt, the attending physician, is retired but still maintains a position on the board of the directors."

"That was forty years ago. He's got to be—"

"Eighty-seven. And judging from the conversation I had with him over the phone a few minutes ago, still in full command of his mental faculties." Winter opened the driver's door and slid into the seat. "When you're researching something like this that has an extensive history, you hope to find someone like Alan Bernhardt. I can't pass up this interview."

"You're sure this is what we're looking for?"

Winter had to be honest with him. "No. But it's the most intriguing aspect I've seen in Marion's journals so far."

David didn't appear convinced.

"Come along for the ride," Winter said. "I'll explain on the way. I'll even buy you a drink."

For a moment she thought David was going to turn down her offer. The possibility stung more than she wanted it to and she was mad at her weakness. *You don't have to keep going back for second and third helpings of disappointment.*

"I could have Henry drive us," David offered.

"I prefer to drive myself." Part of that was from living out in L.A. It was hard to get anywhere in that city without a car.

David frowned at her. "And if I prefer to drive myself?"

"Then you can follow. Or have Henry drive you."

Grimacing, David took a final look back at the house, then he opened the passenger door and sat. He looked for the seat belt and pulled it over his shoulder.

As she drove back into Phoenix through the barren, mountainous countryside, Winter told David about Amanda Weaver and the visit from the "FBI" agent. The story was more complicated than David had thought, even with everything the people at Athena Academy had been involved in.

That I knew about, David amended.

"You think that woman was a hired assassin?" David asked when Winter finished relaying what she knew. He couldn't help looking at Winter. She'd retracted the convertible roof. Her black mane flew in the wind and sunlight showed hints of red. He discovered that he liked looking at her far more than he should have.

Despite his sister's best efforts, and those of other acquaintances here in Phoenix and in Washington, D.C., David hadn't found a woman who'd caught his eye for more than a few days. Plenty of them had been introduced at social events in Washington, D.C., because there were always political events to attend.

They were all beautiful, vivacious women. With the way so many of his family and friends had set him up, it had been like attending a standing buffet. The problem was that he just didn't have an appetite.

Whatever it was inside him that had been drawn to the idea and the promise of relationships had died the day Rainy had walked out of his life. The fitful starts and stops that occurred afterward were even worse. He'd wanted to find someone else to love, and wanted to allow someone else to love him. But it just hadn't happened.

After Rainy had been killed, a couple of years ago, he'd shut down completely. He knew that. But it didn't bother him.

As he watched Winter talking and driving, though, he felt the vaguest hint of stirring interest. That was completely asinine, though. The woman got under his skin on a molecular level. The work that she did, the exposés and muckraking, was dangerous to the work that he did.

David worked in an arena filled with secrets and confidential information that couldn't be made public, not even for the good of the public. Winter Archer made a career of bundling those secrets into attractive packages and selling them to the highest bidder.

"Are you listening?" Winter asked.

"Yes." David had to think for a moment to remember he had been listening while he'd been looking at her.

"Well?"

David tried to remember what she'd obviously asked him. "Do I know someone at Langley that might be able to go through the CIA's files regarding Amanda Weaver?"

Winter looked at him and frowned. He couldn't see her eyes behind the dark lenses.

"Stalling, Counselor?"

"Trying to keep up," David admitted. But he didn't tell her that she was as much food for thought as the story she'd been spinning. "I do have someone that might be able to check into Amanda Weaver's background. If there is one."

"Is he good?"

"She," David said. He was thinking of his sister Allison. She did encrypting for the National Security Agency. A lot of that work involved computer hacking. If Allison couldn't do the job herself, she would know someone who could.

"Oh. She." Winter returned her attention to her driving.

"Allison," David said. "My sister." He didn't want Winter to get the wrong idea. And where the hell had that thought come from?

He opened his cell phone and dialed Allison's work number. After three rings, he was switched over to Allison's stash. He left a message detailing what they wanted her to do. He added his mobile number at the end.

If she was relieved, Winter didn't show it. She kept her attention on the twisting highway. "Just make sure she's careful."

"She's careful. Not only that, but it's been forty years. I doubt anyone cares."

"Really?" Winter's right eyebrow arched over her sunglasses. "Is that why you and Christine called me in to have a look at this? Because no one cares?"

"That's not what I meant. We care."

"Whoever wrote that threatening note cares."

David nodded. She was right.

"One of the things I've discovered in doing the work that I've done," she told him, "is that people fight the hardest to keep buried the secrets they've hidden the longest. People tried hard to keep the truth from your mom and dad. Your father was nearly killed by someone he believed worked for one of the federal government's clandestine espionage organizations."

Surprised, David could only stare at her.

Then she told him what she'd discovered that morning that had prompted her visit to Dr. Bernhardt at the hospital.

Chapter 12

Maricopa County Courthouse
Phoenix, Arizona
Tuesday, May 21, 1968
The Past

"Good morning, A.D.A. Hart."

Drawn by Adam Gracelyn's voice, Marion glanced over her shoulder and saw him coming from the same parking lot across Washington Street where she'd parked. He wore a dark blue tailored suit that was a big change from the casual dress she'd seen him in over the last couple days. His black-lensed Ray-Bans made him look Hollywood cool.

"Good morning, Counselor Gracelyn." Marion never broke stride.

Adam had to hurry to keep up. "You have a long-legged stride for someone in heels."

"I exercise every day. I ran track when I was in high school."

"Trying to stay away from all the boys that must have been chasing you?"

Marion shot him a look. Her cheeks burned with something more than the clear morning sunlight. She wore a business suit and skirt. She hated the skirt but District Attorney Turnbull had instructed her to wear it. The bail arraignment for "Amanda Weaver" was this morning and Judge Dodds was presiding. Everyone knew that the judge was a letch and preferred women to dress like women when they were in his court.

"I withdraw the question." Adam held up his hands defensively. His slim attaché case dangled from one thumb. He did look sincere, but Marion reminded herself that might have been a practiced appearance long before Adam went to law school. "I intended no foul. It was strictly a compliment."

"I'd prefer we keep this on a professional level." Marion heard herself saying that but she knew she didn't entirely mean it. She had good legs and the skirt she'd chosen showed them off. She paused at the curb and waited for traffic.

"That was a professional opinion," Adam said. "I think a woman should be complimented on her beauty."

"That's *so* kind of you, Counselor. What about her mind? Do you think a woman should be complimented on her mind? Or do you prefer a steady diet of mindless beach bunnies?"

Somehow Marion could imagine Adam Gracelyn living at the big house in Gracelyn Ranch with a dozen or more women that would have been at home in the pages of *Playboy* magazine. Of course, if he had been, the scandal would have been all over Phoenix.

"I find that…*beach bunnies* run disastrously short on conversation," Adam replied.

"Oh? Are you a fan of conversation?"

"I wouldn't say that. Some people just don't know when to shut up. Although I have to admit that I like talking to you."

Marion didn't know how to respond to that. She was grateful the lights changed and she could cross the street. Her sudden departure caught Adam flat-footed and he lost ground.

He trotted to catch up again. "Are you in a hurry?"

"I don't like to be late." More than that, though, she knew that Adam Gracelyn made her uncomfortable.

Adam shot his cuff and glanced at the stainless steel Rolex Daytona. The watch was expensive. After graduating law school, Marion had priced one, hoping to be able to afford it for her father as a thank-you for all the help he'd given her while in college. There was a waiting list for the new ones, and the price was way out of her budget.

"It's twenty of," Adam protested. "We have time for a cup of coffee before we enter the courtroom."

The idea sounded inviting. Over the weekend, Marion had talked with Adam on several occasions to make sure he had copies of everything he needed to prepare for the arraignment. He was charming and intelligent, qualities that she usually found mutually exclusive in the male species. At least, she'd found them mutually exclusive of each other in the men who'd approached her.

Business meetings to exchange papers and testimonies had turned into two lunches and dinner last night. She didn't want it turning into anything else, but she couldn't help wondering what it would have been like to meet Adam Gracelyn under other circumstances.

Don't fool yourself, she chided. *You don't even come close to the league Adam Gracelyn plays.*

But he didn't come off as a snob. He didn't act superior or talk down to her. In fact, until that crack this morning about outrunning the boys in school—which truly might have been a compliment—he'd acted like the perfect gentleman. He hadn't even protested too much about her paying for her meals even though they both knew he could easily afford them.

"I don't think coffee's a good idea," Marion replied.

Adam gave her a boyish grin beneath the dark-lensed glasses. "Why?"

Because it's far too easy to let my defenses down around you. Marion started up the steps leading to the tall, stately courthouse. Built of sand-colored blocks, the multistoried building stood out against the downtown area as an imposing bulwark.

Trees and shrubs filled the planting boxes on either side of the steps. At the top, the arched doorway looked like a gaping maw. The four doors across the front looked like rectangular teeth.

Above the door, the huge engraved letters proclaimed:

Maricopa Covnty
Covrt Hovse

When she'd been a girl and seen the courthouse for the first time, Marion had insisted they'd spelled the words wrong. Her parents were teachers. She knew how to spell, and she knew that spelling was important. Her mother had explained the use of the V instead of the U but it hadn't made any sense then. It still didn't. It was one of those things that needed correcting.

"We're not exactly colleagues," Marion said.

"No. But I think we're going to be seeing each other a lot. I just want a chance to get to know you."

Marion liked the promise in his words. He sounded so sincere. But then, as she'd learned in law school, attorneys practiced sincerity. She'd gotten burned by a handful of them before she'd learned her lesson.

At the top of the steps, Marion glanced at Adam. "Are you sure you're going to still be interested in knowing me when I prosecute your client and put her in prison for murder?"

Adam smiled even more broadly at that. "There's not a chance of that happening."

"When I do," Marion told him, "I'll buy you dinner as a consolation prize." Before he could reply, she turned and left him standing there.

She passed through the doors and pretended that her heart wasn't beating like a snare drum. She honestly didn't know if the reaction was from the impending arraignment or the thought of seeing Adam Gracelyn again.

"Do you know what you're doing, Gracelyn?"

The harsh voice broke into Adam's thoughts as he stood in the hallway and watched Marion speaking with District Attorney Geoffrey Turnbull. He hadn't even noticed the large man who'd stepped up beside him.

Conrad Ellis looked formidable. His six-feet-two-inch frame was broad and heavy. His iron-gray hair stood in a rigid crew cut. His face was florid and his nose showed the broken veins of a constant drinker.

He'd played as a linebacker in professional football for five years, then gone into the private business sector. He'd played the markets and ventures with the same hardnosed attitude he'd brought to his game.

These days the gridiron hero was worth several million dollars. Ellis wasn't old money like Adam's father, but the respect was more intense. Conrad Ellis was still molding his world around him, and he molded the people he needed, too.

"Mr. Ellis." Adam stuck out his hand and pasted a smile on his face. He didn't particularly like Conrad Ellis or his cronies. All of them were people that Adam was gearing up to take on over environmental issues.

Ellis ignored the proffered hand. "What do you think you're doing? Running for office? Put your hand back in your pocket."

Embarrassed and not exactly sure what was going on, Adam did.

Ellis took a cigar from inside his jacket and popped it into his mouth. "What the hell did you think you were doing taking on this case?"

"My job," Adam retorted.

"'Your *job?*'" Ellis snorted. "Your job is working for your daddy and keeping all the money you can at home. That's what you should be doing. Not this shyster for the poor and tree-huggers crap."

"Maybe we could have this conversation at a later date," Adam suggested. *Like never.*

"Why? You gonna come to your senses and recuse yourself from this case?"

"No."

"'Cause that's what you ought to do." Ellis pinned Adam with his bleak, unfriendly gaze.

"Why?"

"Because that woman's a killer."

Adam struggled to keep his composure. All his life he'd been around his father's friends. Most of those people—though not all of them—tended to look at the world as their oyster. They didn't look much past their own needs, and often only contributed in fund-raising events to get something—either attention from the press or television, or favors from political candidates—for themselves.

"A jury will decide that, Mr. Ellis. You have a good day." Adam started to walk away.

Ellis grabbed a fistful of Adam's suit coat. "I didn't dismiss you."

Adam gripped the man's little finger and peeled his hand back. If Ellis felt any pain, he didn't show it.

"I dismissed myself," Adam stated quietly. He stepped forward, almost nose to nose with the bigger man. "I don't work for you."

"Your daddy has a political career in mind for you," Ellis said. "You might want to remember that when you start high-hatting people that can help you achieve that."

"My father's intentions aren't always mine." Adam kept himself under control, but his mind was spinning. Conrad Ellis was a friend of his father's. Adam didn't think he'd exchanged a hundred words with Conrad Ellis during that time.

"You're making a mistake representing this woman," Ellis said.

"What interest is that of yours, Mr. Ellis?" Adam asked.

"Colonel Tom Marker was a friend of mine," Ellis said. "That man brought my son home from Vietnam. A lot of other soldiers, too. He was a hero. He didn't deserve what happened to him in that motel."

"Talk to the D.A.'s office," Adam suggested. "They could always use you for a character reference for the deceased." He paused. "In the future, keep your hands off me."

"If it came to it, I'd break you in half."

"Maybe. But however it came out, I'd tie you up in litigation and sue the ass off of you. You've rode roughshod over so many people in this town that I bet you'd be hard-pressed to find twelve jurors that would be inclined to let you off scot-free."

Ellis's nostrils flared in surprise. Then he cursed vehemently and stalked off.

Releasing a pent-up breath, Adam watched the big man go.

Voices rose as sudden excitement filled the hallway. At the far end, sheriff's deputies brought Amanda Weaver into the courthouse. She wore the jail jumper and had shackles on her wrists and ankles.

Sheriff Keller walked beside her and ignored the members of the press as they begged quotes.

Adam went to meet them and felt like he'd stepped into the middle of a three-ring circus. "Dammit, Sheriff," he said to Keller. "Do you think maybe you could have tied a Guilty sign around her neck, too? There could be a couple of people in the crowd that didn't get the message."

"Not my fault, Counselor," Keller whispered. "She wouldn't change clothes."

Adam looked at his client. She refused to meet his gaze.

Still feel like the great protector of the disadvantaged and down-trodden? Adam asked himself bitterly. He stood at his client's side and looked as supportive and confident as he could. After all, no matter how she looked, he still had a plan.

"My God, Marion," District Attorney Geoffrey Turnbull said quietly, "would you look at that?"

Marion was already watching the press vultures gathering around Adam Gracelyn and his client. Amanda Weaver stood out among them in the orange jumpsuit.

And she looked guilty as hell.

"I do believe I've given you a slam dunk," Turnbull gloated.

To Marion's surprise, Turnbull had given her the first chair assignment. As such she was going to present the case and lead direct and cross interviews on the stand.

"If this is how Gracelyn is going to conduct his defense," Turnbull went on, "you might not even have to try this thing. They might plea-bargain this one out."

Marion didn't think so, but she didn't tell Turnbull that. From what she'd seen of Gracelyn, he was a fighter. Not only that, he was intelligent and passionate about what he did. Selling him short would be a mistake.

As she watched, Sheriff Keller and his deputies herded Adam and Amanda Weaver into the courtroom. The press flowed after them but grew immediately quieter. Judge Dodds was known for tossing out media people who disrupted his proceedings.

One of the last people she noticed entering the courtroom was FBI Special Agent Bruce Tarlton. He wore a black suit and looked freshly shaved. He carried a hat in his hand.

"All right, Marion," Turnbull said. "Let's do this. We get finished quickly enough, maybe we can go out for drinks to celebrate."

"Sure," Marion replied. She tried to sound like she was relaxed, but the whole time butterflies swooped through her stomach.

"All rise," the bailiff called out. "The Honorable Judge Roy Dodds presiding."

Marion almost jumped up from her seat. Adrenaline spiked throughout her body. For the first time, she sat at the prosecutor's table alone. Not as support. Not as second seat. But as primary. It felt good. But it was also nerve-racking.

While she'd been waiting, she'd pointedly avoided looking at the defense table. She'd thought she felt Adam's eyes on her, but that might have been wishful thinking.

He's a wreck right now, she told herself. *He has to be. I'd be if I was defending someone and that someone showed up looking like that.*

Dodds stepped out of judge's chambers in a swirl of black robes and took his seat at the bench. Lean and wiry, Dodds was well into his sixties and looked like a ferret due to his sunken eyes and hollow cheeks. He lifted a hand and waved everyone into their seats.

The charges were read, indicating that the district attorney's office wanted Amanda Weaver held over for trial for murder.

"What does the district attorney's office have for us this morning, Counselor—" Dodds had to look at the papers in front of him "—Hart?"

That's okay, Marion said. *He's going to know my name soon enough.*

She stood and made a short summation of the evidence and eye-witness accounts that tied Amanda Weaver to the murder scene at the Kellogg Motel. When she was finished, her breath a little short due to excitement and a touch of anxiety, she resumed her seat.

"Defense counsel," Dodds called out, looking over at the opposing table.

Adam Gracelyn stood up and buttoned his coat. "Present, your honor."

Dodds laced his hands and peered over them at Adam. "Well, Mr. Gracelyn, it appears the district attorney's office has their affairs in order. Are you prepared to go to court?"

"No, your honor."

"Well, then, I'd suggest you get ready because that's where you're headed." Dodds scowled in irritation as he reached for his gavel.

"The district attorney's office hasn't provided me with all the information I need to mount an adequate defense for my client, your honor," Adam said.

Silence filled the courtroom.

Turnbull leaned up from the seat behind Marion and asked, "What's he talking about?"

Marion shook her head slightly and whispered back, "I don't know."

"You've been talking to him for the last few days."

"He didn't lay out his strategy."

"You think you'd have at least gotten to that somewhere over lunch or dinner. You're a woman, Marion. Men love to talk in front of women when they want to be clever or seem powerful." Turnbull leaned back.

Marion's cheeks flamed. Her gender had nothing to do with how Adam conducted himself. And she was angry that Turnbull had suggested that it would matter. She wondered if he'd deliberately assigned her the case thinking she would gain insight as to how Adam would proceed.

Dodds poised with the gavel held between his hands. "What information would that be, Counselor?"

"Your honor," Adam said, "the district attorney's office has failed to provide me with my client's true name."

Turnbull leaned back toward Marion. "What the hell is he trying to pull?"

Despite the situation she found herself in, Marion almost smiled. Adam's argument was totally out of left field. The attempt was inspired. She waited to see how it was going to play out and racked her brain for a way to get the proceedings back on track.

Chapter 13

Maricopa County Courthouse
Phoenix, Arizona
Tuesday, May 21, 1968
The Past

"Mr. Gracelyn," Dodds said, holding up the court record, "according to this document, your client's name is Amanda Weaver."

"Yes, your honor. But that document may be in error."

Desperately, the sick feeling in her stomach roiling now, Marion glanced around the room and spotted FBI Agent Tarlton along the back row. The man sat quietly and watched with avid interest.

"When my client was arrested," Adam hurried on, "she had no identification on her. Nor has the district attorney's office been able to substantiate my client's identity."

"Hasn't your client confirmed her name, Counselor?"

"No, your honor. At this point she hasn't aided me in her defense at all. She barely talks to me."

Dodds leaned back and frowned severely.

"I need to know my client's true identity, your honor," Adam said.

"Why?" Dodds asked.

"She's accused of premeditation in the murder of Colonel Thomas Marker. Premeditation would include a prior history with the deceased. I need to know the nature of that relationship if I'm going to properly defend her."

Seated, her handcuffs evident as she rested her arms on the table, Weaver looked up at Adam with curiosity. Then she must have felt Marion staring at her because she turned to Marion and smiled broadly. It was like she didn't have a care in the world.

Where does she get that confidence? Marion considered her options as she listened to Adam continue.

"If my client—whatever her name is—did shoot Mr. Marker, which I'm not ready to concede at this point—"

Conversation rose in the seats behind Marion as the audience came alive. None of the regulars who attended court functions or the press had expected this.

Neither had the district attorney's office.

"—it remains to be seen if she had just cause," Adam said. "If her prior history with the deceased was of an abusive nature—"

"Then I submit that she wouldn't have willingly gone to that motel room that night," Dodds said.

"Unless she was being blackmailed, your honor. Or coerced in some other way."

"The man was a damned hero!" a loud voice proclaimed. "Don't you dare drag his name through the mud, you son of a bitch!"

Startled, Marion glanced back into the crowd and saw Conrad Ellis standing defiantly behind the prosecutor's table.

"Colonel Marker brought my son home from Vietnam!" Ellis continued. "He did so at great personal risk to himself! And my son wasn't the only prisoner of war the colonel brought home!"

The furor inside the courtroom increased.

Dodds banged his gavel. "Order. Order in this courtroom, by God, or I'll have the lot of you cleared from these proceedings."

The crowd turned meek at once. None of them wanted to leave before the final outcome was reached. Reporters wrote furiously on pads.

Dodds glared at Adam, then at Marion. "Counsel will approach my bench," the judge declared.

Feeling like a schoolgirl called into the principal's office, Marion stood and walked toward the judge's bench. Her knees shook slightly and she willed them to be strong enough to support her.

Get a grip, she told herself. *You can handle this.*

Adam fell into step beside her. She discovered that she suddenly didn't quite feel so friendly toward him. He was taking away her chance to prove she could do her job, a man's job.

Dodds spoke in a harsh whisper as he pinned Adam with his gaze. "You are not going to turn this courtroom into a circus sideshow, Counselor."

"I'm not trying to, your honor," Adam said. "I need the information I'm asking for."

"Then ask your client."

"She refuses to tell me."

"She has to take part in her own defense."

"It would be better if she did," Adam agreed. "But until she's willing—or able to—I need to protect her as best as I can."

Dodds was silent for a moment. "I concur. Why would she not agree to help you?"

Adam shook his head. "I don't know, your honor."

"If I may, your honor," Marion interrupted. Her voice cracked a little and embarrassed her. It wasn't exactly the impression she wanted to make.

"Yes, Miss Hart." Dodds looked doubtfully at her.

"I can provide identification for the defendant."

"Well, then, why haven't you done it before now?"

"There's a man in the courtroom that can provide positive identification."

"Your honor," Adam said, "the man she's referring to is an FBI agent—"

"Whose position makes him an officer of the court, your honor," Marion said. "His testimony is unimpeachable. That should be all the proof we need."

Adam gave up seemingly in frustration.

Marion silently congratulated herself. She'd been fortunate Tarlton had chosen to come to the courthouse. She hadn't even known he was still in the city. He hadn't been in contact with anyone for days.

"Point him out," Dodds instructed.

Marion did.

Dodds waved the big bailiff over. "Bring me that man."

The bailiff nodded and crossed the courtroom.

FBI Agent Bruce Tarlton didn't look happy about becoming part of the courtroom drama. He stood, hat in hand, rigidly at attention.

Adam waited tensely. He'd felt good so far about springing the surprise. He'd caught Marion and the district attorney's office off guard. He felt bad that Marion had gotten whipsawed by it. That hadn't been his intention. He'd figured Turnbull would have taken lead on the prosecution.

The positive identification had been a good delaying tactic, but he hadn't counted on Tarlton being present in the courtroom. He flailed mentally, seeking another weakness in the chain of evidence against his client.

"Who are you?" Dodds demanded.

"Special Agent Bruce Tarlton of the Federal Bureau of Investigation, sir." Tarlton rattled off the reply like he'd been doing it for years.

"I presume you have identification, Agent Tarlton."

"Yes, sir." Tarlton reached inside his jacket and produced it.

Dodds glanced at the badge and identification and passed them back. "Everything looks in order to me. Can you identify that woman?"

"Yes, sir. Her name is Amanda Weaver."

"Very well then."

"Your honor," Adam said, and hoped he wasn't about to spend the night in a jail cell for contempt of court for interrupting the judge. It wouldn't be the first time.

"What, Mr. Gracelyn?"

"Special Agent Tarlton has provided substantiating documentation as to who he is, but I haven't seen any on my client."

"Special Agent Tarlton is an officer of the court," Marion stated. "His testimony—and his identification—is admissible."

"My client is on trial for her life," Adam countered. "I don't think it would be inappropriate to ask for more concrete evidence."

Marion turned back to the judge. "We have a file, your honor.

"With you?" Dodds asked.

"Yes. I can get it."

"Those documents are unsubstantiated, your honor," Adam said. "Special Agent Tarlton brought them to us. Although the district attorney's office—" he didn't want to accuse Marion of being at fault "—has tried on several occasions, they haven't been able to confirm the nature of those documents. Neither have I. For all we truly know, Special Agent Tarlton had them printed just to frame my client."

"I didn't put her in Marker's room," Tarlton snarled. His anger was raw and terrible. "That bitch killed Marker without giving him a chance. She needs to pay for that."

Adam got the impression the man was barely under control. "Furthermore, your honor, I don't think Special Agent Tarlton is performing his duties from an entirely unbiased point of view."

"Is this true, Miss Hart?" Dodds asked. "Have you been unable to confirm those documents?"

"It's true."

Dodds pursed his lips and turned back to Adam. "Mr. Gracelyn, I understand your position, but—"

"Your honor, I need to know why Special Agent Tarlton has been conferring with my client. He's ordered me out of the room during his interviews with her, and he's refused to tell me the nature of those interviews."

Tarlton glared at Adam with murderous rage in his eyes, but the emotion never touched the man's face.

"I need to know why the federal government is interested in my client," Adam said.

"Did that bitch put you up to this?" Tarlton growled. "Or are you just being cute all on your own?"

Adam was too stunned to respond. He hadn't even imagined he would elicit that kind of reaction.

"Calm down," Dodds ordered.

Tarlton took a deep breath.

"Special Agent Tarlton?" Dodds prompted.

Without a word, Tarlton reached inside his jacket again and came out with the presidential letter. He passed it over to the bailiff, who in turn handed it up to the judge.

Dodds took out a pair of reading glasses and quickly read the contents. He handed the letter back to Tarlton.

"Why did you want me to see that, Special Agent Tarlton?" the judge asked. He regarded Tarlton in a whole new light.

"Because I can't answer any more questions in this matter, your honor," Tarlton replied evenly.

"I see."

"Why is the president interested in my client?" Adam asked.

"I can't answer that."

"How did you know my client had been placed under arrest?"

"I can't answer that." Tarlton's voice sounded more strained.

"What was she doing there that night with Marker?"

Tarlton's face purpled. "She went there to kill him, you jackass. It's what she does."

"How do you know that?"

"I can't answer that."

Adam framed his next question carefully. "Why do you think my client would want to kill Colonel Marker?"

Tarlton closed the remaining distance between himself and Adam. "Back off, Counselor. Before you get in over your head." He glared at Adam.

Adam felt the man's hot breath on his face and smelled his mouthwash. Panic flared inside him and he had to resist the impulse to back up or punch Tarlton in the face.

The bailiff's hand dropped heavily onto Tarlton's shoulder. Tarlton shrugged it off and stepped back. He glanced up at Dodds.

"We're through here, Judge. You can work out your dog-and-pony show any way you want to." Tarlton turned and walked away.

Not believing what had just happened, Adam watched the man go.

"Mr. Gracelyn."

Adam glanced up at the judge. "Yes, your honor."

"I'm going to grant your continuance. Miss Hart."

"Yes, your honor."

"I suggest you muster the forces of the district attorney's office to discovering exactly who it is we've got seated in my courtroom."

"Yes, your honor."

"Now step back and I'll deliver my ruling officially. And let's get this damned mess taken care of before the press decides to crawl up our asses. Excuse me, Miss Hart."

Adam stepped back from the bench and listened to the judge's continuance and direction, but his mind was reeling with the implications of what had just happened. Had he really been threatened by an FBI agent in an open courtroom?

"Why are you trying so hard?"

The question surprised Adam even though he thought nothing could after what had happened in the courtroom only minutes ago. He sat at the table in the center of the interview room he'd requested in the courthouse. Shadows of two deputies on the other side of the translucent glass showed as dark, ill-formed shapes.

They have guns, Adam reminded himself. He tried to take comfort in that, but the feeling was elusive.

"What?" He tried to focus on the woman's question.

Weaver, or whatever her name was, stood on the other side of the room. She smoked a cigarette. Her handcuffs required her to raise both arms to manage the task, and the chains clinked together as she did.

"Why are you trying so hard to defend me?" she asked.

"Because it's what I do."

"You don't even know me."

"It would help if I did." Adam searched that hard exterior and wondered if she were only now starting to get scared. Maybe after today she was finally admitting to herself how much trouble she was in.

"Do you always put your life on the line for strangers?" she asked.

"I wasn't aware that I was doing that."

"You're crossing Tarlton."

"Is that really his name?"

Weaver took a hit off her cigarette, blew out a stream of smoke and shrugged. "I don't know. Those guys are always changing names."

"Who? The FBI?"

Weaver smiled. "I talk too much around you. I think maybe I'm starting to like you."

Adam's face suddenly felt hot.

"Maybe you're a little interested in me?" Weaver crossed over to him and reached for him.

Adam caught the chain between her handcuffs and held her hands down so they wouldn't slide around his neck. Her face was only inches from his and he would have sworn he'd never seen bluer eyes. Despite her refusal to change clothes, she'd used makeup. Her ruby lips gleamed.

"Good boys always like bad girls," she whispered throatily. "Have you ever noticed that?"

Adam's physical responses suddenly went on overdrive. She leaned against him harder and her strength surprised him.

"I liked the way you stood up to him," Weaver whispered. "I liked the way you outthought your little girlfriend."

Mentioning Marion curbed Adam's rising desire. For a moment he'd forgotten where he was and who he was with. All he knew was that he had a hot, willing woman in his arms. It had been a while since that had happened. Not through lack of opportunity, but through disinterest. Too many women he met were interested in his father's money.

And what was Amanda Weaver interested in?

"I don't think I've met a guy like you," she whispered to him. "Growing up the way I did in the Combat Zone, you didn't get chances to meet guys like you. Most of them were hoods or made guys."

The words barely registered on Adam. He was captivated by the proximity of the woman. She leaned in hard enough that he could feel her breasts pressed against his arm. All he had to do was move his arm and she'd be in his lap. It was tempting, and almost undeniable.

"Do you wonder what it would be like?" she whispered. "What *I* would be like?" She leaned in farther and tried to kiss him.

Adam turned his head and her lips grazed the side of his face.

"Don't," he whispered hoarsely.

She drew back. Amusement lighted her dark blue eyes, but there was something else in there that looked twisted and razor-edged.

"Why?" she asked. "Aren't I good enough for you?"

"It's not that."

"Then what is it? Is it muffin? That little lawyer got you all in a twist?"

"No."

"Or maybe you're not man enough."

Adam's anger slipped his control before he could get a handle on it. This morning had been completely screwed up. He'd woken and found himself looking forward to seeing Marion again even if it was in a courtroom at opposite ends of the arraignment. He just wanted to see her.

And if that wasn't confusing enough, his brilliant defense of his client had probably gotten Marion jammed up because he hadn't been expecting her as primary. Adam had planned on taking Turnbull apart with his end-run involving the identity issue.

Then Tarlton had virtually come unwound in the courtroom and threatened him right in front of Judge Dodds. And he'd gotten away with it because of that mysterious letter from the White House.

Now he had a lapful of woman—practically—that he wouldn't have turned away any other time. Well, except for the fact that she'd cold-bloodedly shot a man several times in the face and killed him.

He didn't blame himself for getting upset. But it still wasn't professional.

"You know," he growled, "you try really damned hard to make sure no one likes you."

She smiled at him and took a drag on her cigarette. Then she scratched him under the chin like a cat. "A lot of people don't like me, Counselor. They never have."

Adam jerked his head back, then used his hold on the handcuff chain to pull her back from him. She continued walking away till she reached the other side of the room.

"I can help you," Adam told her. "If you'll let me."

She gazed at him and breathed out a stream of smoke. "I can help myself, Boy Scout. You just make sure you stay out of the way when things go to hell."

"What are you talking about?"

She dropped the cigarette to the floor and crushed it underfoot. "I'm through talking. Why don't you have someone take me back to my cell now. I'm feeling a little homesick."

Out in the hallway, Adam instructed the deputies to escort Amanda Weaver back to jail. He looked around for Marion Hart, but she was gone. He assumed she had another hearing or had beat a hasty retreat back to the district attorney's office. Geoffrey Turnbull wasn't going to be happy about what had happened in court.

But Adam did spot FBI Agent Tarlton lounging in the hallway.

The man never looked at him, but Adam had the distinct impression that the man knew he was there.

Tarlton pushed away from the wall, walked down the hallway and entered the men's room.

Adam followed. Part of his decision to pursue the man was stubbornness, but a lot of it was pride. He hadn't liked how frightened he'd felt when the man had threatened him.

There had been other clients that had come through the public defender's office that had gotten irate over Adam's inability to get them off, even though he'd managed to get them lesser sentences or fines. There had been bikers and jealous husbands, blue-collar men and others.

But no one had ever made him feel that vulnerable.

Adam stepped through the doorway and was immediately hit by the astringent smell of the pine-scented cleaners. The fluorescent bulbs glowed overhead. The stalls stood empty on one side of the room and the white porcelain urinals on the other.

He didn't see Tarlton till the door swung shut behind him. Movement drew Adam's attention to his right. He turned just in time to get a glimpse of the hard fist that slammed into the side of his throat.

Chapter 14

Maricopa County Courthouse
Phoenix, Arizona
Tuesday, May 21, 1968
The Past

Pain ballooned inside Adam's head as he slammed back against the closed men's room door. Black spots whirled in his vision. He tried to breathe and couldn't. Panic welled up inside him as he fought to remain standing.

Tarlton hit Adam in the stomach and doubled him over. Another blow, this one to Adam's jaw, drove him to the ground. Before he could recover, Tarlton kicked him twice in the ribs.

Calmly, as if he had all day, Tarlton took a wooden wedge from inside his jacket and slid it under the door. When he tugged on the door, it stayed put.

"Now," Tarlton said, "let's have a chat about how things are going to go."

Certain the man was going to kill him, Adam resisted the impulse to curl up into a fetal position and reached for Tarlton's feet. He caught hold of one of them and yanked. Tarlton fell backward.

Adam's lungs opened up in a rush. Gasping for air like a drowning man, he forced himself to his feet. Tarlton got back up at the same time. Adam blocked Tarlton's next punch with a forearm and responded with a punch of his own. He drove his fist into the man's face and snapped his head back. However, that only earned a brief respite.

Tarlton stepped forward, grabbed Adam by the lapels and slammed him back against the wall. What precious little breath Adam had pulled into his lungs fled again as the impact emptied them. He forced himself to stand.

"You've got some sand in you. I'll give you that." Tarlton wiped his bloody mouth with the back of his hand. "I didn't expect that." He worked his jaw. "Punch pretty good, too."

If he could have caught his breath, Adam would have told the man he'd boxed at home on the ranch under the supervision of one of his father's ranch hands. He'd also boxed in college.

"That was just a taste of what you're going to get if you don't learn to play ball." Tarlton stepped over to one of the sinks. He examined the damage in the spotless mirror, then wet a paper towel and dabbed at his lip.

Adam sucked in air and worked on getting a full breath. It didn't feel like it was going to happen anytime soon.

"You're lucky I was told not to hurt you, Counselor."

This? This is not *getting hurt?* Adam couldn't believe it.

"You can defend Amanda Weaver, Counselor," Tarlton said. "Just don't be really good at it. The woman is a killer dozens of times over. We've even paid her to do it."

"Who's *we?*" Adam gasped.

Tarlton took a comb from his pocket and pointed it at Adam. "Now see? That's the kind of question that'll bring you a lifetime of pain. Or maybe not. It doesn't have to last a lifetime." He calmly parted his hair with the comb and raked it into place.

"Who is she?"

"It doesn't matter who she is." Tarlton wet the comb under the faucet and pulled it through his hair again. "We've read up on you."

We again. Who was *we?*

"You've got all your daddy's money—"

"It's not my money." Adam thought maybe his legs were a little stronger under him.

"—and you got some kind of hero complex. You want to save the world." Tarlton put his comb away. "I could tell you who's really saving the world, but you don't want to hear it. Your kind never does. It's guys like you that's going to cost us the war in Vietnam. And I'm going to tell you right now, buddy, that Amanda Weaver can get you killed."

Adam launched himself at Tarlton. Tarlton turned toward Adam but didn't get clear. As Tarlton closed his right hand into a fist, Adam seized the man's wrist and shoved it into the mirror.

Gripping the back of Tarlton's jacket, Adam rammed the man's face into the mirror as well. Adam lifted his knee into the man's side hard enough to make Tarlton cry out.

Tarlton tried to fight free, but Adam had him bent over the sink. Growling with rage, Tarlton reared back. Adam saw his opponent open his hands and shove against the mirror to break free. Adam tried to hold the man but couldn't. He was still groggy and Tarlton was too strong.

Overcome, Adam stumbled back and lost his hold. Tarlton was on him in an instant. Blows rained down and drove Adam to the ground. Finally, mercifully, Tarlton backed away. The man breathed as loud as a bellows pump.

"Give it up," Tarlton advised. "You'll only get hurt—or worse—if you try to play in this game. You hear me?"

Adam tried to get to his feet but his arms and legs barely held up upright.

Tarlton walked to the door and slid free the wood chock he'd dropped in place. The fact that he'd come prepared for such an enterprise told Adam the man was used to taking advantage of men's rooms and whatever else came along.

"Get to the hospital," Tarlton advised. "You look like you need it."

Slowly Adam worked on breathing. Then he worked on standing. He was almost to his feet when a man entered the men's room and stood flat-footed in shock.

Adam felt blood running down his face.

"Are you okay, buddy?" the man asked.

"I'm fine," Adam croaked. "I slipped."

"How many times?"

Moving slowly, Adam walked over to the sink. He leaned against it, letting it hold some of his weight. With a surge of triumph, he gazed up at the fingerprints captured on the mirror's surface and smiled.

"Can you do me a favor?" Adam asked.

"You want me to see if there's a doctor out here? Probably one somewhere. Doctors are always getting sued. I don't know if I'd want a quack working on me, though."

"I need some Scotch tape," Adam said, ignoring the man's offer. "See if you can borrow some from one of the secretaries downstairs in the records room."

"Hey, Marion."

Glancing up from the files in front of her, Marion saw Jacob Meyers, one of the interns, standing in the doorway. Meyers was young and his hair was longer than Turnbull was comfortable with.

"There's a guy out here to see you. He looks like a bum or a mugging victim."

"Does he have a policeman accompanying him?"

"No."

Marion doubted that Turnbull would run another case at her at the moment. The D.A. had been adamant about the murder investigation taking up all of her available time for the foreseeable future.

So if it wasn't a victim coming to report a crime, who was it?

"What do you want me to do?" Meyers asked.

Marion stood and walked around the desk. "I'll take care of it, Jake. Thanks."

Adam Gracelyn sat perched on a desk in the outer office. And he did look like a mugging victim. His suit was disheveled and his face was bloody and bruised. His left eye had nearly swollen shut.

The silence in the office was immediately noticeable. Normally the typewriter keys banged incessantly as reports and forms were filled out and filed. Every eye in the room was on Adam.

Marion went over to him, started to touch him, then drew back because she was afraid she'd hurt him if she did.

"It's not so bad." Adam tried to grin, then winced in pain. "Okay, it's pretty bad."

"What happened?"

"Long story. But I need to tell it. If you've got time."

Across the room, Turnbull glared at Adam from the doorway of his office. The district attorney chewed on an unlit cigar with grim determination.

"Maybe I should have called ahead," Adam said. Pain tightened his mouth. "But I wasn't sure if you'd have taken my phone call."

"After that stunt you pulled this morning, I probably wouldn't have." Marion folded her arms and stared at him. She knew she wasn't going to win any friends in the district attorney's office by taking Adam in.

"That's why I came instead." Adam's eyes softened. "This is important, Marion. To me and to you."

Marion believed him. She sighed. "All right. Come into my office."

Adam got up painfully and limped through her door.

"Betty," Marion called to one of the receptionists.

"Yes, ma'am," Betty replied. She was in her early thirties, plump and prim, with her hair pulled back into a bun that made her look even older and more severe.

It had been odd for Marion being called *ma'am* by someone who was just a few years older than she was. But that was part of the respect that fueled the district attorney's office.

"Do we have a first-aid kit?" Marion asked.

"Yes, ma'am. A good one."

"Could you bring it to me?"

"Yes, ma'am." Betty got up from her desk and headed for the storeroom.

Although she knew she was going to regret it, Marion glanced at Turnbull. The district attorney shook his head in disgust, turned and stalked back into his office.

Just when I thought things couldn't get any worse, Marion thought glumly.

"All right, mister. You'd better talk and talk fast. Otherwise I'm going to throw you out of here on your ear."

Adam wasn't surprised by the attitude, but he was surprised at how naked it was. Judging by the obstinate set of Marion's jaw and the look of cold fury in her eyes, he figured she meant what she said.

Unfortunately, instead of being intimidated or threatened, Adam found himself gazing at Marion's slim hips and high breasts. She wore stockings that made her skirt swish as she crossed the room. God, how could a woman keep getting better looking every time he saw her? That had never happened before. He was suddenly glad he was sitting down in the chair in front of her desk. Otherwise his interest would be evident.

He decided his present state had to be the result of a near-death experience. He'd read somewhere that a near-death experience could heighten the senses and…other urges. Based on the pain and excitement he was feeling, he'd been very close to death.

"I was attacked," he said.

Instead of sitting, Marion remained standing. She kept her arms folded and her chin lifted. The sunlight staining the Venetian blinds over the window behind her painted her in light and shadow.

"By who?" she asked.

"Whom," he corrected automatically.

Marion frowned. "I don't need a grammar lesson. I'm still digging out from under that pile of steaming horse—"

Adam thought it would have been interesting to find out if that pretty little mouth was actually going to say what she'd started to say. However, Marion was interrupted by a voice from the door.

"Ma'am." A receptionist stood in the doorway holding a small metal box marked First Aid.

"Thank you, Betty." Marion took the kit.

Betty continued standing in the doorway. She gazed at Adam with hungry eyes.

"You can go, Betty," Marion said.

"Do you need some help, ma'am?" Betty's eyes never left Adam.

"No," Marion said. "I can take care of this." She ushered the woman back through the doorway and closed the door after her.

"I'm fine," Adam protested.

"You need a second opinion on that." Marion put the kit on her desk and rummaged through the contents. She took out a bottle of antiseptic and some cotton balls.

Adam didn't relish the prospect of being touched. The pain had finally muted to a dull roar and he didn't want it stirred up again.

"Seriously, I don't want you to do this. I've got a doctor."

"Then why aren't you there?" Marion came closer and stood next to him.

Adam suddenly realized that letting Marion tend to him put him closer to her than he'd been since he met her. He breathed in the delicate fragrance of her perfume and felt the heat of her body against his face. She'd left a couple of buttons undone at the top of her blouse and the view was—

"Ow!" Adam protested when she touched his face with the cotton ball. Despite the exotic lure of her scent and the sight before him, he tried to pull away.

"Don't be a baby," Marion ordered. She cupped the back of his head and held it still while she ministered to him.

Adam kept his groans to himself and tried to concentrate on Marion's elusive and rolling cleavage. He suddenly realized the throbbing in his face was being echoed in another particularly insistent part of his anatomy. He decided to tough it out. Getting thrown out of the office in his present condition was out of the question.

"Do you know how swollen it is?" she asked.

"What?" For one insane moment Adam wasn't sure what Marion was talking about.

"Your eye," she said. "Do you know how swollen it is?"

"Almost shut," he replied, grateful they were talking about his eye. "I can barely see through it."

"You may need to see that doctor you're so proud of."

"The very next thing," Adam promised. "I had to come see you first."

"Why?"

"Because I need to file charges against the person who did this."

Marion looked down at him. Unfortunately she noticed where he was staring. She moved back and took a moment to button her blouse.

"Whom?" she asked.

"Who," Adam corrected before he could stop himself.

Marion scowled.

Adam held up a hand in surrender. "I know, I know. No more grammar lessons." He cleared his throat. "And I didn't mean to stare. I just—you were just—"

Scarlet flamed Marion's cheeks, but Adam wasn't sure if it was caused by anger or embarrassment.

He opened his mouth to explain what happened and heard himself say, "You're really pretty."

Marion took a breath. The effort tightened the buttons across her blouse.

"Thanks. I think. But w-*what* happened to you?"

"Special Agent Tarlton jumped me in the men's room at the courthouse."

"Why?"

"I don't think he was satisfied that the threatening look he gave me at Judge Dodds's bench was going to do the job. I think I was supposed to be more intimidated."

Instantly Marion became totally focused. "Tell me what happened."

Adam did. At the end of it, he brought out the index cards with Scotch tape on them. He showed them to Marion.

Marion was still stunned. "This doesn't make any sense."

"J. Edgar Hoover's boys aren't always known for their winning manner and fair play attitude," Adam said. "I've talked to a few people who've been manhandled by them on different occasions. Not to mention illegal wiretaps and other flagrant violations of rights."

"Why would the FBI be interested in Amanda Weaver?"

"That's probably not her name," Adam pointed out.

Marion frowned at him. "I got enough of that this morning, thank you."

"Sorry. I thought I was going to be dealing with Turnbull."

"Because, as a woman, I wasn't competent enough to handle prosecution in this case?"

"Because Turnbull likes to grab headlines and easy cases. This murder investigation has started to gain national attention. And, if I may be so bold, until this morning the case looked like a cakewalk."

"It still looks like a cakewalk."

"Not with FBI agents laying for public defenders in the men's room."

Marion let out an angry breath. "No, not with FBI agents ambushing public defenders anywhere."

"Want to see my Scotch tape? I'm rather proud of these."

"What are they?"

"During my struggle with Special Agent Tarlton, I managed to press his hand up against the mirror in the men's room. I used graphite from a pencil sharpener to make a poor man's fingerprint powder. I pulled the fingerprints off the mirror with Scotch tape. I've seen crime scene guys do that. I didn't figure the prints would last long, so I took them myself. I thought maybe you could have someone try to match them up."

Marion took the cards. "You may have compromised the integrity of these prints. Do you have a witness that can verify you took these prints where you say you did?"

"I got a bailiff to observe me. He signed the back of both those cards. He's willing to testify."

A quick flip of the cards revealed the promised signatures and date.

"Impressive," Marion said.

Adam grinned ruefully. "It would have been more impressive if I'd dragged Tarlton in after me."

"Yes," Marion agreed.

Some of Adam's spirits dropped a little at her frank response.

"But you did what you could." Marion reached into her desk and brought out a tablet of lined legal paper and a pen. "Write your statement down."

A look of surprise filled Adam's face. "Can't you get someone in here to take dictation?"

"No."

"You're deliberately being obstinate."

"I'm not going to feel sorry for you. You have a way of frustrating people, Counselor."

"Then can I borrow your typewriter?" Adam pointed at the Underwood manual on her desk.

"You know how to type?" Marion arched a brow.

"Eighty words a minute. Not great. But I do my own papers."

Marion hesitated for a moment, then nodded. "Get it typed up. I'm going to see if I can find Special Agent Tarlton."

Adam walked behind the desk and sat down. He laced his fingers, cracked his knuckles, and winced. His right hand ached and was somewhat swollen from hitting Tarlton.

"Finding Tarlton isn't going to be easy," he said.

"What makes you say that?"

Adam fed paper into the platen and slapped the carriage return lever. "I called his hotel. He's checked out."

Marion opened the door and went out. Adam typed quickly,

getting into the rhythm in seconds. But he couldn't help thinking about Marion Hart, her warmth, her scent and that delightful view down her blouse. It took his mind off the pain and how scared he was of what he'd gotten into the middle of.

Chapter 15

Dr. Bernhardt, dressed in a shirt and tie, black slacks and his lab coat, met David and Winter at the nurses' station on the fourth floor. After a brief greeting, he guided them to an office in the back and closed the door.

"My one and only asked-for indulgence from the board of directors," Bernhardt said, waving toward the cramped office. Photographs, black-and-white and color, took up all the available wall space that wasn't covered in books. "It's not much of an indulgence, but I like to feel as though I'm keeping my hand in."

Winter sat in front of the desk and took out her iPAQ. "From what I saw, you've more than kept your hand in. You regularly publish articles in leading medical journals."

Bernhardt shrugged as if anyone with half a brain could accomplish the same thing. He laced his fingers before him, elbows resting on the desk and gazed at her through thick horn-rimmed glasses.

"Now what's a pretty girl like you want with an old fogie like me? I do have to admit that I have a compelling bedside manner." Bernhardt waggled his bushy gray eyebrows suggestively.

In spite of the seriousness of what had brought her there, Winter couldn't help laughing. The years had been kind to Bernhardt, and he obviously had no confidence problems.

"I'm doing research on a book about Marion Gracelyn," Winter said.

"Ah." Bernhardt's eyes widened. "So I was right. You're *that* Winter Archer."

"Is that a good thing or a bad thing?"

Bernhardt smiled. "I enjoy your work, but I don't think I'd want you writing about me. You…like to use your magnifying lens a little too much for my taste."

"I don't create the dirt I find, Dr. Bernhardt," Winter said defensively. "And I don't make it any more than it is."

"I understand that, Miss Archer. As I said, I'm a fan of your work. I also believe that you do good things and you make discriminate choices. But I think most people have something they'd rather not disclose."

"Some people and corporate entities don't have that luxury. I like to think that I do more good than harm."

"Actually I believe that you do." Bernhardt leaned across the desk to get down to business. "I have to admit that the primary reason I agreed to see you was that I thought I knew who you were. I enjoyed your interview on *Larry King Live*."

"Thank you."

"Now…about what brought you here. I'm eighty-seven. I'm not going to last forever."

Winter leaned forward as well as she responded to the physician's body language. He wanted to talk. And he was curious.

"I want to speak to you about a woman you treated back in 1968," Winter said.

"That's a long time ago."

"It is. But I think you'll remember this one."

Bernhardt smiled. "Let's see if you get a mental bingo. At my age, I can't always guarantee results."

"Amanda Weaver," Winter said. "She murdered Colonel Thomas Marker in the Kellogg Motel."

Bernhardt leaned back in his chair. The move was designed to create space and time to think. "Ah. That one."

"You examined her the morning the sheriff's office arrested her," Winter said.

Bernhardt looked past Winter. "You're David Gracelyn, President Monihan's handpicked attorney general."

"I am."

Winter never took her eyes from Bernhardt. These were the stressful moments when interviewees often revealed a lot about themselves and how they would continue to handle stress and questions.

"Are you here in an official capacity?" Bernhardt asked.

"No. I'm helping Miss Archer with her research. I want to make sure my mother is represented fairly in this."

"I see." Bernhardt shifted his gaze back to Winter. "That was a long time ago. My memory's not what it used to be. Although it was before you were born, you might have heard how turbulent 1968 was. Elvis made his comeback that year and soon moved off to Las Vegas."

"I'll take what I can get."

"That could be precious little."

Winter was stymied. She tried to figure out whether she should retreat till another day when she found a lever to prise at Bernhardt's hard exterior or throw herself on his mercy. Personally she hated the mercy angle. Once weakness was shown people generally didn't forget that.

"Dr. Bernhardt," David spoke up before she could say anything. "We have reason to believe that the events that happened forty years ago might have something to do with my mother's death."

"I don't see how—"

"This isn't for public consumption, but my mother was being blackmailed by a person we're trying to identify. That blackmail has only lately come to our attention."

A perplexed look twisted Bernhardt's seamed face. "You think she was being blackmailed over something that happened forty years ago?"

"Old secrets never die," David said. "People just try to hang on to them more tightly. The blackmail took place over several decades. Miss Archer has been going through my mother's journals. The story of that murder caught her attention. I have to admit that it's done the same with me."

"You're not doing a book on Marion?" Bernhardt looked at Winter.

"Not yet."

"Pity. She was an amazing woman. I was very fortunate getting to know her. I enjoy lecturing out at the academy when I get the opportunity."

Winter mentally kicked herself for not checking for Bernhardt's name on the staff roster. She was too tightly focused on the mystery and not seeing the big picture.

You gotta loosen up, she told herself. *You're going to miss too much.*

"As to your murderess, and I remain firmly convinced that she did indeed kill that man in that motel," Bernhardt said, "I suppose you're the reason my nurse pulled these old files." He reached for a folder on top of a stack of books behind the desk. "These are copies, but—at this point at least—they're not to leave my possession."

"May I?" Winter asked.

Bernhardt pushed the files over to her.

Winter opened the files and quickly went through them. "They're very well organized."

"Thank you."

The reports were handwritten, as they would be in the examination rooms, but they were backed by typewritten pages that Bernhardt had initialed. Winter found the initial examination pages that detailed the bruising Amanda Weaver had shown.

Winter also found the follow-up pages regarding Bernhardt's thoughts on the scars that Amanda Weaver had over her body. The list of damage and the physician's guesswork about when it had occurred was carefully delineated.

"You made a time line for the injuries Amanda Weaver received," Winter said.

David had come up behind her and read over her shoulder. She was too conscious of his warmth and the smell of his cologne.

Focus, Winter reminded herself. She did *not* want to get lost in a schoolgirl crush that should have died years ago. She had enough things in her past that occasionally spilled out and made her life difficult.

"I made the time line," Bernhardt said, "in case Marion and Sheriff Keller needed to try to track the woman. Given the state of intelligence reports from abroad at that time, especially with the fact there were few women assassins in the world back then, I thought it was feasible they would be able to establish a history for her based on possible events."

"You seriously believe she was an assassin?" David asked.

Bernhardt laced his hands on the desk in front of him. Small tremors passed through them. "I do. The kind of violence she had done to her body—the knife wounds and the permanent tattooing caused by gunfire only inches from her flesh—spoke of a constant and close proximity with death. You don't find that kind of lethal intimacy without hunting for it."

"You were in the OSS," Winter said.

"And later the CIA," Bernhardt agreed. "I'd seen men who enjoyed that kind of lifestyle. It takes a special breed to do what they did, constantly staring death in the eyes behind enemy lines." He held up a finger. "But in all my life, I truly believe I've only met one woman like that."

"This one," Winter said.

Bernhardt nodded. "They tried to kill her, you know. Amanda Weaver? They tried to kill her while she was in custody."

"I know," Winter said. She'd read that in Marion's journals.

"When?" David asked.

Winter hadn't yet told David about that. She'd wanted to tell the story in as chronological a fashion as she could. Telling it that way kept her mind clear and focused.

Except for the way she kept noticing him.

"I'll tell you later," Winter said.

"I treated her burns after that attack," Bernhardt said. "She wasn't seriously harmed. And she was totally calm. She could have burned to death in that cell, but she was calm when I saw her. That couldn't have been more than thirty minutes later."

The entry in Marion's journal that day had been exceedingly descriptive. Winter had gotten a chill just from reading it. Considering that she'd done a book on Billy Clyde Taylor, the Iowa hunter who had killed seventeen people over a six-year period—including children—and she had been present when four of those bodies had been reclaimed from the earth, she didn't often get spooked.

"She killed the man that almost killed her," Bernhardt said.

Winter nodded. "That was another side of Weaver's life that spilled out of her past."

Bernhardt smiled. "Because of the Queen of Hearts playing card. I've always felt that if anyone ever found out the truth of that woman's past it would make a hell of a story. It's something you would write, Miss Archer."

"I know. I'm tempted. But there are too many missing pieces. You were talking about your concerns the day Amanda Weaver was attacked in the jail."

"Like I was saying, I knew she was all right when Marion called me. She and Adam were both at the jail just a few minutes after the attack."

"My father was there?" David asked.

"He was. He'd been in a meeting with your mother. Afterward, he felt responsible for not insisting on tighter security. But that wouldn't have stopped the assassin."

"Why?" Winter asked.

Bernhardt shook his head. "He had a court order. It was forged, of course. I don't believe Marion or Adam ever found out who made it. They weren't talking too much to me, but I know they suspected the *FBI* agent that pulled rank on them of being behind the attack. Of course, they found out that the attack came from a whole new quarter. Amanda Weaver, whatever her name really was, had made a lot of enemies."

"But she was all right?" Winter asked.

"She was. Marion arranged for them to bring her into the E.R. to see me. When I arrived, she was just sitting there like she hadn't a concern in the world. Handcuffed, of course, because by then they'd seen her in action a couple of times. I wasn't worried about her, though. I was worried about the baby. There had been a lot of smoke in the jail from the reports I'd gotten. Smoke cuts down on oxygen to a baby."

The announcement caught Winter by surprise. "A baby?"

"Yes."

"What baby?"

"Amanda Weaver's baby. She was pregnant at the time. Only a

few weeks." Bernhardt leaned forward and sorted through the files. "It's here." He pulled out a sheet of paper and passed it to Winter. "She was definitely pregnant at the time she killed Colonel Marker in that motel room."

Chapter 16

"What's Gracelyn doing here?"

Marion resented the tone Turnbull was taking with her, but she knew she had to be careful handling his rancor. Turnbull was a team player as long as everyone remembered he or she was on Turnbull's team.

"He's reporting a crime," she said.

"What crime?"

Pausing in her search of the filing cabinet, Marion looked at Turnbull. "I'm going to open up with assault and battery. Maybe bump it up to aggravated assault because there's a definite indication of premeditation. Given the look of Gracelyn's face, what do you think my chances are of securing a conviction?"

"A damn sight better than they are at nailing Amanda Weaver for murdering Colonel Marker," Turnbull growled. "Who did the deed?"

Marion decided to drop the bomb and see what happened. "FBI Special Agent Tarlton."

Turnbull stopped chewing his cigar and took it out of his mouth. He cursed. "There's something screwy going on with this case."

"I think that was Gracelyn's point this morning." Marion pulled a camera from the filing cabinet.

Turnbull didn't take the bait. "Where's Tarlton now? Isn't he staying somewhere in town?"

"He was," Marion agreed. "He left us the number of the hotel he was staying at."

"Why do you say *was?*"

"Gracelyn says Tarlton skipped."

"Did he?"

"I've got Betty checking now."

Turnbull cursed some more. "My phone is ringing off the hook. The mayor wants to know what I'm going to do with this case because he wants it shoved off the front page of the papers and shelved as the lead on the evening news."

"Why?"

"Guess who he plays golf with."

"Conrad Ellis."

"Got it in one. And Ellis is a big fan of Marker's."

"Because Marker brought his son home from the war."

"Yeah. All this pressure means that I'm not a happy man. And when I'm not a happy man, nobody else gets to be happy, either."

"Rule number one," Marion said automatically.

"Exactly. Make me happy, Marion. Get to the bottom of this."

"I will," Marion promised. She hoped that she could.

"Betty, have you checked on Special Agent Tarlton?"

The secretary looked up from the paper she was working on diligently with a Wite-Out brush. "Yes, ma'am. He checked out of the hotel."

Marion checked the film in the camera she was carrying and found there were still eighteen unexposed shots on the film. "Was there a forwarding address?"

"No, ma'am."

"I assume Special Agent Tarlton was driving a car while he was in the Phoenix area."

"I wouldn't know, ma'am."

"You would if you'd call the desk clerk at that hotel back and ask him."

"Yes, ma'am." Betty reached for the phone.

"See if you can find Sheriff Keller for me, too."

"Yes, ma'am."

Marion took one of the fingerprint cards from her jacket pocket and placed it on the desk. "Get someone in the research department to get these fingerprints photographed. I want copies sent to Washington, D.C., immediately."

"To whom?" Betty grabbed a shorthand pad and held a pencil poised in readiness.

"You're sure it's not 'to who'?"

"Yes, ma'am."

Marion sighed. Why was it the office secretary spoke more grammatically correct than she did, and she was supposed to deliver stunning orations that would leave juries ready to deliver a maximum judgment against a lawbreaker.

"Send copies to the FBI, the military branches, and the Washington, D.C. Police Department." Marion felt that was a big enough spread to start with. If she had no luck getting information on the prints in those places, she'd start with the next people on the list she planned to put together.

"Yes, ma'am."

"In fact, pull file copies of Amanda Weaver's fingerprints and let's get them circulating in that area as well." So far they'd stayed close to home in their investigation.

"Yes, ma'am."

Satisfied she had the camera in proper working order, Marion went back into her office.

By the time Marion reentered her office, Adam was reading the neatly typed pages with a pencil in hand. Although he tried to keep the pages clean, he also tried not to Wite-Out mistakes too much. He preferred catching his mistakes in the raw copy and retyping the necessary pages.

"You're already finished?" Marion looked surprised.

"Just checking it over. I'll probably have to retype a couple pages. I like my reports neat. That's part of why I type them."

Marion placed the camera she was carrying on the edge of her desk and picked up the sheaf of papers. The document was seven single-spaced pages long.

"You said you typed eighty words a minutes."

"Yeah, but I do it every minute till I'm done."

"You need to sign it."

"As soon as I'm happy with what I've got."

Marion put the document back on her desk and took up the camera. "I need photographs."

"For what?"

"Evidence. If this gets out of hand and it takes us a while, those bruises are going to heal. If I get the chance to prosecute Special Agent Tarlton, I want to do it right. It's hard to show a jury where a bruise *used* to be."

Irritated and embarrassed, Adam allowed himself to be posed while Marion took shots. It was bad enough that a few attorneys he knew had seen him leaving the courthouse, but the pictures would possibly be seen by a larger share of the local populace.

"Take off your shirt," Marion said as she advanced the film.

"What?" Adam was certain he hadn't heard her right.

"Your shirt," Marion repeated. "The way you're moving, I know he worked over your upper body, too. I've prosecuted domestic abuse cases. I recognize the careful way you're twisting and turning." She gestured for him to hurry up. "Let's get this done. It's practically painless."

For you, Adam thought angrily. He hadn't counted on this aspect of the encounter. It was one thing to come in wearing bruises and marks on his face, but it was another to reveal the extent to which he'd gotten beaten. It was embarrassing.

"I got a few good shots in," he said.

"I'm sure you did."

Adam still didn't move. He couldn't.

When Marion spoke again, her voice was softer. "This isn't a contest, Adam. Everybody can get beaten up. There's no shame in what happened to you. Nobody was keeping score. All I want to do is prove my case."

Reluctantly Adam stood, but he didn't reach for his shirt.

After a moment, Marion came over without a word. She placed

the camera on the desk and reached for Adam. Slowly and gently, she took his jacket and tie off, then unbuttoned his shirt.

Adam stood there hypnotized. The scent of her was overpowering. He felt intoxicated. As she worked, she concentrated on what she was doing. He looked down at the top of her head and felt the heat of her body radiating against his own.

She peeled his bloody shirt off him and revealed the T-shirt beneath. Working together, carefully, she pulled it over his head with his help.

Even though she had to have expected what lay beneath, she gasped in surprise. Adam knew the bruises and abrasions showed. The T-shirt had stuck to dried blood underneath.

She ran her hands along his torso to explore the battered flesh. Her touch felt like fire. Desire detonated inside Adam's head and thundered through his veins. Unable to stop himself, he reached for her.

He caught her chin with his fingers and tilted her head up while his other hand cupped the back of her neck and pulled her toward him. She resisted, a little, and he had to step toward her in the end. But her lips parted when they met his.

The kiss nearly took off the top of his head. The burning contact with her lips, the delicate and quick embrace of their tongues and the way she smelled swept over him like a wave. He was on fire, buried alive in sensations he'd never before experienced.

This is insane, he told himself. *You can't do this here.* But his hands explored her body. His fingers gently traced the valley between her breasts. She shivered against him and kissed him more fiercely. Her hands tenderly held his face, pulling him more tightly into her as if she was going to absorb him.

For one impulsive moment, Adam fantasized about lifting her up onto the desk, shoving her skirt up past her hips and—

Marion abruptly broke the contact and shoved him back.

"I'm sorry," Adam mumbled through numb lips. "It's my fault. I shouldn't have—" He stopped speaking when he saw the ruby-red that stained the fingers of her left hand. For a moment he thought it was blood, but it was too bright. Then, with a sickening lurch of his stomach, he realized what the color was.

Amanda Weaver had marked him with her lipstick when she'd kissed him. He hadn't gotten it all off.

"I can explain," Adam said. He stepped toward her.

"Don't." Marion held up a hand. "Don't. Talk."

Helplessly he stood there. He didn't know what to say. Words wouldn't come.

"The mistake was mine." Pain showed in Marion's eyes. "I knew what you were the first time I laid eyes on you. I just forgot. But just for a minute." She reached for the camera. "Now hold still and let's finish this up."

"Marion—"

"No." She spoke from behind the camera as she took pictures. "If you keep talking, I'm walking out of here and one of the other assistants can finish taking these."

Cursing himself and his client, Adam put his hands behind his head as he was directed and turned around so she could shoot him from all sides. He closed his eyes and swayed as the pain filled his body in an overwhelming rush.

The man who'd been calling himself FBI Special Agent Bruce Tarlton stopped the Ford sedan he was currently driving at a truck stop outside of Tucson. He still hated the idea of turning tail and running from Phoenix. He should have kept his cool, but that lawyer was mucking things up.

He'd been tempted to just kill Adam Gracelyn there in the men's room and vanish. He'd done that a few times in other parts of the world. It was easy.

Except that killing one clever lawyer hadn't been what he'd been sent to do. He'd been after bigger game. If Weaver was in Phoenix, it stood to reason that Evaristo Melendez was there, too.

After all, Weaver hadn't been in the city on a vacation. She'd gone there to do a job.

It was just Marker's bad luck that she'd cut his trail. Of course, it was kind of hard to miss him. Marker had been living up his war hero shtick lately. He'd been a speaker at a Rotary Club the night before.

Marker had gotten incredibly stupid. He hadn't gotten that way till after he'd come back from the war. Something had changed there and the agency that Tarlton worked for still didn't know what it was.

They'd gotten lucky when one of the agents following Marker

had spotted Weaver. They'd let her kill him, of course, because it saved them the trouble. But they'd counted on her getting away and leading them to Evaristo. In fact, they'd been surprised when Evaristo hadn't shown up at the Kellogg Motel.

But Weaver's luck had turned sour, too. Something had happened inside the motel and Marker had gotten in a lucky punch that had left her dazed just long enough to get her captured.

She'd gotten her revenge, though. Tarlton didn't begrudge her that. He'd read her file. He'd known how Marker had betrayed her in Vietnam. He just didn't know why Marker had betrayed her. For a handful of years, Weaver—or whatever her name really was because Tarlton was used to working in a world where no one wore their right name—had been one of the Agency's top assets.

He glared at the truck stop through the dust-covered windshield. He hated the fact that he had to call in to report his failure. Usually in his line of work a man didn't have to call in to report such things. People usually just found the body—or sometimes not—and knew.

He left his tie off as he clambered out of the car, but he slid the .45 he'd kept under his thigh on the seat into the waistband at his back. The heat beat into him as he crossed the dusty lot. He hated the desert.

Inside the truck stop, air-conditioning, the only thing that made Arizona habitable, kept the heat at bay. Only a handful of patrons were scattered through the booth seats at the windows. Long-haul truckers, waitresses and the short-order cook glanced at Tarlton as he entered.

He walked to the counter. "Can I get a beer? I want to cut the dust."

The cook pulled tap beer into a glass and slid it across.

"And some change for the phone," Tarlton added.

"How much?"

"Couple dollars' worth."

The cook opened the register and took out quarters, dimes and nickels.

Tarlton dropped money on the counter and picked up his drink and the change. At the back of the room, he stepped into the telephone booth and dropped quarters into the slot. He dialed and sipped his beer. It was cold and refreshing, and it finally took the edge off the anger he'd nursed at Adam Gracelyn for spoiling things.

"Hello," a female voice answered.

Tarlton gave his code name and that of his supervisor. Booker came onto the line a moment later.

"I hear we hit a snafu out there," Booker said. His voice was flat and mid-Western.

"Things got complicated," Tarlton agreed. He set his beer on the shelf in front of him and took out his cigarette pack.

"I'm surprised you left the lawyer alive."

"That was a real piece of self-control." Tarlton struck a match and lit his cigarette. "Guy was screwing with what we had in play. He was gonna have everybody digging into her past." He spoke obliquely because there was no way of telling when J. Edgar's real boys were tapping phone lines. Even the Agency wasn't safe from them.

"Well, we couldn't have that, could we?"

"No."

"You did the right thing. It's just going to be harder."

Tarlton let out a stream of smoke. "I think it's a bust. Her friend's a no-show. Maybe something happened to him."

"I believe we'd have heard about that. He isn't the type to go quietly into that good night."

Tarlton figured the weird words were a quote for something, but he didn't know what. Quotes didn't kill people. Guns did. Tarlton knew guns. And knives. And fists.

"Either way, I think leaving the woman in play is a mistake," Tarlton said. "She's become more of a disadvantage."

"She's bait," Booker pointed out.

"She knows too much about what we've done. She knows where the bodies are buried." Tarlton snorted with mirth. "She buried some of them herself and never told us where they were. Do you really think the upper brass wants that landing in their laps?"

Booker didn't answer for a moment.

Tarlton smoked quietly. He knew Booker would see it his way. The man had no choice.

"All right," Booker said finally. "The team is still in place there in the city?"

"Yes."

"Then they can—"

"There's another way," Tarlton interrupted.

"I'm listening."

"She dropped her calling card in that motel room."

"I'd heard that. Awfully presumptuous of her."

"She's always been...*possessive* about her work." Tarlton didn't blame her for that, either. Weaver had a solid rep in her craft. People might not have known her name, but the right ones knew her calling card. He palmed a Queen of Hearts from his pocket and studied it. "So far the locals have kept that out of the news."

"They always hold something back."

"I know. I was thinking that she's got a lot of enemies."

"Maybe the right words in the right ears?" Booker asked.

"She's got a history in Boston," Tarlton said. "If we make sure the trail leads back there, I think we can come out of this clean. No one will know to look any further than that. They definitely won't be looking in our direction."

Booker hesitated for a moment.

Tarlton practiced shaking the card and making it disappear. When it came to small objects, he was as adept as any stage magician.

"All right," Booker said. "Get it done. Do you have a number to call?"

"I know it by heart."

"Monitor the situation. Let me know if you need anything."

"Sure," Tarlton agreed. He cradled the phone, then lifted the receiver again and dialed another number. He changed his voice so that he sounded more nasal and flattened out his A's.

"Yeah," a gruff voice answered.

"I need to talk to Uncle Sal," Tarlton said.

"Who's this?" the voice demanded.

"Just a guy who knows something."

"Everybody knows something."

"Tell Uncle Sal it's about the Queen of Hearts." Tarlton stared at the playing card in his hand. "Tell him I know where he can find her."

"Hold on."

Tarlton listened as the houseman yelled at someone to get Uncle Sal. Sitting in the phone booth, Tarlton felt better. Things were going to work out. He shook his wrist, snapped his hand and popped his fingers.

The Queen of Hearts disappeared as if she'd never been.

Chapter 17

District Attorney's Office
Phoenix, Arizona
Friday, May 24, 1968
The Past

"Ma'am."

Marion looked up from the court reports she was going over in preparation for a trial that afternoon. Betty stood in the door.

"Yes, Betty?"

"That man." Betty pointed. Then she whispered. "He's back." She pointed again with more urgency.

It took Marion a moment to realize what man the secretary was referring to. *Oh. That man.* Marion sat up straighter and tried to figure out what she should do.

She hadn't seen Adam Gracelyn since the debacle in her office three days ago. He'd tried calling and had even left messages, but she'd ignored them. That had been hard to do, but every time she thought about giving in she remembered the crimson lipstick that had stained her fingers while he'd been kissing her.

While you were kissing him back, she chided herself. *You don't have to take that away from him.* But she wanted to. She didn't want to admit any interest in playboy Adam Gracelyn.

Except that she kept being impressed by the way he'd gone to bat for his client. Of course, now Marion knew why he was working so hard. There were fringe benefits other than the low pay the public defender's office offered.

"Ma'am?" Betty prompted. "What do you want to do?"

Marion steeled herself. She'd actually wondered how he was doing. He had been badly beaten. Resolutely she returned her attention to the court report.

"Tell him I'm busy."

"What if he wants to make an appointment?"

"Tell him I'm busy."

Betty hesitated.

Marion looked up at her. "What?"

"Well, I think he *really* wants to see you." Betty smiled hopefully. "It couldn't hurt to talk to him for a few minutes. After all, he's handsome and rich and smart and—"

Marion glanced past Betty at Adam, who had come up behind the secretary.

Betty looked mortified. "—and he's standing right behind me, isn't he?"

Marion nodded.

"I'm going to be sick." Betty clapped a hand over her mouth, turned away and fled the doorway.

Adam's face was a multicolored patchwork of bruises. His eye had resumed its normal size, but deep purple ringed it.

"Sensitive, isn't she?" he asked as he watched after Betty.

"Some things just turn her stomach," Marion said. "I'm incredibly busy right now."

"I've heard that you were. I keep getting that message."

"Some of us have to work for a living."

"Ouch," Adam commented. He stepped into the room anyway, then closed the door behind him.

"I'd prefer that the door remain open," Marion said.

"Okay." Adam opened the door and turned back to face her. "I came to apologize. I didn't mean to kiss you the other day. That kind of happened before I planned for it to."

"Wait." Marion held up a hand. "I don't want to hear—"

"You're going to hear me," Adam said. "The question is, do you want the secretarial pool to hear as well."

Marion sighed and leaned forward to rest her elbows on the desk. "All right. Close the door. But if you try to come around to this side of the desk, I'm going to put you into the hospital."

Adam held his hands up, closed the door, then sat in the chair in front of her desk. They stared at each other for a moment.

"This is awkward," he admitted.

Marion didn't say anything. It was awkward for her, too, and she wasn't going to make things any easier for him.

"You're not like any other woman I've ever known," he said.

"And how many women have you known, Counselor?"

"I'll plead the Fifth on that one. My point is that I don't know how to approach you."

"Judging from what little I know of your track record, which is documented in the society pages—"

Adam frowned. "The *gossip* pages, you mean."

"—you've been successful at approaching a lot of women."

"Did you know that before or after I kissed you?"

Marion's irritation grew. He seemed to know exactly the right thing to set her off. The truth was that after that kiss she *had* gone to the library and read through recent back issues of the papers to find mentions of him. She just hadn't been able to get him off her mind.

"That was crass," Adam said. "I apologize. I came to try to make amends."

"You don't have anything to apologize for," Marion said. "You were hurt and, quite possibly, not in your right mind."

"The truth is I've wanted to kiss you from the moment I first saw you," Adam said. "I'm not apologizing for that. That kiss was one of the best I've ever had."

"'One of the best?'"

Adam grinned at her. "You never forget your first kiss. I was thirteen. Amy Franks was fifteen. Later I told my buddies she kissed me. She, of course being two years older and incredibly cooler than me, denied everything. They never believed me. So I looked like a jerk because I couldn't stop trying to convince them for months."

In spite of the tension, Marion laughed.

"I have to admit," Adam said ruefully, "that isn't the reaction I was going for."

"I've found that thirteen-year-old boys don't change much over the next twenty years."

"I'm not trying to convince anyone that I kissed you."

"Thank God for small favors."

"I'm trying to convince you," he said, looking her straight in the eye, "that I kissed *you*. Not some target. Not some sex object." He paused. "I kissed *you*."

A warm feeling spread throughout Marion. She hadn't expected this at all. Not his words and certainly not her reaction.

"And it was one of the best kisses I've ever had," Adam said.

"So we're back to that."

"Well…" Adam grinned. "You can always try to improve your standing."

"Why should I want to?"

"We could go with Betty's list. I'm handsome…"

"So is a golden retriever."

"…I'm smart…"

"Debatable."

"…and I would like the chance to get to know you better."

Marion was so tempted she couldn't believe it. *Surely you're not going to be stupid enough to fall for this.* But she wanted to.

"You came to me wearing your client's lipstick," she said. "That's not exactly endearing."

"She tried to kiss me," Adam said.

"You were wearing her lipstick."

"I turned my head. That's why the lipstick was behind my ear. I thought I'd wiped it all away."

"So how did the kiss—the *almost* kiss—happen?"

"After the arraignment I was trying to talk to her, hoping she'd open up—"

"I bet you were."

"—and tell me more about Special Agent Tarlton and why the FBI would be interested in her. I think she tried to kiss me to shut me up."

"Or maybe she thought you were handsome and smart."

Adam nodded confidently. "Maybe so. I am. But it doesn't mean I'm easy."

Even though she told herself she wasn't going to, Marion laughed. "You definitely don't have a confidence problem."

"I never have," Adam admitted. "But there's something about you that makes me just the teeniest bit uncertain."

"How uncertain?"

Adam spread his forefinger and thumb a fraction of an inch. "This much. But it's way more than anyone else ever has. You're at the top of that list."

"Maybe it's not so good to be at the top of that one."

"Yeah," Adam said. "It is. I love being challenged and intrigued."

"I'm not here for your personal amusement, Mr. Gracelyn."

"Would you like to have dinner with me? It seems to me that we had some good times over lunch and dinner while we were working this case before the arraignment. I'd like to see what that was."

The earnestness in his voice caught Marion's attention. He was handsome and he was smart. And she could back out at any time that she wanted to. He definitely wasn't irresistible.

Keep telling yourself that, she thought. *Maybe you'll believe it.*

"I've got a full weekend planned," Marion said. It wasn't a definite answer either way.

"That's fine. I've got a proposition for you."

Marion waited, but she was irritated at her own level of interest.

"My parents usually throw a big Memorial Day event," Adam said. "Memorial Day is next Thursday. I thought maybe you'd like to go as my guest."

Marion knew she was going to accept. She'd already gone through her closet mentally and figured out that she didn't have anything to wear.

"It's a public event," Adam said. "It's not like we're on a date. You can drive yourself if you want."

"Nice to know that I have an option."

"I just don't want you to feel trapped. If you drive, you can come and go as you like."

"Is there a dress code?"

Adam smiled.

"I haven't said yes yet," Marion pointed out. "I'm just asking."

"It's my mother's event," Adam said. "Of course there's a dress code. Casual wear, jeans and golf shirt, until seven. Dinner is black tie. Do you want me to pick you up?"

Before Marion could answer, the intercom buzzed for attention. Grateful for the respite, she punched the button. "Yes, Betty."

"I'm sorry to interrupt, ma'am," Betty said. "But the jail just called. There's a problem over at the jail that Sheriff Keller wanted you to know about."

"What?"

Adam sat up straighter on the other side of the desk.

"There was a fire in Amanda Weaver's cell."

"Who are you?"

Marco Fanelli lied through his teeth. Twenty-seven years old, dark hair and dark eyes, he'd been lying since he could talk. It was his second-best skill. He was about to employ his best.

"Farmer," Fanelli answered. "Michael Farmer." He smiled.

"What's your relationship to Amanda Weaver?" the female jailer asked.

"I'm her brother."

"You've got different last names."

"She was married. It didn't work out." Fanelli put on a sad face. Women loved his sad face. The female jailer was no exception.

"She's not supposed to have any visitors."

Fanelli knew that, too, and he'd come prepared. He reached into his jacket and took out a piece of paper. "I've got a court order."

The jailer looked at the document, which looked as real as the forger could make it. According to the paper, Michael Farmer was allowed to visit his sister, Amanda Weaver.

"I need to see some identification," the jailer said.

"No problem," Fanelli replied. And it wasn't. He showed the jailer the forged Nevada driver's license and social security card.

"I've got orders that she's not to be let out of her cell," the jailer said.

Fanelli already knew that. "That's okay. I'll talk to her there."

"She's got an attorney. Adam Gracelyn. Have you talked to him?" The jailer made a note of the driver's license and passed the documents back.

"My next stop. I heard he was a nice guy."

* * *

Minutes later, Fanelli stood in front of Amanda Weaver's cell. He didn't know the woman by sight and she only kind of resembled the few pictures he'd been shown.

She sat on the bed in her prison uniform with a book cradled in her lap. She was alone. It wouldn't have bothered Fanelli if the woman hadn't been. Whoever was inside that cell today was going to die.

The jailer introduced Fanelli as Weaver's brother.

"Hey, sis." Fanelli smiled.

"If you need anything, let me know."

Fanelli said he would, thanked the jailer and watched her walk away.

"I don't know you," Weaver said quietly. She didn't get up from the bed.

"Uncle Sal wants you to know he sends his regards." Fanelli knew from the woman's reaction that she knew the name. She didn't over-react or act frightened, but her shoulders squared slightly. He'd heard she was dangerous but she sure didn't look it at the moment.

"Tell Uncle Sal he can go to hell," she said.

The woman sounded like she had ice water in her veins. The loathing in her voice was pure and unforgiving. But it was easy being brave on the other side of iron bars. Which side didn't matter.

Fanelli took the Queen of Hearts from his pocket and flicked it at Weaver. The playing card fluttered through the air and landed face-up on the bed.

"Get ready to burn, baby," Fanelli said. He took a Zippo lighter from his pocket and struck it to life. "I'm about to light up your world."

Fanelli pulled out the rubber tubing hidden up his sleeve. The jailer's quick pat down had been for weapons. He pointed the tube into the cell and squeezed the rubber bladder under his arm.

Amber liquid streamed out of the tube in a rush. The sweet smell of gasoline tainted the tepid air. He'd aimed at the woman and hoped to douse her. But she was up and moving incredibly fast. In the end it wasn't going to matter. Fanelli had done this before.

He'd never seen anyone as fast as the woman, though. She ducked and came at him. The amber stream shot over her shoulder.

More quickly than he'd thought possible, Weaver reached

through the bars and caught his coat. She hauled him into the bars so quickly he couldn't brace himself. His head thudded against the bars and his knees went out beneath him.

The hose fell into his lap. Weaver squatted in front of him as he tried to escape. She pressed on his elbow like she knew about the gasoline bladder trick. The amber liquid pooled in Fanelli's lap.

Somehow he'd managed to hang on to the Zippo. The flame wavered but still held. He tried to slide away from Weaver, but her grip was inexorable. She grabbed his hand with the lighter and bent it back toward his body. His elbow didn't bend that way. He wanted to tell her that but the pain turned his words into screams.

Something in his elbow shattered. He felt it come apart. Then the lighter dropped onto his lap. The pooled gasoline caught fire immediately and raced up his body.

She let go of him then, but it was already too late. The joke was going to be on her in the end. The Zippo dropped into the line of gasoline leading to the bed. Flames raced along the floor and greedily latched onto the bed.

In the next instant flames filled the cell.

Agony claimed Fanelli, but there was no solace in knowing he was taking the woman with him. His next breath was filled with flames that burned the life out of him.

Chapter 18

By the time Adam and Marion reached the jail, the danger had passed but the excitement was still at fever pitch. Over the years inmates had tried starting fires inside the jail to trigger escapes in the confusion. The jailers had set up fire suppression equipment throughout the building.

Marion walked toward the knot of people in front of Amanda Weaver's cell.

The stench of burned material and overcooked pork filled the stale air. Other inmates screamed and cursed as they demanded to be moved or told what was going on. The jail was a madhouse.

For a moment Marion thought the burned corpse in front of the cell was that of Amanda Weaver. It was burned that badly. Then she realized the corpse was dressed in street clothes. The fatality was also a dead *man*.

His face was nearly burned off on one side, but his mouth was open in a silent scream.

Amanda Weaver lay facedown in the hallway as jailers used fire extinguishers to hose down the bedding, which was erupting into flames again. Two jailers knelt in the center of the woman's back.

The orange jumper was burned in place. Scorch marks showed on the fabric and her arms, legs and face. Her hair was singed. But she didn't show any pain.

A sheriff's deputy put his hand in the center of Adam's chest and blocked his approach to Weaver.

"Stay back, mac," the deputy warned.

"That's my client," Adam protested.

"Right now she's our prisoner," the deputy said. "We let her out of that burning cell and she attacked us. Almost got away."

Adam looked at Marion. "Do something. She needs medical treatment."

Marion showed her identification. "Marion Hart. District attorney's office. I want that woman transported to the hospital."

"Ma'am," the deputy protested.

"Get it done." Marion's voice was chipped ice. "You people almost got her killed today. Call in whatever personnel you need, but make it happen."

Reluctantly the deputy nodded.

Marion stared at the burned jail cell and the charred corpse on the floor. Who had this woman angered?

A white rectangle caught her eye. She moved to the soot-covered bars and pointed at the rectangle.

"I want that," she said.

One of the deputies bent toward it.

"Pick it up by the edges," Marion directed. "There may be fingerprints. It's evidence."

The deputy hesitated, then did as he was told. Marion tore a sheet of paper from her legal pad and folded it into a makeshift envelope. The deputy slid it inside and she pocketed it.

"What's that?" Adam asked.

Marion showed him the Queen of Hearts playing card.

"Did she have a deck of cards in her cell?" he asked.

"I don't think so."

Adam looked back at the corpse. "Then this guy brought it in as a calling card."

"Some call," Marion said.

By the time Amanda Weaver arrived at the hospital, Marion had gotten in contact with Dr. Bernhardt over the phone. He signed on as attending physician and treated Weaver.

Marion was given access to an office. She used the phone to alert Turnbull and the medical examiner's office. She also called Sheriff Keller for a team to process the crime scene.

No one she talked to was happy. Turnbull and Keller didn't need the added aggravation, and the medical examiner complained that he had a full docket as it was.

Marion ignored all of it, conscious that Adam was watching her and taking notes. She wrote notes of her own, covering pages with precious little information and a lot of questions.

"You know," Adam said when she finally hung up the phone, "you're good at what you do."

The compliment irritated Marion in ways she didn't understand. "Do you mean, 'for a woman'?"

"No." Adam shook his head. "I've known a lot of guys who couldn't get things organized the way you just did. I didn't think of half the questions you did. The part about having the sheriff's deputies search for any unclaimed cars in the neighborhood? I wouldn't have thought of that."

"They're looking for a Ford," Marion said as she glanced at her notes. "Probably a rental."

"How do you know that?"

"I called the medical examiner's office and asked about the contents of the dead man's pockets. There was a single Ford key on a ring."

"Motel or hotel key?"

Marion shook her head.

"The guy probably didn't intend to stay in Phoenix long," Adam said. He stretched his legs. From the careful way he was moving Marion knew he was still hurting from the beating he'd taken.

"How bad is it?"

Adam looked at her suspiciously. "You didn't call to find out for three days. Now you want to know?"

"I didn't have your number. It's unlisted, remember?"

"You work in the district attorney's office. You could have found out."

"I try not to mix professional business with personal business."

"So I'm elevated to personal business?" Adam smiled.

"I figured you were going to live."

"And I figured you'd be able to read my unlisted number off my complaint form if you were concerned."

Marion sighed and closed her eyes. *Way to go, Nancy Drew.* "I didn't even think about it."

"Then I guess you're not infallible."

"Hardly. I get reminded of that on a regular basis." The men in the district attorney's office were constantly searching for her mistakes. That was one of the reasons she had to get there before they did and leave after they left. She couldn't afford to make mistakes that might be attributed to her gender. In the end, she'd had to be better at the job than they were.

And that only added fuel to the fire when it came to the prejudice that remained low-key in the office. Even some of the secretaries were quick to point out her failings.

"For what it's worth, I think you're pretty incredible. I don't know anyone—male or female—who could have kept focused with everything that just happened."

Marion blushed a little and got angry at herself for reacting that way. She didn't need nice words from Adam Gracelyn as validation. She was capable of validating herself.

However, it felt good to hear it. It would be nice to hear it more.

"You can pick me up," she said.

Adam looked confused.

"Next Thursday," Marion said. "Memorial Day. You can pick me up."

He smiled that boyish smile of his again. "Great. Not afraid of consorting with the opposition."

"Given everything that's going on, I'm not entirely convinced that we're on opposite sides of this thing. I'm still going to prove that Amanda Weaver—or whatever her name truly is—killed Marker in that motel room. But I think both of us need to know why she was there."

* * *

A few minutes later, Dr. Bernhardt entered the room. He took in Adam and Marion at a glance, then looked at Marion.

"It's all right," Marion said. "He needs to know everything I know at this point."

Adam shot her a troubled look. "You've been keeping something from me?"

"Nothing that we can document," Marion said. "Dr. Bernhardt is something of a local expert when it comes to wounds and European dentistry."

"I don't understand."

Bernhardt glanced at Marion.

Marion hesitated a moment, then nodded. Adam deserved to know what they were thinking.

Claiming a nearby chair, Bernhardt sat with his hands between his knees. "We believe your client is an operative who's been operating outside of this country."

"Why?"

Bernhardt went through his findings again, included a brief and modest history of his own experience in the espionage field. Adam took notes.

"And you didn't tell me any of this?" he protested when Bernhardt had finished.

"It's all conjecture," Bernhardt insisted, "and based on a past I've had that I can't talk about in detail."

"It also doesn't have anything to do with what Weaver was doing in Marker's motel room," Marion pointed out. "But it does offer testimony to a degree of experience and callousness on the part of your client."

"If you can prove that."

Marion almost smiled. Adam was already thinking like an attorney again.

"How's your patient?" Marion asked.

"She's resting." Bernhardt rubbed his hands together. "I'm somewhat bothered by her pain threshold."

"What do you mean?"

Bernhardt frowned at the wall. "Although the burns she suffered aren't life-threatening, several of them are quite painful. She's showing no signs of discomfort. She's got a degree of willpower I'm not certain I've ever seen before." He paused and let out a breath. "I'm not sure if it's something she's learned or if her ability to shut off pain is the result of some traumatic experience she's been through."

"You think she's psychologically damaged?" Adam asked.

Marion leaned forward. "Insanity isn't a defense."

"If she didn't think what she was doing was wrong at the time she did it, it could be. The Durham Rule."

"Judges and attorneys have argued over the Durham Rule since it came out in 1954," Marion said. Her law school class spent some time on the *Durham v. United States* case study. Some students and professors felt that the insanity defense might gain in popularity due to the drugs becoming more prevalent in the world and the pressures from the Vietnam War.

"You pulled your hidden expert out of the woodwork," Adam reminded. "I'm only playing off the conjectures you've established. He's probably seen firsthand what posttraumatic stress disorder does to people who are involved in war."

"We don't know that she's been involved in a war. And posttraumatic stress disorder isn't a defense, either."

"According to the information you intentionally derived from Dr. Bernhardt, she's certainly wounded like she's seen combat."

"You'll have to prove that, and with the closemouthed way your client has been conducting herself, I don't think that's going to happen."

"That closemouthed attitude is just what you'd expect of someone who's done what you think she's done."

Marion didn't say anything. Adam was right. If she had been a spy, Amanda Weaver wouldn't talk about anything she'd done.

"Then there's the matter of verification," Bernhardt said. "If I'm right, and let's say for the sake of argument that I am, neither that woman nor her employers are going to readily admit to anything that she's done."

Marion made herself relax and sit back again.

"He's right, you know," Adam said. "Proving it either way is going to be a problem."

"I don't think she's psychologically unsound," Marion contended.

"If she's an assassin," Adam said, "she's been trained to kill. For all you know, someone paid her to kill Marker in that motel room that night. She could just be a tool."

"I'm afraid it's worse than that," Bernhardt interrupted. "I don't think that woman's moral compass is wired the same way ours is. She doesn't recognize good and evil the same way we do."

"You think she's a sociopath?" Marion asked. Her class had looked into that field as well, as a result of the Charles Whitman and Richard Speck mass murders. The idea of an inhuman monster that looked like an average person left her unnerved.

"Perhaps."

Marion glanced at Adam. "That's not a prognosis that's going to help your client."

"Maybe we could concentrate on keeping her alive long enough to try her," Adam replied.

"Whatever you do," Bernhardt said as he got to his feet, "I want you to know that she and the baby are both fine."

That caught Marion's attention immediately. "'Baby?'"

Bernhardt nodded. "Your prisoner, your client, is with child. Since she's not showing, I assume she's only a few weeks along. I don't have a scientific way of knowing that time frame."

The announcement seemed to yank the ground from under Marion. *I'm trying to put a pregnant mother away for life?* Since women were rarely executed in Arizona, capital punishment was pretty much off the table. She knew that children were sometimes born in prison, but she'd never imagined that she would trigger that.

"You're sure she's pregnant?" Adam asked.

"I just got the results from the pregnancy test," Bernhardt said. "The rabbit died." He smiled a little at his joke. "Of course, every rabbit dies as a result of the process."

"What's the process?"

"I injected a small amount of the woman's urine into the subcutaneous fat of a female rabbit," Bernhardt said. "Yesterday I harvested the rabbit and examined its ovaries. They showed the change that indicated the presence of a pregnancy. If there were no hCG, human chorionic gonadotropin, hormone available those changes wouldn't have taken place." He paused. "She's pregnant."

"Does Weaver know?" Marion asked.

Bernhardt held up his hands. "I don't know. I haven't told her."

"It seems like a woman would just know," Adam said.

"That," Bernhardt said, "is because you're thinking like a man. I've seen cases where women came into the hospital with what they thought were severe stomachaches and went home a few days later with a baby. I've delivered a few of those."

Marion thought about the complications the pregnancy would present. But it also provided her with a lever that she hadn't had before.

If she was callous enough to use it. She knew Turnbull wouldn't have hesitated one single heartbeat. But she wasn't Turnbull. More than that, she was a woman who'd learned to fear being in exactly the same condition Amanda Weaver was now in.

Hours later, Marion looked through the observation window into the interview room Amanda Weaver occupied. The woman wore chains again, but this time they were over white bandages. She'd refused to change out of the scorched jail jumper. One of the legs and the sleeves had been cut away so Bernhardt could tend her wounds.

She sat in her chair and looked totally in control despite the handcuffs. The coal of her cigarette glowed orange briefly, then she released a stream of smoke toward the nicotine-stained ceiling.

Geoffrey Turnbull leaned against the side of the window. A heavy frown dragged down his whole face. He smelled of cigarettes, coffee and aftershave.

"So what's the plan?" Turnbull asked.

"I'm going to try to identify the man who tried to kill her," Marion said. "I don't think I'm going to get much out of her."

"Neither do I. Look at her." Turnbull cursed. "She's acting like she has all the time in the world."

"Maybe she thinks she's safer inside than she is outside."

Turnbull shook his head. "She's not gonna live that fantasy. That guy that came at her today had her cold. If she'd been anybody else. She isn't. So she's gotta be thinking that she's safest if she's up and running. If Bernhardt is right and she's been traveling the world, she's got thousands of places to run to."

"What would you do?"

"Go at her with the baby. See if that doesn't shake her up a bit. My wife and I have had three kids. We talked about how we wanted them before we found out we were gonna have them. I can tell you from experience that nobody—and I mean *nobody*—takes the announcement of a baby coming calmly. It makes you crazy."

But what if you started out that way? Marion wondered. *Would you get crazier? Or would you get saner thinking for two?*

"I do have some good news for you," Turnbull said.

"I'll take it."

"The way that guy tried to kill her? With the gasoline-filled bladder? That's a signature."

Like the playing card.

"I'm betting there aren't too many people who try to kill in that fashion. I've passed your identification kit—the photographs and particulars that you nailed down—to some contacts I have in organized crime investigations back East. I think we'll get a hit from that direction."

Marion couldn't believe it. Every step seemed to lead her farther and farther into a surreal world.

"The Mafia?" she said in a low voice. "You think the Mafia was behind this?"

"According to your report, the assassin stated that 'Uncle Sal sends his regards.' Sal could be short for Salvatore, which is definitely an Italian name. Maybe I'm making too big a leap here, but I think we'll find out soon."

But will it be soon enough? Marion wondered.

Chapter 19

Standing in front of the big marker board she'd had brought into Marion Gracelyn's office, Winter surveyed her handiwork with a touch of pride. She'd spent the whole day organizing the material she'd gathered regarding Marion's investigation of Amanda Weaver in May of 1968.

Five days had passed since she and David had talked with Dr. Bernhardt. She was getting frustrated with her lack of progress.

She'd gone to the court clerk's office and spent most of the next day rooting around in records buried in the basement. After wading through mountains of dust and mold and being stalked by the biggest rat she'd ever seen, she'd gotten her hands on the court transcripts. They hadn't added much to her current knowledge base, but she liked having all the pieces.

Winter sipped water and watched how the various time lines connected to the investigation came together. Everyone involved was in Phoenix that final day. She knew that, but she didn't know for sure what had happened.

Only three people still lived that knew what had happened that day. Winter had access only to two of them, and she wasn't ready to talk to either of them.

"Hey."

Turning, Winter found David at the doorway.

"Got a minute?" David asked. He held out a sheaf of papers.

"Sure." During the last few days, Winter had started looking forward to his visits.

Lunch with him was a customary thing now, and they'd gone to dinner in Phoenix the last two nights. He didn't interfere with her work time, and he didn't ask a lot of questions except over meals.

"I just got this from Allison." David proffered the papers.

Winter scanned them. "These are all CIA documents."

"I know." David sat on the edge of the desk. "Most of them are about Marker and soldiers like him who were in the Phoenix Program over in Vietnam."

Surprise settled into Winter as she looked at the documents. There were reports and photographs. "Most of this is sensitive information."

"I know. Allison told me we couldn't go public with this."

"These are classified reports on American military activity in Vietnam that still haven't been released under the Freedom of Information Act."

"I know. I told you Allison could get that information."

"Remind me to call her the next time I have reluctant interviewee or one I think is lying to me." Winter sat at the desk and spread the papers out. She brought out her iPAQ and jotted notes to herself to keep everything organized. "You've read this?"

David hesitated.

"I'll know if you lie," Winter warned, but she smiled to take the sting out of it.

David smiled back and rubbed his chin. "I read through some of it pretty quickly as it printed out. A lot of it is redundant."

"Some of the best research is. If you do it right, you're overlapping on nearly everything you work on. Surely you do the same thing in court cases."

"Not so much. Generally we work with evidence. If that gets redundant, the plea bargaining gets easier to negotiate. Allison is *extremely* thorough."

"She always was."

"Does it help?"

"It gives me a better picture of Marker. He was part of a Sensitive Operations Group. That's a euphemism for assassination team. They hunted political and military targets among the Vietcong."

"I got that. In some of those reports it mentions that Marker and his team worked with a woman."

"I see that. But she's not identified. That makes me wonder if Marker ever identified her to anyone."

"You think it was Weaver?"

"It fits the profile I've established for her. And it would definitely account for the wounds she's suffered that were mentioned in Dr. Bernhardt's report."

"But it might not be her."

Winter shrugged. "If it's not, it's someone like her. Still, I'd feel better if I could conclusively say it was her."

David ran a hand through his hair. The gesture was so natural that Winter could remember how he'd been as a teenager. "Who else could it be?"

"Other women were used. They always are in wars. In one capacity or another." A reference caught Winter's eye. She folded the page over and picked up a yellow highlighter. When she finished she pointed out what she'd highlighted.

The reference in the report noted that one of the Vietcong commanders had been slain in the middle of the night. A Queen of Hearts playing card had been impaled on the knife that had slid into the man's heart.

"I didn't see that." David frowned. "But was it left by Marker or by the woman?"

"I'm betting on the woman," Winter said. "She had a history with that card. Evidently it all started in Boston."

"Boston?"

"New information I found today. Since your mom figured out who the arsonist in the jail was, I did some digging into the Boston crime family scene. We've got more assets, history and computer files than she ever dreamed of. I called an OrgCrime agent I've gotten to know over in Massachusetts. As a favor to me, he dug through some old files prior to 1968."

David waited. "Must be some friend."

Was that a hint of jealousy? Winter wondered. Then she got irritated with herself. *You shouldn't even be thinking like that. He's still carrying a torch for a dead woman. You can't compete with that.*

"I'm godmother to his daughter. Paul helped me with the Crittenden Kidnapping book."

That had been a high-profile crime back in 1987. Winter had lit a fire under the cold case team working the kidnapping and provided new thinking with the information she'd dug up. Eventually they had found the little girl's body, which had been buried and returned to the family.

"Oh," David said.

Now that looks like relief, Winter thought. *Or maybe you're just wanting him to look relieved.* She wasn't sure.

"There were murders in Boston that involved the same crime Family," Winter said. "Each of them was marked with a Queen of Hearts playing card."

"You think it was Weaver?"

"I don't know. For all we know, there were a number of government-sponsored assassins crawling through the jungles over there that used that playing card to claim their kills."

"Kind of like 'Kilroy was here,'" David said.

Winter nodded. *Kilroy* was a fictitious soldier in World War II. Servicemen and others drew graffiti that perpetuated the myth of an invincible warrior that hunted the Axis military and often showed up in military engagements to lend a hand.

"The Phoenix Program was big on psychological warfare," Winter said. "They could have promoted that aspect."

"Except that you found evidence of the card used as a signature in Boston before it showed up in the war."

Winter passed the files over. "Paul just sent these today."

David read through the files. "No one came forward to say who the killer might have been?"

Winter shook her head. "Back in the early 1960s, the Mafia didn't talk to anybody. The RICO laws were tearing them apart, and people were starting to break the code of silence."

"So where do you go from here?"

"I'm working up information on the Mafia angle. I think we can put something together there. But I want to dig more deeply into Marker."

David pointed at the CIA files. "You've got a lot there."

"Not from the CIA end," Winter said. "From the personal side. I want to know what Marker was doing in Phoenix in 1968. From what I've been able to find in the newspapers, Marker was frequently a guest at Conrad Ellis's home."

"Marker did bring back his son from Vietnam when everyone else thought he was dead. If that hadn't happened, Brian Ellis wouldn't be a House Representative for Arizona."

"Conrad died nine years ago," Winter said. "His wife preceded him in death. Brian was their only. He's the only one to ask."

"Then ask him."

"I've tried. I can't get him to return my calls."

"You should have told me." David checked the time on his cell phone. "It's four o'clock in Washington. Let me make a call." He left the room.

Winter turned her attention back to the marker board. The answer had to be up there somewhere. One of the things she'd learned in her writing was that the best answers always came from asking the best questions. She just had to find the question that would unlock the puzzle.

David returned less than an hour later. "We're on for lunch on Thursday."

Winter automatically checked the calendar on her computer. Today was Tuesday. "You got through to him?"

The boyish grin framed David's lips. "Sometimes it's good to be the United States attorney general."

"I'm impressed."

"It wasn't totally me. I had to call Gabe to help me twist Ellis's arm."

Gabe was Gabriel Monihan, the current president of the United States.

"You called in the big guns."

"You said you needed to talk to Ellis. Now you'll have the opportunity."

"That doesn't mean we'll get any answers."

"One thing I learned in the courtroom," David said. "You only have a real problem when you run out of questions."

"I'll have to make travel arrangements." Winter pulled out her iPAQ and punched up her phone database.

"It's already taken care of."

She looked at him in surprise. "You didn't have to do that."

"If you wanted to get there on time, with a decent room in Washington before you meet Ellis, I did. These things don't just happen."

"Thank you."

"It's going to cost you, though," David said.

"I'd be happy to pay my way. Just let me know how much—"

"Not financially. I've got that covered. After all, technically you're working on my problem so I'm picking up the expenses."

"Then what?"

"I'm coming with you."

Winter thought about that and wondered what she was supposed to say.

"'Thank you' would be appropriate," David suggested.

"Thank you," Winter said automatically. The prompt irritated her on a certain level, but she knew she had it coming. "Why are you going?" She curbed herself just in time to keep from asking if he didn't trust her. Over the last few days, he'd been nothing if not supportive.

"You told me a few days ago that people hang on to their oldest secrets the tightest. But those secrets also make them dangerous. Right now you're dealing with something involving the Mafia, the CIA and potentially an assassin-for-hire. I don't think I'm being paranoid when I think you might be in danger."

"I can take care of myself."

"Probably. I know you've had to defend yourself in the past."

The outlaw biker she'd shot while writing an expose on the link between Chinese sex slaves and cocaine roaring into the United States up Interstate 35 had grabbed headlines for months. *Court TV* had even shown a computer-generated sequence of events that had justified the shooting. They had invited Winter to be on the show, but she had declined.

However there had been some fallout over the situation because some people insisted that if Winter hadn't been in the bar that night she'd never have had to shoot that man. Sometimes Winter had thought those people might be right. But her book had broken the back of the Vipers biker gang and the Black Dragon Song Triad that had worked that supply route.

The civil case had been a nightmare that had lasted ten months. The publishers had picked up the legal tab because the extra news coverage had resulted in unexpected publicity that kept the book on the bestseller lists.

"But two people can watch over each other better than one," David finished.

"What about the men you've had watching me since I left L.A.? Did you book them on the flight, too?" Winter almost laughed at David's surprised look.

"You knew about that?"

"Yes. I had a friend run their rental car plates when I spotted them. She traced the plates back to you."

David looked uncomfortable. "I didn't know what Christine was starting when she asked you to look into this."

"Were you scared of me? Or of what we might find?"

He hesitated. "I don't know. Both, maybe."

Winter appreciated his honesty. They'd come a long way in the last few days.

"Morning's going to come early," David warned. "You'd better get some sleep."

"I will." Winter watched him as he walked away. But she knew it wasn't going to be restful sleep. Lately he'd been in her dreams a lot.

She couldn't wait to get this wrapped so she could get back to her life. David Gracelyn was definitely out of her reach. She didn't want to hang around till she forgot that.

Seated in first class the next morning, David read through the material Allison had sent to him the previous day. Beside him, Winter worked on her notebook computer. Her fingers flew across the keys.

He also had a time line that Winter had prepared regarding the events back in 1968 and how they might have led up to the present day. There were a lot of holes and a lot of creative leaps of logic that he wasn't entirely happy with.

But it felt right.

His cell phone vibrated and he answered it.

"Did you make your plane all right?" Allison Gracelyn's voice was clear and strong as always.

"We're here now," David answered. He enjoyed talking to his younger sister, but they'd both been so busy lately it was hard staying caught up.

"I've looked over the material you sent me."

David cupped the phone closer to his ear so the conversation wouldn't bleed over. Winter wore earbuds and listened to blues music off her computer while she worked, but he didn't want a patch of silence to inadvertently betray his call.

"And?" he asked.

"I think she's onto something."

"So do I."

"Why didn't we ever pick up on this before?"

David knew Allison was berating herself for what she perceived as an oversight. "This happened forty years ago, and Mom and Dad didn't ever talk about it that I can recall."

"They didn't. I would have remembered."

That was true. Allison had a mind like a steel trap.

"But forty years? Come on," David said.

"I see that you're on the plane with her." The smirk carried in Allison's voice. "You must at least think it's possible."

"Anything is possible. Though I still have trouble believing there's some boogeyman out there waiting to bring the academy down."

"If Winter's right, it's a bogey*woman*."

"Whatever."

"Oh ye of little faith," Allison chided.

"This isn't a game, Allison."

Her voice hardened. "I know that, David. I knew that even before those girls were kidnapped from the academy."

"We don't know that your bogey*woman* was behind that."

"Someone was."

"What if we're chasing shadows?"

"Then we'll move on to the next shadow. From what I see in Winter's work, she's hooked on this."

"I know. Getting her to shut down about it afterward could be a problem."

"I don't think so."

"Why?"

"All you have to do is ask her."

That surprised David. "She doesn't listen to me."

"She will."

"You sound awfully confident."

"Winter had a crush on you back at the academy. I'll bet you that hasn't gone away."

"I'll bet you're wrong." As David spoke, he gazed at Winter. She wore simple jeans, T-shirt and loose blouse today. Her black hair was pulled back. Her fragrance haunted him.

She looked up at him without warning and caught him staring at her. She smiled uncertainly and pulled the earbuds out.

"What is it?" she asked.

Despite years of courtroom experience, David froze. He didn't know what to say. He was afraid he was going to say the wrong thing and turn the trip into a long and uncomfortable thing.

"Tell her you were confirming dinner reservations," Allison prompted.

"I was making dinner reservations," David said.

"Where?" Winter asked.

It's a surprise? David thought.

"Charlie Palmer Steak," Allison said. "As I recall, Winter likes to keep things simple."

"Charlie Palmer Steak." David knew the restaurant. It was one of his favorites. Allison knew that.

"I've eaten there before," Winter said. "It's good."

"It's also hard to get reservations," David said, more for Allison than for Winter.

Winter frowned at him in confusion. "So, do you *have* reservations?"

"Yep," Allison said. "Eight o'clock. I just confirmed them through their Web site. You gotta love the Internet."

"I do," David said in amazement. "At eight o'clock."

"Enjoy," Allison said. "Let me know how everything works out, and if you need any further help."

The phone clicked dead in David's ear. He slid it into his pocket.

"I thought you answered the phone," Winter said. "I didn't see you call."

She was observant. David nodded. "I just had someone confirm reservations."

Winter smiled. "When I see Allison again, remind me to thank her."

"Sure." David sat back in his seat and felt confused. He didn't know what had happened, but he was pretty sure he'd been manipulated.

However, the anticipation of dinner tonight with Winter tonight wiped out any anxiety he had about that.

Chapter 20

"Do you see him?"

Marion peered through the courthouse window as she stood next to Adam. His proximity was more than a little distracting. She followed Adam's line of sight, though, and looked at Washington Street.

"The red Chevrolet," Adam said. "Four cars up from the corner. See the two-way aerial mounted on the back?"

Spotting the car and the aerial then, Marion studied the occupants. Two men sat in the front seat. Both smoked. Neither talked. They just sat there and watched the street. Both wore dark suits that were out of place in Phoenix at this time of year. They also wore dark sunglasses.

"All right," Marion said. "They're there."

"The second group is across the street," Adam said. "In the parking lot. Blue Chevrolet this time."

After a quick search, Marion found the second car. The occupants were similarly attired.

"You think they're federal agents?" she asked.

"I do," Adam assured her. "But I don't think they're FBI agents."

Marion didn't bother asking what kind of agents Adam thought they were. Whatever they were, they were the same kind as Tarlton.

She also didn't ask why they were here. So far there was only one truly mysterious prisoner in all of Phoenix.

"I noticed them on my way into court this morning," Adam said. "There are more cars around the building. They're not taking any chances."

"If they want Weaver, why don't they just come and take her?"

"Because she has me for a lawyer," Adam said. "I wouldn't let them take her without positively identifying each one of the men that showed up. That could be complicated for whoever sent them."

"They could have a writ."

"And I'd challenge it." Adam looked at her. "Surely you're not going to tell me you'd just turn her over at this point?"

Marion wished it were that simple, but she knew it wasn't. She folded her arms and thought. She wasn't going to risk Weaver or her unborn child.

"No," she said. "I wouldn't."

"We need to get rid of those men."

"How? They're not disturbing the peace. They're just sitting in their cars."

"Marion, those men are dangerous. They're not sitting out there to protect Amanda Weaver. You're not going to convince me of that."

"I know." But she didn't see what she was going to be able to do about them.

Growling inarticulately, Adam stalked off.

Marion started to go after him, but she didn't know what she would say. Instead she decided to go in search of Sheriff Keller.

Less than five minutes later, Marion was out on the street with Sheriff Keller in tow.

"I don't know what you expect me to do, A.D.A. Hart," Keller said as he kept stride with Marion.

"They're loitering."

"There's no law against loitering in front of the courthouse."

"The parking spaces are reserved for people on court business," Marion said stubbornly. "Unless they're waiting for someone, they're just occupying space."

"That's not illegal," Keller pointed out.

"No, but given the attempt on Weaver's life, I'd say we'd be remiss in not checking them out."

Keller might have objected further, or he might even have dragged his feet entirely. Marion didn't know and she wasn't going to get the chance to know.

Ahead of them, Adam stepped toward the car with a news photographer in tow.

"Oh, now this should be interesting," Keller said.

Marion halted beside the big sheriff.

Adam leaned on the Chevrolet and stared through the window at the men inside. "Hi. I'm with the local paper. We're doing a study on government agencies. You know, where they hang out, who they hang out with, why they hang out there. That kind of thing." He turned to the cameraman. "Take their picture."

The photographer took the picture.

"Hey," the driver protested. "You can't do that." He flailed for the camera.

"Sure he can," Adam said. "This is public property. In fact, if you want you can come in and check on that. I'll have a judge verify it for you."

The big man tried to get out of the car. Adam slammed a hip into the door and forced it closed again. The man reached down and came up with a snub-nosed revolver.

Marion's heart leaped into her throat. *You fool!* She turned to Keller, but the sheriff was already in motion. Keller pulled his own service revolver as he calmly approached the vehicle.

"You want to back off," the driver snarled, "before you get yourself into a world of hurt."

"I've already been there," Adam said. "Your buddy Tarlton, or whatever his name is, worked me over before he headed out of town." He didn't flinch from the pistol only inches from his face. "This time I've got witnesses."

Keller stopped only a few feet from the car and pointed his pistol at the driver. "Sheriff's office. Put the weapon down. *Now!*"

The driver didn't move.

"Interesting situation we have here, isn't it?" Adam asked. Incredibly he was still smiling like he was out for a walk in the park.

He's insane, Marion thought. But even though she was worried about him and his mental health, she couldn't help admiring his courage.

The photographer took another picture.

"That's Sheriff Keller." Adam nodded at the sheriff. "You can tell because he's got the uniform, gun and handcuffs. I can also tell you he's a crack shot. If I were you, I'd put the gun down."

Growling curses, the man put the pistol on the dash and grabbed the steering wheel when Keller told him to.

"I still think the sheriff should have arrested those guys and verified their identification," Adam said as he followed Marion through the district attorney's office. "At least we'd have known who they were working for."

"Keller called the number those men gave him. The man at that end said they belonged to the FBI." Marion pulled her keys from her purse and opened the office door. She followed it inside. The heat of the day had baked into the office.

"But nobody vouched for the guy at the other end of the phone connection."

Marion put her purse on the desk and opened the window. The circulation didn't improve much, but she thought the breeze cooled the room.

"You know, I bet a smart defense attorney could have gotten them out of the sheriff's jail before we could have gotten enough verification to suit you," Marion said. "It happens to the D.A.'s office a lot."

Adam leaned against the wall as she sat behind the desk.

"Probably," he admitted. "Just for the record, though, I also didn't care much for the way they refused to answer why they were staking out the courthouse."

"They said there was a threat against it."

"From who?"

"Are you sure that's not 'whom'?"

"I'm sure. From who?"

"They didn't say."

"Convenient." Adam cocked an eyebrow. "Do you believe anything they said?"

"No. By the way, just so you know, you're an idiot."

That brought a big smile to his face. "Why?"

"Walking over to those men that way. They could have shot you."

"In broad daylight?" Adam shook his head. "I didn't think so."

"And if you were wrong?"

"You could have called me an idiot and I wouldn't have argued."

"Because you'd have been full of holes."

Adam crossed the room and leaned on her desk. He slid his face to within inches of hers. "Were you worried about me?" he asked in a husky voice.

Marion looked at his face. The bruises from the beating Tarlton had given him were fading but still there. She couldn't believe his attitude.

"You're not just an idiot," she said, looking into his brown eyes. "You're mentally deficient."

His grin widened. "Do you know I've done nothing but think about kissing you again since the last time we kissed?"

Even though the chance for a return engagement had been constantly in her thoughts, Marion would never have admitted that.

"Good," Marion said.

Adam looked hopeful.

"When we get to court next week to begin the trial, you won't be at your best."

The smile faded. "You've got a mean streak in you, A.D.A. Hart."

"I do. You'd be well off to remember that." Marion turned her attention to the papers before her. More court cases were pending.

"I hate to break this up," Geoffrey Turnbull said from the open doorway, "but I've got some news."

Feeling guilty that her boss had found Adam in her office, Marion stood to be on more equal footing.

"What news?" she asked.

"I think we've identified your arsonist." Turnbull looked at Adam. "You might as well come along. You're going to need to know this at some point, too."

* * *

Marion's stomach lurched as she surveyed the pictures Turnbull had brought out of the folder he'd carried in with him. The photos were all eight-by-ten glossies depicting the man who had tried to burn Amanda Weaver alive in her cell.

Normally pictures entered into evidence in murder trials—and only those shown to the jury after the judge agreed that the prosecution had made its case to show the grim brutality involved with the murder—were in black and white. The thinking was that no jury should be subjected to how horrific the murder scene actually looked.

These were in color.

"Are you okay?" Turnbull asked.

Marion nodded. "I've seen pictures like this before. Just not from a murder scene that was so…fresh."

The pictures of Tom Marker lying in the Kellogg Motel had been bad, but they hadn't been this bad.

"One of the guys I know in racketeering out in Boston identified this guy for me." Turnbull struck a match and lit a cigarette.

The sulfur smell of the match took Marion back to the county jail that day. She opened her mouth to breathe instead of taking in the scent.

Adam moved a little closer to her.

"Who is he?" Marion asked.

"A little weasel named Marco Fanelli," Turnbull answered. "He's a torch. Specializes in burning buildings and businesses for the insurance money. He does a lot of work in Boston. Every now and again, he'd step out of the box and murder somebody." He took a drag on his cigarette. "The story I got said Fanelli burned a mother and her two daughters to death in their car. The father had skipped town owing money on a deal that went south."

Marion wrapped her arms around herself. *What kind of animals are we dealing with?*

"Who did Fanelli work for?" Adam asked in a cold, hard voice.

"A mobster named Salvatore Giambi. He's a young guy, but he's a made man in the Mafia. He's been pretty untouchable so far, according to my source. But he'll slip up one day."

"Is there any way to tie Fanelli to Giambi?" Marion asked.

Turnbull shook his head. "There's no paper trail. Just word on the street."

"What about Amanda Weaver?"

"We don't know. My source has never heard of her."

"She could have had another name."

Turnbull shrugged. "Maybe we'll find it."

Staring at the pictures of the dead men, Marion had the feeling that Amanda Weaver had been careful about her past. Or maybe someone had been careful about it for her. But all of that was about to come tumbling down.

"This is a *little* party?" Marion stared out across the lawn at the huge group of people that had gathered at the Gracelyn home. She sat in the passenger seat of the limousine Adam had picked her up in.

"According to my mother," Adam said dryly, "this is just a soiree. Anything they can do at home classifies as an *intimate* gathering."

The huge, sprawling expanse of the ranch allowed for a lot of room for gatherings. Marion would have bet her eyeteeth that there were at least a thousand people at the party. Tables had been set up across the manicured grounds. There were several croquet areas, two tennis courts, and—in the back by the guesthouses and long garage—a helipad for a small helicopter.

The main house was three stories tall and looked like a fortress seated in the shadows of the White Tank Mountains. Catering crews and bartenders worked constantly to replenish drinks and appetizers. Lights were already strung for the evening's festivities.

"This isn't an intimate gathering," Marion whispered. She suddenly felt incredibly out of place.

"What would you consider an intimate gathering?"

When Marion looked at Adam, he was all innocence. He'd deliberately loaded the question. Before she could make a response, the driver opened her door.

Adam walked around the car and joined her. "Mother has assigned you a room. You're one of the few that got one." He offered his arm.

"I'm not going to be staying the night."

"I explained that to her," Adam said as he led her into the madhouse of confusion that was the Memorial Day party. "She said she wanted you to feel comfortable. I told her that I could drive you back home to change into evening attire."

"I could have changed in the bathroom," Marion said. She'd packed a bag just to do that. She worried that the little black dress she kept for such occasions wasn't going to be enough. She was definitely underpowered when it came to the crowd of social elite packed around her. She recognized many of them from the society and business pages.

"Mother wouldn't hear of that."

Marion stopped and looked at Adam. "Seriously, I mean no offense, but this is a bit much for me. This many people—*these* people—in one place like this makes me nervous."

"What?" Adam mocked. "No sense of adventure?"

"I know when I'm out of my depth."

Adam stared at her in disbelief. "You're serious?"

"This isn't my playground, Adam. I didn't grow up around this."

He smiled. "I did, and I have to admit that I don't care for it much." A mischievous look glinted in his eyes. "Want to escape?"

"I think maybe I want to go home."

Some of the fun and excitement drained from Adam's gaze, but he never lost his smile. "If that's what you want to do, sure. But I do have a better idea. At least hear me out."

Marion stood for a moment and tried to figure out how to respond. She really didn't feel comfortable at the party, and she knew she should have because she would be running into some of the same people occasionally while she was working in the district attorney's office.

More than that, though, she didn't want to lose the chance to be with Adam. Ever since she'd agreed to come, she'd been looking forward to being with him. Memory of the kiss they'd shared hadn't been far from her thoughts.

That was ridiculous. She'd been kissed before. It wasn't like men were some big mystery. Or even complicated. She'd been around enough of them to know that. They were easy to figure out. At least, most of them were.

Adam Gracelyn, though, equal parts irritable predictability and stubbornness as well as charm, cleverness and bravery, was outside of anything Marion had ever known. Well, the bravery part was debatable. Stupidity often masked itself as bravery. But Marion believed Adam would do whatever he could to defend his client and her rights.

In the end, her desire to be with Adam won out.

"What's your big escape plan?" she asked.

"Have you ever been to the top of White Tank Mountains?"

Chapter 21

The motorcycle was a surprise. Marion hadn't imagined Adam Gracelyn, either the playboy or the public defender, on one. But there had been one in the garage and he handled it like he'd been born to it.

Marion held on to him as the motorcycle zoomed up the narrow, winding road. She felt the warmth and strength of his body against her, and it was as exciting as the trip up the mountain. The noise of the loud engine prevented talk, so all she could do was hang on to him until they reached the top.

Finally Adam pulled to a stop and killed the engine. He took off his helmet and grinned at her. "Surprised to be alive?"

Marion removed her borrowed helmet and said, "Frankly, yes." When she saw the road grit on Adam's face, she regretted her impulsive decision to accompany him. The dust had to have ruined her makeup. The offer of a room at the Gracelyn home was suddenly more appealing.

Adam left his helmet dangling from the motorcycle's handlebars. He walked to the nearest edge and looked down at the sprawling urban area of Phoenix below. He held his arms out at his sides and for a moment Marion thought he might actually jump and try to fly down.

"I love it up here," he said. "I've been coming since I was fourteen, old enough to ride a motorcycle up here."

"Your parents let you?"

Marion couldn't imagine a fourteen-year-old boy loose in the mountains with a motorcycle. But somehow she could see Adam Gracelyn doing that.

"I've walked most of the hiking trails that go through the mountains, and I've seen all of the archeological digs. The Black Rock Trail leads right to one of the Hohokam villages." Adam turned to look at her. "This is where I fell in love with nature, Marion. This is where I finally figured out what I wanted to do."

His voice sounded so different in the stillness that enveloped the mountaintop. Marion couldn't help laughing at the excitement she heard in his words.

"What?" Adam looked embarrassed.

"You," Marion said, and couldn't say anything more.

"What about me?"

Marion shook her head. "I just never expected this."

"This—" Adam swept a hand over the mountain range "—is what I want to do with my life, Marion."

"You want to live on a mountain?"

"No," he said softly. "I want to protect this. Before air-conditioning was invented, people chose not to live in Arizona. This place, and others like it, would have remained pristine, frozen in time."

Marion loved listening to his words. They held fire and passion. He was talking about his dreams, and it was powerful.

"Now you look down and Phoenix is lapping at the foothills," Adam said, pointing at the city below. "I have to wonder how much longer it will be before those houses and office buildings start climbing the mountains."

"I don't think that'll happen."

"There are people already planning residential areas all around us. Even if they don't build, a lot of damage has already been done to the environment and the wildlife. Things have changed up here since I was a kid. The park area was only declared and set aside in 1954. More work needs to be done—laws written to protect these areas—and I want to help do that."

A hawk skirled silently by as it rode the wind.

Marion watched Adam watching the bird. His fascination gleamed in his eyes.

"That's a tall job," Marion said, "protecting the world."

Adam shoved his hands in his pockets and shrugged. "Maybe it is. Maybe it's even a little foolish. Tilting at windmills." He looked a little sheepish. "But I want to bring my kids here one day, Marion. A son. A daughter. Both. It doesn't matter. I want to know that they'll have this, and places like it, just like I did."

Marion walked over to him and took him by the hand. "It's not foolish. It's not going to be easy, but it's not foolish."

His eyes searched hers.

"You really don't think so?" he asked.

"No," Marion whispered.

Then he leaned down and kissed her. She was surprised at how hungry she was for the taste of him, and how much she desired him. Her head swam and she felt like she was falling, like she'd stepped over the edge and was dropping toward Phoenix.

Only he wrapped his arms around her then and pulled her close. She felt totally safe.

After a while, Adam kissed her forehead and looked down with her. "So what do you want to do, Marion?"

"Me?" Marion hesitated. She didn't like talking about her dream. She'd never discussed it with anyone. She rarely even talked about it to herself these days because it seemed too big, too impossible.

But you're talking to a guy who wants to save the world, she reminded herself. "What do I really want to do?"

"Yes."

Marion took a deep breath as she looked into his eyes. "I want to build a school," she said. "A school for girls."

"A finishing school?" Adam shook his head as if he couldn't believe it.

"Not a finishing school," Marion said. "A school where girls get every edge they need to survive in the world. I don't want their thinking to be clouded by society or convention, or even restricted by economics. I want this to be a school with a student body that's invited to participate. The best of the best. I want them to be women who'll grow up to be attorneys and federal court judges. Pilots and astronauts. Political and military leaders. I want them to be women that other girls can look up to." She paused. "And I want my daughter, or daughters, to go to school there."

When she finished speaking, she realized how scared she was. Adam was going to think her whole idea was—

"Then do it," he said softly.

"It's impossible," she replied. "Every time I think about how much money is involved—"

"There's something my father always told me," Adam said. "If it's a good idea, people will step up to buy it. The smartest thing you can do is figure out how to see what you think up. If you want it badly enough, Marion, make it happen. Just keep on pushing till you get there. In the end, that's the only way we're ever going to get anywhere." He smiled. "If I'd told you I was going to bring you to the top of White Tank Mountains when I picked you up, would you have believed it?"

"No."

"And yet—" Adam swept his arm out over the high desert landscape "—here you are."

"Miss Hart."

The woman's voice startled Marion. She ran her fingers through her hair again to make sure everything was in place, then walked to the door of her borrowed bedroom.

She and Adam had arrived back at the Gracelyn estate with barely enough time to get dressed. Marion had showered and changed into the little black dress she'd brought, but she knew it was going to be drab compared to what she'd seen the other guests wearing.

She opened the door, expecting a maid come to tell her she was late.

Instead Mrs. Evelyn Gracelyn stood in the doorway. She was tall and elegant. Her henna-colored hair drifted across her bare shoulders. Her smile was wide and generous. She wore a simple black dress but had accessorized it with jewelry. She carried a slim wooden case in her left hand, but she offered her right.

"Good evening," she said. "You must be Marion Hart."

"I am," Marion said.

"Pleased to meet you. I'm Evelyn Gracelyn."

"I know."

Evelyn waited for a moment, then asked, "May I come in?"

"Of course. I'm sorry." Marion stepped back from the door and allowed her entrance.

Evelyn entered and looked around the room. "I hope you found everything in order."

"I did. Thank you very much for your hospitality."

"I didn't get to meet you earlier. I expect Adam took you up into the mountains?"

Marion didn't know what to say to that, but suspicion formed in her mind even though she didn't want it to. "Does he do that with…everyone he brings here?"

"No. Adam doesn't even take his guy friends up there." Evelyn regarded Marion with a speculative glance. "He must think you're something special."

Marion blushed. The woman was a lot more forward than she would have thought.

"You're going to have to forgive me," Evelyn said. "It's my country showing. Jim and I haven't always lived like this. And to tell the truth there's just some parts of me that I don't think will ever be completely citified. I know for a fact that Adam thinks you're something special because even when he isn't talking about you, I know you're on his mind."

"Thank you," Marion said.

"Adam asked me to give you this." Evelyn passed Marion the small wooden box she held. "Just for the night, mind you, because those are something special. I can't let them out of my hand till my dying day."

Curious, Marion opened the box and found a string of black pearls so beautiful they took her breath away.

"After Jim and I started making money," Evelyn said, "I bought those for my mama. She and my daddy never had much, and I wanted her to have something truly grand before she passed on. Mama wore them only a few times, more to make me happy than anything else, I suppose. At the end, I was going to bury them with her, but she told me to keep them for my first granddaughter."

"I can't," Marion said, offering the box back.

"Yes, you can, honey. Adam has always been an independent child. He's never asked much of me or his daddy. And he thought enough of you to ask me a week ago if you could borrow these." Evelyn folded the pearls into Marion's hands.

Marion didn't know what to do.

"Come over here." Evelyn waved her over to the full-length mirror in the corner. "Let's put those on you."

Quietly, feeling just a little like a princess, Marion stood in front of the mirror and watched as Evelyn draped the pearls around her neck.

"You have a good complexion, honey." Evelyn smiled into the mirror over Marion's shoulder. "Those pearls make you look—"

"Beautiful."

Startled, Marion turned toward the door and saw Adam standing there. He was dressed in a tailored tux and looked like he'd just stepped out of a Cary Grant movie.

"She is beautiful," Evelyn agreed. She patted Marion on the shoulder. "Now I gotta be running along. Big Jim always sets up a huge fireworks show, but I'm the only one that can rein him in so he doesn't set the pasture afire."

"Thank you, Mother," Adam said as they passed. He walked over to Marion and took her hand. He kissed her fingers tenderly. "You really do look stunning."

"It's the pearls," Marion said.

"Even before the pearls," Adam told her.

"Your mother said you asked to borrow these." Marion touched the pearls.

"Because I knew if I bought you something you wouldn't like it."

"No," Marion said. "I wouldn't have."

"And you aren't going to find pearls like that just anywhere."

"I wouldn't think so." Marion squeezed his hand. "I really didn't know what I was getting into when I agreed to come out here. I was scared that I wouldn't measure up." If it hadn't been for that trip up the mountain, if he hadn't told her everything he had, she wouldn't ever have admitted that.

"You?" Adam raised mocking eyebrows.

"Oh, don't get me wrong," Marion said. "I intend to kick your butt in court, but this whole family thing just—"

Adam leaned in and kissed her and took her breath away. Her head spun.

He was smiling when he pulled back. "Want to go watch my father's fireworks? Or do you want to stay here and make some of our own?"

"You're really confident, aren't you?" Somehow, though, Marion didn't take offense at the suggestive offer. It was more than a little tantalizing. *No,* she told herself. *There'll be better times and places.* And she was surprised at how much she believed that.

"Sorry," Adam murmured. He blushed a little. "Lost my head there for a minute."

"Me, too. Now let's get out of here before we create a scandal at your mother's party."

It was almost three in the morning before the party wound down. Adam brought Marion home shortly after that. They sat together in the privacy of the limousine and talked for a little while. It was mostly idle chatter. Both of them knew they were avoiding conversation about the court case and about any kind of future.

Marion almost asked Adam in but she knew she couldn't. She wasn't ready to deal with that. And she didn't want their first time together—and she knew there was going to be a first time—to be in her apartment at the end of a long day. They deserved better than that.

Goodbye seemed to last forever and was over in a split second at the same time. He walked her to the door and placed her bag inside.

"We have a date tomorrow," Adam said.

Marion smiled at him. "I don't recall you asking."

"A court date," Adam reminded. "To start selecting jury members."

Marion nodded, remembering. Disappointment gnawed at her.

"What about dinner tomorrow night?" he asked.

"It wouldn't be good to be seen in Phoenix together with the trial going on."

"We could go to Tucson."

"That's a long way to go just to eat and turn around."

Adam smiled. "We could spend the weekend."

"Let me think about it."

"Sure." Adam kissed her again, lightly, and turned to go.

"Hey," Marion called softly.

He looked back at her.

"I've thought about it," she said. "Tucson sounds great."

"I'll pick you up." Adam slid back into the limousine as Marion stepped inside her apartment and locked the door. She figured she'd be able to see herself glowing in the dark from happiness.

"Did you have a nice time?" an accented voice asked quietly out of the darkness.

Panic screamed through Marion. *Someone's in the house! Someone's in the house!*

She reached for the lock and tried to fumble it open. Before she could work the mechanism, two strong arms wrapped around her from behind. The man lifted her from her feet and carried her backward.

She opened her mouth to scream. The man clapped a rag over her mouth. A bittersweet smell flooded Marion's nostrils. She took a breath, two, then she slid over into total blackness.

Chapter 22

Charlie Palmer Steak
Washington, D.C.
Now

Dinner was a mistake.

Winter knew that within minutes after they'd been seated at a table in the elegant restaurant burgeoning with patrons. The only thing they had to talk about was Marion's murder, the kidnapping and the events of the case back in 1968. It wasn't anywhere near the casual dinner conversation that it should have been. Back at the Gracelyn Mansion, such talk would have been easy and even expected. But here, in the elegant beauty of the steak house, talking about any of that would have been objectionable.

Instead they tried to make small talk about their careers, and that wasn't working, either. Both of them knew too much about the other because both of them were in the news. Neither of them was much for hobbies, either.

And the shadow of Rainy Miller somehow lingered between them.

Winter felt the void created by Rainy's death. They'd discussed a lot of events that had led up to the recent kidnappings that had triggered the investigation into Marion Gracelyn's background, but David glossed over the details of Rainy's murder.

'I'm sorry," David said after the conversation had stumbled to a halt again.

The sound of the other conversations—personal and professional—around them sounded loud. He wore a nice suit and she wore a black dress. Winter knew that to anyone else in the restaurant they looked like a couple.

"For what?" she asked.

He gave her a lopsided grin. "This has turned out to be a first date. I blame my sister."

"For trapping you?" Winter hadn't intended to say that, but it was out before she knew it. She was tired and jet-lagged.

"No," David growled. "For setting this up so it feels like a first date."

"I didn't think it was a date," Winter said.

"Exactly. It's a shared meal between two people. It's no big deal."

Well, there's no sense in staying for dessert and coffee, Winter thought.

"Allison…meddles. She can't help herself, I suppose. She's had this tendency for a long time."

"Dinner's about over." Winter gestured at her nearly finished plate. She was suddenly looking forward to the hotel room she'd been dreading.

"Don't get me wrong," David went on. "I love talking to you. You've got a great mind."

So we can be friends? Winter sipped her wine and was disappointed to realize that the glass was almost empty.

David heaved a sigh of disgust. "See? I've developed foot-in-mouth disease. I'm no good at stuff like this."

"What *stuff?*" Winter couldn't help herself. She wasn't going to let him wriggle off the hook.

"One-on-one conversation with a woman."

At least he'd noticed her gender. "I'm sure in your work you talk to women every day."

He scowled at her. "Yes."

"So maybe it is the company."

"No, it's not. It's the atmosphere. Let's get out of here." David signaled for the check. Then he looked back at her. "Are you too tired to go for a walk?"

The question caught Winter completely off guard. "A walk?" *Wow. Aren't you the scintillating conversationalist? No wonder he's fleeing the dinner table.*

"I'm too wound up to go back to the hotel and lock myself inside four walls. I thought we could go see the Lincoln Memorial. I like to walk there when I need to think."

"'We?'" Winter echoed. "So you're not making an escape?"

David smiled. "No. I'm trying to give you a break. I feel like I'm the most boring dinner partner in the world right now. If we were just getting to know each other, maybe this would be a good place to come. But we can't talk here." He shook his head. "I feel like I'm about to explode. I need to move, to talk."

"A walk sounds good," Winter said, suspecting she was going to regret her decision.

David parked their rental car in the visitor's area at the Lincoln Memorial. They walked down to the Reflecting Pool. At 9:15 p.m., with full dark swaddling the city, the Memorial stood to the west and the Washington Monument was at the other end of the two-thousand-foot expanse of the pool. Moonlight glimmered on the water and gave it a silvery sheen.

"Do you come here often?" Winter asked.

David looked at her. "When I can. I keep a full schedule."

"With everything there is to see in Washington, D.C., why come here?" Winter walked with her arms wrapped around herself.

"You're cold," David said.

"I'll be all right."

"Take my jacket."

"It's okay."

But David knew it wasn't. The wind was up and brought the early spring temperature down to a near-uncomfortable level. He shrugged out of his jacket and offered it again.

She hesitated.

"I seem to recall a time when you would have gladly worn my jacket," David said. He regretted the words as soon as he said them.

Anger glinted in her eyes. "That was a long time ago."

"I apologize. That was out of line. Please wear the jacket. Otherwise we're going back to the car. I'm not going to walk around out here with you freezing."

With obvious reluctance, Winter pulled it on. It hung nearly to her knees, but David supposed that was a good thing because it helped block more wind.

David walked toward the tall spire of the Washington Monument. "I come here, usually about this time of night, when all the tourists are gone, to stretch my legs and enjoy the openness. If you walk close to the treeline, sometimes you can't see the city at all."

"So you're still just a country boy at heart?" Winter smiled a little in good-natured teasing.

"I was *never* a country boy," David said with a grin. "With my mom and dad, how could I be? They were constantly involved in political functions, always at one party or another. Your parents were the same way."

"No." Winter looked away. "My parents were always gone. Europe. Asia. The Middle East. Wherever Dad had business. I usually stayed at a boarding school or at home with an au pair. I had a very small life, all things considered. I think having a child was inconvenient for them. They never had another."

"Ouch."

"It wasn't all bad. After I was accepted at Athena Academy, my life got a lot bigger. Those were the good times."

"I hear that a lot. Allison still talks about her time at the academy. She's got a lot of friendships from school that she maintains."

"A lot of the graduates do."

"What about you?" David asked. "Anybody you keep in touch with?"

"A few people. I've always tended to be a loner."

"I see your name in the entertainment section of the newspapers and magazines."

"It's in the tabloids occasionally."

David smiled and nodded. "I've seen it there, too."

"Don't believe those stories. Especially the one about me trying to track down Bigfoot's child for a paternity test."

David laughed and it surprised him. "Now that one I didn't see."

Winter looked up at him and her eyes sparkled mischievously in the moonlight. "It was great. One of my favorites. I was researching an exposé on Klaus Darber, the movie director from the 1970s who got tried and convicted for cannibalism."

"He's the one that kidnapped and ate McKenzie Tyler, right?"

"Yes. But that wasn't why I was researching him. Darber was also allegedly involved with a sex and drug ring responsible for taking young girls off the street who arrived in L.A. with stars in their eyes."

"I remember the book. It caused quite a stir when it came out."

"It was my third book, and it was the one that hit the *New York Times* and other bestseller's lists." Winter grimaced.

"What's wrong?"

"It wasn't exactly my best book."

"Why do you say that?"

"My agent suggested the story to me. I wanted to stay away from it. She said it was the perfect vehicle to push my career to the next level. And it was. But the whole thing was too gratuitous and sensational for what I wanted to do."

"What do you mean?"

"Normally I try to expose injustices perpetrated by people or corporations. Shine my light on the dark things."

"A Hollywood sex and drug ring sounds pretty dark."

"It was, but the book didn't really change anything. Hollywood is still all about power, and power is all about taking advantage of other people. In the end, I didn't write about Hollywood devouring young hopefuls. I wrote about a cannibal."

"Power doesn't always take advantage of other people," David said. "I like to think I do some good as attorney general. And I know Gabe feels the same way as president."

"I didn't mean any offense. I know you've done well with your work. I've followed your career."

That surprised David. They rounded the end of the Reflecting Pool near the Washington Monument. Lights made the structure stand out against the night.

"Well," Winter said after the silence between them stretched out for a moment. "That was maybe a little more revealing than I'd intended."

"No," David said. "It's kind of flattering, actually. And to balance the sheet, I had copies of all your books even before Christine suggested bringing you into this."

"You did?"

He nodded.

"But did you read them?"

"Every word. I didn't always agree with you, but I found your perspective…intriguing."

"Very polite and noncommittal."

"I'm an attorney. I've learned not to say anything that can be used against me."

Winter laughed and the sound was warm and honest. She had, David couldn't help thinking, a great laugh.

"I was a fan of your writing even before you were published," David said.

"Now there's a lie."

"Not a lie. Allison and Rainy would bring home the stories you wrote for creative writing class and read them in their rooms. Sometimes I listened. You were a popular writer."

Embarrassment darkened Winter's cheeks. "Hopefully those have all been destroyed. I really don't deserve to be punished like that."

"Rainy really enjoyed your stories."

"She was always sentimental."

David nodded. His throat tightened just thinking about her.

"I know you didn't want to talk about Rainy earlier," Winter said.

"I still don't."

Winter fell silent as they walked.

David looked up into the dark sky. With the chill around him and the sounds of the city muted, it felt like he was in a different world. "I don't want to, but I probably need to. I haven't talked about her as much as I should."

"I didn't mean to pry. I guess it's just the storyteller in me. I always want to hear the tale." Winter smiled encouragingly at him.

David concentrated on walking and breathing. Just those two simple things. Whenever life got complicated, and it often did, he'd slow things down to just those two processes.

"It's no secret I carried a torch for Rainy," he said. "That didn't go over well at home when Rainy and Allison were competing with each other at the academy."

"You had to choose family loyalty or romance."

"Something like that. Simple, but so damned complicated, you know?"

"The near-misses for relationships are the absolute worst."

"Sounds like you know something about that."

"I do. Painful stuff. You don't know whether to try to stick it out or run for cover."

"I guess you've always run for cover."

Winter nodded. "Ugh. I'd rather have a root canal."

Despite all the pain talking about Rainy caused, David found himself laughing. "It wasn't like that with Rainy. I just never really had the chance. I went away to college, tried to stay in touch, but something happened and when I got back she was engaged."

"But you still waited."

Uncomfortable, David didn't answer.

"I saw the yearbooks on your desk a few days ago," Winter reminded.

"I don't like to think I was waiting," David said. "She was married. But no one else ever measured up to her." He shook his head. "You probably think that's incredibly stupid."

"No," she said quietly. "I understand."

David looked at her to see if he was just getting the sympathy vote. "You're waiting for someone, too."

She smiled at him as if in jest, but sadness lingered in the expression. "I don't like to think so."

It was funny and sad that she was returning his words to him.

"The truth is," Winter said quietly, "I've always been kind of hung up on you."

That caught David totally off stride. He stopped at the foot of the Lincoln Memorial and looked up at the giant figure of Abraham Lincoln. The lights tinted the white stone slightly blue.

"Me?" David asked.

"Yeah. Allison wasn't playing matchmaker in the dark. She knew how I felt even if you didn't."

Hesitantly David looked at her. Part of him wondered if she were putting him on.

"I probably shouldn't have said that. But you're not the only one with issues here. Researching your mom's story, hearing about how she fell in love with your dad in spite of the differences in their worlds, it's left me a little more open about my feelings than I normally would be."

"They really weren't that different. It may seem like it in Mom's journals. But they weren't."

"I know. I've gotten to know them quite well from reading about them. And I've seen how you and Allison have turned out. I'd say they were really good together."

David thought back to all the Christmases and family vacations, the way things had been in the Gracelyn home when his mother had been alive. "What they had was amazing."

"I believe you."

David pointed to the steps at the foot of the Lincoln Memorial. "Do you mind if we sit?"

"Not at all."

He offered his hand and helped her sit, then sat beside her. He gazed out at the Reflecting Pool. "Seeing me brought back all those old feelings you had."

Winter laughed. "They weren't that far away."

"So that's the tension I've been feeling?"

Winter held her forefinger and thumb a fraction of an inch apart. "A teeny bit." She was smiling, obviously enjoying herself at his expense. "I think your biggest problem with me has been your reluctance to share your mom's story."

David placed his forearms on his knees and laced his fingers in front of him. He tried to sort out his feelings. Of course, he'd known she'd been interested in the past. It was hard to miss the interest of a high-school-aged girl. But he couldn't help wondering if she was still interested now.

And if she was—what was he prepared to do about it?

You don't need any entanglements in your life, he told himself. But all night he'd noticed how sexy she'd looked, how she'd smelled, how she moved so gracefully and how she'd paid attention to him when he was speaking.

She was a beautiful and engaging woman. And if he told the truth, he'd started noticing all those things about her back in Phoenix.

"This probably isn't the best time for this to have come up," Winter said. "Moonlight walks tend to bring out a poetic side of me I try to keep locked away." She shrugged. "If you hadn't been honest about Rainy, maybe I wouldn't have been honest, either."

"Honesty isn't always the best policy," David said. "That's why they wrote the Fifth Amendment."

"Actually they wrote the Fifth Amendment for bad people to hide behind."

"Allison didn't help by scheduling dinner for two."

Winter shrugged, and she looked like a little girl inside his jacket. "She probably thought she was helping."

David was silent for a long time while he tried to decide what to do. He was aware of her heat beside him, her full lips and her appraising gaze. Her perfume gently prodded his senses.

He might be able to take her to bed if he tried, he thought. Then immediately he felt incredibly egotistical. She'd said she was crushing on him, not that she was willing to act on it. There was a world of difference between impulse and intent. As a lawyer, he knew that.

He was surprised at how much her interest spurred his physical reaction. The cold didn't touch him anymore. He felt hot all over. Giving into his impulse would have been foolish, though. Neither of them had time for the aggravation.

After a quick glance at his watch, he said, "We should probably be heading back to the hotel. I've got an early morning to put in if I'm going to make lunch with you and Ellis."

She placed her hand in his and allowed him to pull her to her feet. Her eyes met his boldly. Looking at her, he was filled with desire. It flooded every piece of him and became an almost overwhelming rush. All he had to do was pull her a few inches closer and he could taste her lips.

Instead he released her hand and took a step back.

Winter smiled and before she turned away, she leaned into him, and pressed her lips against his. David responded to the kiss before he knew he was moving. He put his arms around her and held her tightly. When her mouth opened, his did, too, and he felt the softness of her tongue stroking his. His conscious mind seemed to fragment and he couldn't put a single thought together.

She pulled away before he was ready. He was still hungry for her, but she put the distance between them again.

"Thank you for the evening," she said. "And the honesty."

"Anytime," David said. He had to try twice to get it out. He took her elbow and walked her back to the car, telling himself he didn't need any more problems than he was currently dealing with. But he couldn't help thinking, *That was a thank-you kiss?*

Chapter 23

Mandarin Oriental Hotel
Washington, D.C.
Now

Winter woke still feeling the frustration she'd gone to bed with. She'd admitted too much too freely when she'd spoken to David last night. But seeing him still clinging to the memory of Rainy Miller had brought that honesty out of her.

Or maybe it was just the proximity to the memorial for Honest Abe.

Admitting her interest also seriously ticked her off. There was no way she could compete with a ghost. Winter had kissed David there in front of the Lincoln Memorial with the intention of saying goodbye to that stupid infatuation she'd carried around for years.

The effort had failed. Not only that, it had backfired—big time.

She'd returned to the hotel with her hormones singing in overdrive. She'd tried cold showers, television, and—finally—work on her new book. She hadn't fallen in love with the story yet, so working on it was proving difficult. When she frustrated herself like that usually she could count on getting to sleep early.

Instead she'd just stared at the screen for two hours and didn't get enough sleep as a result. Part of it was the time difference between Los Angeles and Washington. She still hadn't acclimated to Phoenix time, much less the shift to the East Coast.

After a glance at the clock to discover it was 9:48 a.m., she forced herself out of bed. There were no messages on the phone, so David hadn't tried to call. She couldn't help wondering what kind of mindset he was in. Had she totally embarrassed herself? Or had she sparked a little interest?

And he had kissed her back, right? But was that just response? It was hard to tell with men.

A quick check of her e-mail on her notebook computer confirmed there was nothing pressing. She retreated to the bathroom and tried to forget about that kiss.

Feeling refreshed but still not at ease, Winter returned to the spacious room and dressed in business attire. The Mandarin Oriental Hotel was located in downtown Washington, D.C. She'd only stayed there once before and it had been when she'd been dead tired. She hadn't had a morning to laze around and appreciate the beauty.

The five-hundred-square-foot room was located in the corner of the building and on the Mandarin level, the top two floors of the hotel. Standing at the window, Winter had a view of the Jefferson Memorial and downtown Washington. She turned away and took a bottle of water from the minibar.

Taking a seat in the chair, she opened the files she had on Marion Gracelyn and went to the one she'd established for Colonel Thomas Marker. He was a point of uncertainty she hoped to clear up by having a conversation with Congressman Brian Ellis.

She'd also added the files Allison had sent. There were several pictures of Marker, and Winter studied the craggy face of the man. She also had the black-and-white and color pictures of the crime scene. Allison was very thorough.

The room phone rang.

Winter's heart sped up, thinking it might be David. Instead, when she answered the phone, a woman's voice came on.

"Winter? It's Allison Gracelyn. Long time no speak."

"It has been a while," Winter admitted cautiously. Although she'd known Allison back at the academy, they'd never been close friends.

"Am I catching you at a bad time?" Allison asked.

"No." Winter checked the time. It was still over an hour till the meeting with Ellis.

"My brother's not still around, is he?"

"Your brother," Winter replied stiffly, "stayed in his room last night."

"Ah. Okay. Embarrassing moment. I just thought maybe he might have stopped by for breakfast."

"No, he didn't stop by. And no you didn't think that. He told me you were the one who arranged dinner."

"Before I own up to anything, I need to know how that went."

"I stopped short of suicide. But it was a near thing."

"I thought maybe you were still interested in him. Everything I'd found out about you indicated you were still single."

"I am. But David is still in love with Rainy."

"Rainy's dead," Allison said quietly.

"I think he knows that," Winter replied archly. "That's one of the problems he has with relationships."

Allison sighed. "Look, I apologize for that. I just knew you guys had spent the last eight days together—"

"Nine," Winter corrected automatically.

"I've been up all night. It's still yesterday to me. I don't ever let it be tomorrow until I've been to bed." Allison sounded genuinely tired.

Winter was willing to cut the other woman some slack. The investigation into Marion's past, and the recent kidnappings, had to be hard on everyone connected to the Athena Academy.

"Dinner was fine," Winter said. "I just don't think David is ready for anything more."

"What about you?"

Winter laughed. "It's funny how quickly you step over the line from polite to prying."

"It's usually a very thin line. I remembered how you had a thing for David. I thought maybe, under the right circumstances—with a nudge, something might happen. Something good even if it wasn't permanent."

"It didn't."

Allison sighed. "That's too bad. He really needs someone to break him out of the rut he's in."

"I'm not exactly a service."

"I didn't mean to infer that you were. I thought you'd have a good time, too."

Winter checked the time. "Why did you call, Allison?"

"I've been looking over your notes, and I've got to say that I think you're onto something with the Amanda Weaver angle."

"Me, too." Winter took a swig from her water bottle.

"But the real reason I called—"

"Was to pry?"

"No."

The seriousness in Allison's tone gave Winter pause.

"The people that are involved in this are dangerous," Allison said.

"I know. The Mafia guy—"

"Salvatore Giambi."

Winter was impressed that Allison knew. "Giambi is still alive. Potentially the other agencies Marker and the woman, Weaver, were involved with could still want this story kept quiet."

"Yes." A computer keyboard clacked at the other end of the connection. "I checked your licenses and found you have a gun permit."

"I do," Winter agreed, "in the state of California."

"Well you're licensed in D.C. now, too."

Allison's announcement surprised Winter. "Maybe you could slow down and repeat that."

"I said, you're now licensed to carry a gun in D. C."

"I haven't applied for a permit or taken tests here."

"Doesn't matter."

Winter couldn't believe what she was hearing. David had mentioned that Allison worked for the National Security Agency, one of the most secret intelligence agencies in the United States, but she was supposed to be a computer person or something. Not Spy Girl.

"You can do that?" Winter asked.

"It's already done. Go answer the door."

"The door?"

At that point someone knocked on the door.

Cautiously Winter went to the door and peered through the peephole. A well-dressed man stood there holding a package. He looked like he was in his mid-thirties and was well-built. He wore a dark blue suit.

"Do you see the guy at your door?" Allison prompted.

"Yes. But how do you see him?"

"I've hacked into the hotel's security cameras."

"You can do that?" Winter was impressed.

"Yep. You'd be surprised what I can do."

Winter suspected that was true.

"He's going to hold up his ID so you can get a look at it," Allison said.

The man did. His ID card had his picture on it and his name: Simon Talley.

"His name is Simon Talley," Allison said. "He's going to give you a package."

"What's in the package?"

"A pistol. I found out you were licensed for a 10 mm. I sent you the same model that you have at home."

"Why would I need a gun?"

"Because you're with my brother."

"He's been a perfect gentleman so far."

Allison laughed. "Funny. But the idea is to provide you a means to protect yourself. David won't carry a gun."

"Does he dislike them?"

"He can shoot a rifle, but he's never learned how to handle a pistol. He didn't go to Athena Academy."

Winter remembered the first time she'd gone to the gun range at the academy. She hadn't especially liked guns, but over the course of weeks, months and years, Winter had gotten to where she enjoyed shooting. She even shot regularly on a gun range in Los Angeles.

"Open the door and take the package," Allison directed.

Winter did. She also took a five-dollar bill from her pocketbook and tried to tip the man. He just smiled, shook his head and walked away. After locking the door, Winter took the package back to the desk and opened it.

The 10 mm pistol looked sleek and deadly. The box also contained a belt holster that would hide under a jacket and a box of rounds. The smell of gun oil tickled Winter's nose.

"Do you really think this is necessary?" Winter asked.

"I hope not," Allison said. "But if it is, take care of my brother."

"He's got a security team watching over us."

"Then I hope you never have to use your gun. But if you do it'll be easier if you have it."

Winter took out the slim manila envelope and found the gun permit with accompanying photo. The picture was from one of her book jackets.

"You could have found a better picture for the permit," Winter said.

"E-mail me the photo you'd like on the permit and I'll get it done."

Winter smiled. "Kidding."

"Just be careful," Allison said. "I think we've only seen the tip of the iceberg on this thing. Whoever we're up against, they don't hesitate to kill to protect themselves. And we're closer now than we've ever been."

Winter said she would.

"And don't give up on David," Allison added. "He's a good man."

"I know," Winter said softly. She just didn't know what she was going to do about it. Or even if she wanted to chance anything permanent. She'd worked hard to find equilibrium in her life. She didn't want to just throw that away.

Not even for David Gracelyn.

"I suppose the congressman is fashionably late," Winter commented at 12:16. She gazed at her watch pointedly.

"It's the Hill," David said. "Everything out here runs on its own time. Meetings extend. Arguments start. Deals come to term. Getting to everything on time gets impossible some days. And that's without the traffic problems."

Winter sipped her tea. They sat at a table in Café MoZU, one of the restaurants in the Mandarin Oriental Hotel. The menu was primarily Asian and the view overlooked the Washington Channel and the Potomac Tidal Basin.

"He'll be here," David said confidently.

If the tension between them hadn't been so thick she could have cut it with a knife, Winter wouldn't have minded the wait. The view was wonderful and the atmosphere was great. She was also looking forward to the meal. She'd skipped breakfast. However, the pistol riding on her right hip was uncomfortable. Thankfully her jacket concealed it.

"Did you sleep?" David asked.

"I did."

"Me, too." Sighing, he turned to her. "About last night…"

Winter wanted to groan in frustration, but she didn't dare. She wanted to talk about last night, but not right now.

Thankfully Brian Ellis chose that moment to arrive. The gray hair, which had gone that way at an early age, gave the congressman a distinguished look that he made the most of. His suit was elegant and simple. In his early sixties, Ellis moved confidently and sure-footedly across the floor. Two large men trailed after him.

David stood and drew the congressman's attention.

Ellis adjusted his course and waved the two big men off. They walked over to the bar and stood in a position to watch the meeting. Winter knew they were bodyguards.

"Hello, David," Ellis greeted as he took David's hand.

"Congressman," David said.

"Who's your friend?" Ellis asked as he smiled at Winter.

"Winter Archer," David replied.

Some of the confidence slid off Ellis's face, but he offered his hand anyway. "The writer?"

"Yes," Winter replied and took the man's hand for a moment.

Ellis sat across from Winter. He looked up at David. "I don't understand."

"It's nothing really," David said. "Winter is an Athena Academy student. She wants to do a book about my mother."

"Great lady," Ellis said, but there was no real passion in his voice. The remark was more automatic than inspired. "You green-lighted this book about your mother, David?"

"For the moment."

A server came over and took Ellis's order for a drink. He tried an easy smile. "Where do I fit into your mother's biography?"

"Marion Gracelyn investigated the death of Colonel Tom Marker," Winter said. "Do you remember him?"

"Of course I remember him," Ellis said gruffly. "You don't forget the man that hauled you out of a Vietnamese death camp and saved your life. Tom Marker was a hero."

"Except someone didn't think so," Winter countered.

Ellis shook his head. "They were wrong. Guy was a saint in my book." He took his glass from the server and drank half the contents. "Why are you interested in him?"

Winter thought that was an interesting question. "I'm not interested in Marker," she replied. "I'm following up on the murder."

"Why?"

"It was Marion's first big case. The people who read the book about her will want to know more. There are some interesting aspects to the murder investigation."

"Like what?"

"The fact that it never got solved."

"That's because the woman disappeared before she could be tried."

"I know. I'm trying to find out who she was."

"Why?"

"Because the case is interesting."

"It's not interesting when the police fail to catch the guilty party."

"It's interesting when you think she might still be out there."

Ellis shook his head. "If she is, she'd be an old woman now."

"Like Adam Gracelyn is an old man?"

An uncomfortable look tightened Ellis's features. He tried flashing David a grin that indicated he meant no harm. "I'm not much younger than Adam these days, Ms. Archer."

Winter ignored that. "Colonel Marker was a frequent visitor to your father's house. Correct?"

Ellis looked wary. "Yes, he was."

"Why?"

"My father was always grateful to Tom for what he'd done. For the record, so was I. If Tom were still alive, he'd be welcome in my house at any time."

"Do you know who killed him?"

"That woman."

"Had you ever met her?"

"No."

"Would it surprise you to learn that she might well have been an assassin employed by the United States military?"

Ellis's eyes narrowed. "Yes, it would." He turned his attention to David. "This is beginning to sound like some kind of witch hunt."

"Ms. Archer's research into my mother's past has taken some intriguing twists," David replied.

"So you're on the trail of an assassin that's turned forty years cold?"

"I'm trying to reconstruct what Marion Gracelyn was investigating all those years ago."

Ellis frowned and sat back. "As I recall, her investigation all those years ago got intensely dangerous."

"It did. Marion was nearly killed on a couple of occasions."

"All of this for the sake of a story? No, less than that. All of this for the sake of sensationalism?"

"I'm just trying to find the truth," Winter said.

"Whatever that truth is, it's forty years buried."

"Do you think there are people out there today who would want to keep it buried?" Winter closed in for the kill. She was aware that she was pushing the man. Maybe she was even pushing him too hard. Beneath the table David's hand dropped onto her thigh and squeezed in warning.

"How would I know?"

"You were one of the people closest to those events. You were closer to the murder victim than anyone left alive."

"I don't understand how that involves me."

"I'd just like to know what Colonel Marker was doing in that hotel that night."

"I don't know."

"And why he visited your family so often."

"He didn't have any family," Ellis said. "He got divorced while he was in Vietnam. His wife left him. He liked to play golf with my father." He took out his cell phone and glanced at it. Then he dropped his napkin onto his plate. "I've got to go. There's a deal in the works that's just fallen apart. I've got to do some damage control." He smiled at David. "I'm sure you know what that's like."

David nodded but didn't say anything.

"Ms. Archer." Ellis stood and nodded. He didn't offer to shake hands with either of them.

"Could we reschedule this meeting?" Winter asked.

"Why? I've told you everything I know."

"I have more questions."

"Phone my office. Let's set up an appointment next time instead of having me ambushed under the guise of doing a favor for the president. Have a good day." Ellis turned and left. His bodyguards joined him by the time he reached the door.

"Maybe you pushed him too hard." David said.

"Criticism?" Winter arched a brow in rebuke.

"No. Just saying."

"You could have jumped in at any time."

David shook his head and looked thoughtful. "No. You were doing fine. If I'd been asking the questions, I'd have gone after him just as hard. He wasn't exactly forthright. But that may be standard operating procedure after a career on the Hill. Ellis is the kind of guy you won't get a straight answer from unless you use a crowbar. Unless the straight answer is the one he wants to give." He paused. "Did he seem defensive to you?"

Winter didn't hesitate. "Yes."

"Me, too."

"Interesting."

"I was thinking the same thing." David looked at the menu before him. "Should we order?"

"Dinner didn't go so well last night," Winter reminded him.

"Maybe we're more the *lunch* crowd." David smiled brightly.

"All right," Winter said, unable to resist that smile.

Despite trying to beg off to go work, David managed to talk Winter into spending the afternoon with him. Things went better between them when he had the chance to show off the city.

They walked through the historic district and exchanged tidbits of trivia about the people and events that had shaped the nation. Since his father had been a Civil War hobbyist later in life, David had a wealth of stories to share, especially about the Second Battle of Bull Run. Winter's knowledge tended to relate more to political stories, but they spanned decades and often intersected. Several of the stories were ones David hadn't heard before.

After sightseeing and shopping, they had dinner at the Wok & Roll on H Street.

The structure housing the restaurant had also been a boarding-house at one time. Mary Surratt, the proprietor, had been the first woman executed by the United States government. Surratt had been part of the conspiracy to kill President Abraham Lincoln in the Ford Theater. Dinner went a lot easier with the distraction of history and politics.

When they'd finished their meal, even though David was tired and thought Winter probably was as well, he asked her to coffee and dessert. Since everything in Chinatown was nearby, they walked and chatted.

David was surprised to discover that he was enjoying himself, and he was more aware of Winter's sensuality than he had been before. The kiss in front of the Lincoln Memorial had haunted his sleep last night and preyed on his mind all day. It had set something in motion that he'd thought dead and gone.

They walked close together down H Street. He used his body to knock as much wind off her as he could. He was paying such close attention to her that he didn't notice the car slide to a stop beside them until Winter's attention was focused on it.

The car was a sleek Lexus, black or dark gray. That was all he remembered about it later, though Winter assured him it was dark blue. In the darkness with the streetlights, it was hard to say.

Three figures sat in the car.

Wary now, David covered more of Winter's body with his own. Why would muggers ride around in a Lexus?

The man in the passenger seat and the one in the rear rolled their windows down. Guns appeared.

David turned and wrapped his arms around Winter as he drove her back into the nearest doorway. Bullets slammed into the nearby walls and tore glass out of the shop windows. The crescendo of gunfire echoed between the buildings and over the street.

Winter struggled and twisted within his grasp. David tried to hang on to her, but she seemed to know just how to move to get away from him. Incredulous, he watched as she swept a pistol from her hip and took deliberate aim. The pistol bounced in her hand as she fired.

Her bullets punched holes in the side of the car. Then one of them caught the man in the passenger seat and threw him into the driver. Blood glistened on the inside of the windshield. In the next instant, the driver pulled away and wove dangerously through the traffic.

By that time David had his phone out and had dialed 911. He looked at Winter. "Are you all right?"

She nodded. "I think so. What about you?"

"I'm okay."

Winter stepped closer to him. "You're bleeding." She touched his face and her fingers came away stained with crimson.

David felt the pain then, but it was almost inconsequential in the adrenaline haze that had filled his nervous system. He walked toward the street as he talked to the dispatch officer. Sirens echoed in the distance. A crowd had gathered.

As he surveyed the damage, David realized how close the bullets had come to hitting Winter. She would have been gone.

Just like Rainy. Fear ached within him.

Winter knew David was angry with her. She could tell it from the short way he'd dealt with her, and the quick way he'd called in favors from the president to get them cut loose from the Washington, D.C., police. She'd been waiting for him to blow up since they'd arrived back at the hotel.

Without a word, he'd walked her to her room.

Winter swiped the door open with her keycard and turned to face David. "Up until almost getting shot, I thought the evening was going pretty good."

"This isn't a laughing matter." David stepped past her and entered the hotel room.

"Come on in, why don't you?" Winter said sarcastically. She closed the door behind her.

"Where did you get the gun?" he demanded.

Winter couldn't believe it. "People shoot at us on the street and you want to know where *I* got a gun?"

"You didn't have it when we got here. You'd have had to check it through luggage."

"Might I point out, Counselor, that if I hadn't had the gun tonight, things might have ended differently back there?"

"Did you know those men?"

"Now I'm being accused of bringing firepower *and* the villains?" Winter shook her head. "This is ridiculous. You need to go."

"I'm not leaving till I get answers."

"You're leaving when I say you're leaving." Winter made her voice hard. "I *still* have the gun."

"Where. Did. You. Get. It?"

"Where were your bodyguards while we were being attacked?"

David cursed. "I'd told them to keep their distance. I hadn't wanted them breathing down our necks. That was my fault."

"Allison sent me the pistol," Winter said grudgingly. Since he was being honest and forthright, she felt she had to be as well. "She knew I was licensed to carry a gun in L. A. She arranged for the gun permit for D.C., too."

That seemed to stun David. "Allison gave it to you?"

"Yes. She was worried about us. She said you would never wear a pistol, but she knew that I was sometimes in the habit of doing so. To tell you the truth, I even thought about *not* wearing it. But now I'm glad I did." Winter paused. "And, *no,* I didn't know those men. Hopefully the police will find them and we'll learn who they are."

David took a deep breath and let it out. Some of the anger left him then, too. "I thought for a moment they'd killed you."

Winter remember how he'd turned to her, wrapped his arms around her protectively and hustled her to safety. She'd already reached for him and had him by the jacket lapels to do the same, but she'd let him carry them backward while she'd switched her attention to drawing the pistol.

"They didn't," Winter said softly. She looked at the blood dried on his cheek. For just a moment, he looked incredibly vulnerable. "Let's go have a look at your face."

"My face is fine."

"You refused the EMTs at the scene," Winter said. "But you may need to have someone look at it."

"It's just a scratch."

Winter went into the bathroom. "Let's have a look. After you invade my hotel room and accuse me of being a willing accomplice to what happened out there on the street, you at least owe me that civility."

With obvious reluctance, David followed her.

Winter turned on the light and opened the pack of wipes she'd brought for cleaning her face. The dried blood came off stubbornly, but it came off and revealed the shallow cut beneath. She guessed that he'd been hit by a piece of flying glass.

"You should probably have this taped up." Winter prodded at the cut in an effort to see how deep it was. She was way too conscious of his proximity and the small confines of the bathroom. "If it was steri-stripped, there'd be less chance of scarring."

Gently he reached up and captured her chin in his hand. He held her head and stared deeply into her eyes. "I thought they were going to kill you," he said hoarsely.

"They didn't," Winter whispered back. Her gaze was captured by his.

In the next minute, he leaned into her. She met him halfway. His hands rose to her sides and pulled her toward him. Her hands curled around his neck. He pressed his lips onto hers and she answered his urgency with her own.

A moment later, David pulled back. He breathed raggedly. "This," he whispered, "is *so* not a good idea."

"You're right," Winter said. "We should stop now."

"Yeah," he agreed. But he pulled her tight again and kissed her even deeper and longer.

"I've got a bed," Winter said.

"I know."

"Maybe we could—"

"Yeah," David agreed. He lifted her. She wrapped her legs around his midsection to help him balance them as he walked into the next room.

He placed her tenderly on the bed and stroked her through the clothing. His hands squeezed her breasts just enough to take her breath away. She felt his erection pressed against the inside of her left thigh as he lay on her.

Impatiently she pulled his shirttail out of his pants, then took his tie off and worked through his buttons. He ran his hands under her blouse, slid his fingers under her bra and found her nipples. She moaned a little at the rough contact. Her hips involuntarily bucked against him.

All resistance melted away. They undressed each other hurriedly in the lighted room. She loved the sight of him, the hard planes of his muscles and his trim waist. Her desire turned her liquid and his fingers slid easily inside her as he stroked her to intense need. She reached down and gripped him, finding him hard and ready.

Winter tried to breathe, but there didn't seem to be enough air in the room. She kissed him again and again, staring into his eyes as she felt a small orgasm building and demanding release. His fingers never stopped moving as they constantly rewarded her flesh with wanted attention. Only a few minutes later, she peaked. Her climax shuddered through her, setting every nerve on edge.

A few minutes later, when those feelings had subsided, David rose to his knees, slid between her thighs and started to sheathe himself in her. Then he hesitated.

"What's wrong?" she asked, crazed with longing for the feel of him inside her.

"I don't have a condom."

"Top drawer in the nightstand. I bought them from a drugstore yesterday. I was hoping that dinner last night would end later than it did."

David took one of the condoms out, ripped the packet open, and—with her help—slid it on. Then he moved between her legs again and drove himself home. She stretched around him and held him tightly.

He surged against her, giving in to desire, taking her deeply and pounding against her. Winter's head swam. Her breasts felt heavy and full as he caressed them, then kissed them. She slammed against him, then put her hands on his hips and pulled him into her even harder.

She climaxed again, and this time her tightening muscles triggered his release.

Afterward, Winter lay with David's head cradled on her breast. She stroked his hair with the fingers of one hand. He had his arms wrapped around her waist. She wondered if he thought he'd made a mistake in becoming physically involved with her.

"Any regrets?" he asked as if he'd read her mind.

"No," she said.

He was quiet for a moment. "Me, neither. I didn't expect that."

Winter smiled. "What did you expect?"

"I don't know." David rose up on one elbow to look her in the eyes. "I don't know where this is going, Winter. This is a surprise."

"For me, too. But we don't have to figure it out now. There's time."

"I don't want to stay in Washington, D.C., any longer than we have to. It's dangerous here."

"We don't have to stay here any longer," Winter said. "Ellis wasn't forthcoming with any information we can use. But there is one more person we haven't talked to."

"Who?"

"Christine Evans. After the night your mom was attacked in her apartment, Christine and the Army arrived."

"Christine was there?"

"Yeah."

David looked surprised. "She's never mentioned it."

"It's time that she did," Winter said. "I want to hear the rest of the story from her."

"So do I."

"That can wait a little while," Winter said with a small smile. "At least till morning." She rolled him over onto his back and threw a leg across his hips. She at least wanted the night for herself even if this proved only to be momentary weakness on both their parts. Right now, though, feeling David's body against hers, there was nothing weak about him.

Afterward, David lay still and waited for Winter to fall asleep. His mind was restless and thoughts kept getting jumbled up. On the nightstand, his cell phone buzzed for attention. He glanced at the Caller ID, recognized the number, and knew that it wouldn't be anything important.

Quietly, he got out of bed and walked to the window. They'd turned the lights out at some point, although he didn't remember doing it. He'd been too caught up in the moment, in the sheer physical heat of the encounter.

That wasn't like him. Other times he'd been "involved," there hadn't been as much…passion. Tonight, all of tonight from dinner through the shoot-out, had been different. Scary different. He hadn't felt like he'd been in control of anything that had happened. Or of himself.

"David?"

Although he didn't think he was ready to talk to her yet, David turned to face Winter. She sat in bed with her arms tucked around her knees. The sheet shadowed her body but didn't hide the curves.

"Yeah," he said hoarsely.

"Planning on making a fast getaway?"

He heard that note of challenge in her voice. "It's crossed my mind."

"The door's open."

"I know." David wished his mouth didn't feel so damn dry.

"I'm not going to try to hold you here."

"I know that, too." He took in a deep breath and let it out. "The problem is, I don't want to leave."

"I didn't ask you to."

"Do you want me to stay?"

She was silent for a moment. "Yes."

"Good," he said. "Good." Part of that distance he'd tried to keep between them went away and he let it. "Because I really don't want to go."

"Come back to bed."

David shook his head. "It's not about the sex, Winter."

She raised a brow. "Is something wrong with the sex?"

Was she teasing? David didn't know. How could anyone possibly joke at a time like this?

"The sex was great. Everything…was great. That's what scares me. That's why you scare me."

"You don't have to be scared of me."

"Yeah, I do." David swallowed. "This isn't just about having fun. Not for me." He paused to let her speak.

She didn't.

"It would be easier if you talked, too," he said.

"What are you afraid of?" Winter asked.

"Getting close to you and losing you."

"That doesn't have to happen."

David locked his hands behind his neck and tried to think straight. "It happened with Rainy. I came back from college and she was engaged. I watched her walk down the aisle on some other guy's arm. I attended her funeral."

Anger tightened Winter's face. "I'm sorry I'm not Rainy."

"I'm not," David said. "I couldn't ever have Rainy."

"So I'm the consolation prize?" Winter shook her head. "That's not anything I'm interested in. Maybe tonight was a mistake, but it doesn't have to be one that we can't—"

David interrupted her because he knew she'd misunderstood. "Listening to you tell the story about my parents, about how different they were, about all the things that could have kept them apart, I know it couldn't have been easy for them, either."

"No," Winter said. "Your mother's journals bear that out."

"But they didn't let it keep them apart. Not their opposing views. Not their jobs. Not the difference in backgrounds. They just let go of all that…and loved each other."

"I know," Winter whispered.

David walked to the bed and took Winter's hand in his. "Working with you on this has been a strain. Trying to understand how everything that took place back then applies to now has been difficult. But do you know what's gotten easier?"

She shook her head.

"Being with you," David said.

"Even when I was, let me see, 'shooting up half of D.C.,'?"

"Yeah. Even then." David shrugged and smiled. "It made things a little dicey with the police, and my PR team is going to tell me I've presented them with a nightmare, and even the president might not be too happy. But yeah. Even then."

"What about all the hostility earlier?"

"I think that was my last defense." David touched her face. "However this works out, Winter, I want you in my life. I don't want to live my life being scared, and there's not a woman I've met who has ever touched my life like you have these past few days."

"Doesn't mean it's forever," she said quietly.

"I don't think my mom and dad thought it was forever, either," David said. "But it was." He brushed hair from her eyes. "My mom always said I'd know when I was truly in love. What I felt for Rainy, what I've been carrying all this time…this is something new and different. And every bit as wonderful."

Tears glimmered in her eyes then. Without a word she pulled him back into bed and kissed him deeply.

"After all that," she growled huskily into his ear, "you'd better not just fall to sleep."

David laughed and proved to her that wasn't going to happen anytime soon.

Chapter 24

Phoenix, Arizona
Friday, May 31, 1968
The Past

Consciousness slowly returned to Marion. Her head felt incredibly thick and huge. She struggled to open her eyelids and barely succeeded.

"Ah, Miss Hart, you're once more among us." The sibilant voice was unhurried.

Rolling her head to the right, afraid for a moment that it was just going to spin free and fall off, Marion looked at the shadowy shape on the vanity seat beside the bed. She was lying in the bed with no memory of how she got there.

The man lit a cigarette. For a moment the harsh yellow flame lit up his dark features. He looked Indian or Hispanic. His hair was cropped short. A pencil-thin mustache darkened his lip.

"Who are you?" Marion asked. Her mouth felt dry and awkward.

"I've worn many names."

"Like Amanda Weaver."

The glow of the cigarette barely revealed the smile that pulled at his full lips. He was an incredibly handsome man.

"Just so. I want to talk to you about her."

Marion tried to get off her bed but discovered clothesline held her arms and legs to the four posts. The restraints weren't tight enough to cut into her flesh, but she was securely held.

The man smoked silently and waited until she gave up. Marion started to scream again. Before she could shout, he clapped a hand over her mouth. This time there was no rag.

"At this point, Miss Hart," he whispered as he leaned down close enough to touch her face with his, "I feel you're more valuable to me alive than you are dead. Please don't do anything to disabuse me of that notion."

Trembling, her senses whirling, Marion lay back.

"Good," the man said. "Very good. Now…I'm going to remove my hand from your mouth. When I do, you won't scream."

Yes, I will, Marion promised herself. *As long and as loud as I can.*

"If you do," the man stated calmly, "I'm going to cut your pretty little throat and that will be the end of it."

He held up a small combat knife with a single-edged, four-inch blade. The cast-off glow of his cigarette gleamed along the weapon.

"Do you understand?" he asked. "Nod if you do."

Marion nodded.

"Good. We're communicating."

"What do you want?"

"I want Amanda Weaver out of your jail and free to go where she pleases."

"I can't make that happen."

"I think you're selling yourself short, Miss Hart. A pretty young woman like you will have many champions. Tonight you went to the Gracelyn party, on the arm of one of the wealthiest families in the area. I saw you and Adam Gracelyn go up in the mountains today. I get the impression that he would do what he could to save you."

A tight, hard knot swelled in Marion's throat. She couldn't speak. Even in her worst nightmares she'd never imagined being as helpless as she was now. If she ever did create that school—that academy—for girls, if she lived through this night, they were all going to be taught how to defend themselves.

"So you understand when I tell you that I will do anything I can to save…Amanda."

His white smile sliced through the darkness in the room. He reached out to stroke her cheek, and Marion knew it was only to remind her how helpless she was.

"What I want you to do, Miss Hart, is find some way to dismiss the charges against Amanda," he went on. "If you don't, I'm going to kill your mother and your father. Then I will come after you. You have my word on that."

Without a sound, without another word, he leaned forward and cut one of her hands free. Then he laid the knife on her chest and left her apartment.

Tears leaked down Marion's face as she picked up the knife in her shaking hand. *It's a trick. He's going to come back and kill you. This is just a trick.*

She was shaking so badly she cut her wrist as she sawed her other hand free. When she was finally free, she dashed into the bathroom and was sick. Pain thudded at her temples as she threw up. The retching went on for a long time even after her stomach had emptied its contents.

Finally she washed her face and stood on weak knees as she leaned over the sink. *That's not just fear,* she told her dark image in the mirror. But she was too afraid to even turn on the light. *I won't let myself be that afraid. Part of that was the chloroform or whatever he drugged you with. You can't be that afraid. You* will not *be that afraid.*

She forced herself to stand on her own, then she returned to the bedroom. The glowing clock by the bed had been turned to face the wall. The man, Amanda's man, had to have done it.

Fingerprints, she told herself. *Let there be fingerprints.*

She looked at the clock without touching it, though, to note the time. Then she started to pick up the phone.

He might have used the phone, she told herself. *Don't touch it.*

Knowing she had to go outside to find a phone almost made Marion sick all over again. But she forced herself to move. Purse over her shoulder and keys in her hand, she walked out of the apartment on trembling legs and went down the stairs to ground level.

She kept peering over her shoulders as she headed for her car.

Before she knew it, she was running. Her heart pounded so hard she thought it was going to explode.

When she was behind the steering wheel, she locked the door and started the engine. For a moment, when the lights of a passing car struck her back window, she thought she saw someone in her rearview mirror.

A scream almost made it past her lips. Then she calmed herself, put the Mustang in gear, and drove.

Minutes later, her face still wet with tears, Marion took loose change from the coin purse she kept in the car and got out at a convenience store. She made it to the pay phone even though she didn't think she'd be able to.

She hesitated about who to call first. Her parents would be in bed, and she didn't want to deal with the possibility that the man had visited them before he'd visited her. She thought about calling the police, or Sheriff Keller.

But in the end, she called Adam's home number and hoped that he was home.

He answered on the first ring.

"Hello."

"Adam," she whispered. Her voice was hoarse with fear.

"Marion?"

"I need you. Something…something happened."

"Where are you?" Concern sharpened his words.

Marion looked around, in that confused moment not sure at all where she was, and told him.

"I'll be right there," he promised.

"Hurry." Marion couldn't hang up the phone till she heard the disconnect at his end. Then she dropped more money into the slots and called Sheriff Keller.

Minutes later, Adam's MG squealed to a stop in the convenience store parking lot. He got out of the car, his shirt flapping loosely, dressed in jeans and wearing tennis shoes. He carried a large revolver naked in his right hand. His eyes were hard and intense as they locked on her.

"Marion," he croaked.

At first Marion couldn't move from the perceived safety of the phone booth. Adam pushed on the folding door but she wouldn't let him in.

"Marion," he said again.

The sound of his voice speaking her name broke through the fear that held her captive. She opened the door and stepped out into his arms.

Even though the men in her house were crime scene techs working with the sheriff's office, Marion still felt violated. The apartment was her home. The men were going through her life and she didn't want them there.

She sat in the back of Keller's cruiser and watched the investigation. The whirling lights cut through the predawn gloom and drew curious neighbors.

"It's going to be okay," Adam said. He sat beside her and held her hand.

Marion didn't trust her voice. She continued to sit quietly. But she couldn't help glancing around at the surrounding buildings. Only a few hours ago, it would have felt ridiculous to think about a sniper on the roof in the neighborhood. Now it seemed foolhardy not to give serious contemplation to the possibility.

I just want my life back, Marion thought.

"I'm going to take you off this case," Geoffrey Turnbull announced.

Marion sat in one of the chairs in Keller's office. She'd changed into slacks and a blouse in the women's room at the sheriff's department. She didn't know when she'd feel safe going back to her apartment.

"I don't want to be taken off this case," she said in a shaky voice.

Turnbull heaved a sigh. He ticked off points on his fingers. "You're involved with the public defender assigned to this case—"

"We're not involved," Marion insisted. "I went to the Gracelyn Memorial Day party. A lot of other people did."

"Not as Adam Gracelyn's guest."

Marion could have argued the point, but she chose not to. She sipped hot chocolate from the foam cup Keller had ordered in for her.

The big sheriff, his face haggard and drawn, sat behind his desk. Pale morning light illuminated the Venetian blinds behind him.

"The integrity of your prosecution and Gracelyn's defense might be called into question," Turnbull pointed out.

"The district attorney's office has to reveal all the evidence with the defense counsel," Marion said. "We've worked closely together on this thing since the beginning." She looked at Turnbull. "If you're worried about whether or not I'm in it to win it, I am."

"Marion, people are going to wonder if evidence is all you've been revealing."

Her cheeks flamed. She never broke eye contact, though. "It is."

"Not everyone is going to believe that. Especially not when they find out Adam Gracelyn was hanging around the sheriff's office all morning."

Marion didn't address that. It was true that Adam was waiting somewhere else in the building, and it was true that he was worried about her.

"Secondly," Turnbull went on, "I can't guarantee your safety. Neither can the sheriff. Can you, Fred?"

"No," Keller replied. "We got some prints off the clock that aren't Marion's. I'm hoping we'll get a solid identification, but I don't know if that's going to happen. We couldn't get identification on that Tarlton character, either."

At least Marion's parents were safe. The sheriff had sent deputies to take them from their homes and put them up in a hotel until the present situation was resolved. Thankfully the school year had ended so they were able to remain in hiding. She'd talked to them only briefly, long enough to assure them that she was all right.

"The bottom line is, Marion," Turnbull said in a softer voice, "it's too dangerous for you to stay involved with this."

"I know this case," Marion protested weakly. She didn't want to be driven from anything.

"And I expect you to help with it. But you're going to be doing it from the sidelines. I'm not going to change my mind about that."

"I understand," Marion said. And she did. She just didn't like it.

For two days, Marion hid out in a hotel room in downtown Phoenix. She spent time with her parents and she missed Adam.

They talked on the phone, but the promise of the budding relationship seemed to be on hold.

If it isn't dead in the water, Marion thought.

She occupied herself with the case. Turnbull had papers and documents couriered over to her hotel room, all in a circumspect way so whoever the man was that had broken in to her apartment wouldn't be able to find her.

More and more information came in regarding the ties to Salvatore Giambi, but the district attorney's office didn't have a way to act on it. All they could prove was that Giambi *might* have hired Marco Fanelli to kill Amanda Weaver in her cell.

It was all frustrating.

Saturday night at nine o'clock, someone knocked on Marion's hotel door.

Even though she had a sheriff's deputy in plainclothes stationed nearby, Marion still experienced a sudden jolt of adrenaline. She wasn't expecting anyone. She'd ordered a sandwich at five and dozed. She'd declined her parents' invitation to eat with them, telling them that she had a lot of paperwork to put together by the time the trial opened up on Tuesday.

She peered through the peephole and saw Adam standing there dressed in a biker's leathers. He looked like he hadn't shaven for a couple of days.

She opened the door. "What are you doing here?"

"I told the sheriff I was coming," Adam said. "He didn't like it and even threatened to arrest me. He almost had me when he told me that my coming around you could be dangerous for you. But I figured that if I could find you, someone else could, too." He shrugged. "You're probably going to be moved in the morning."

"That's all right." Marion invited him in. She sat on the chair while Adam perched anxiously on the front of the couch. "How did you find me?"

"I hired a local private eye firm as soon as the sheriff told me he was going to sequester you. I've used them to find witnesses in cases before. They're good at what they do."

"I guess so."

"I had to see you. It was driving me crazy not to."

Marion reached over and took his hand. "I know. I've felt the same way."

He leaned over and kissed her. Fire ignited in the pit of her stomach and spread throughout her body. When the kiss finally ended, they were both breathing harder.

"I'll be glad when this is over," Adam said. He dragged his fingers through her hair.

"I know," she said. "Me, too." She left the chair and joined him on the couch.

He wrapped an arm around her and held her tightly. They didn't say anything. They just sat quietly together. Marion put her head on his shoulder and her hand over his heart. Before she knew it, she was asleep. For the first time in two days she slept soundly and without nightmares.

The Army arrived early Sunday morning.

Knocking startled Marion into wakefulness. She discovered she was still asleep on Adam. He lay sprawled across the couch in a seated position, his head thrown back.

Rising from the couch, Marion walked to the door and peered out. Sheriff Keller stood in the hallway. Two people stood beside him.

One was a tall redheaded man in a suit and the other was a young blond woman with startling eyes. The woman looked like she might have barely been out of college. She wore professional attire as well, but there was something about the way that she looked around constantly that told Marion she was extremely competent.

"Miss Hart." Keller knocked again.

"What do you need, Sheriff?" Marion felt awkward about Adam's presence in the room. Having a man stay all night in a hotel room guarded by sheriff's deputies was by no means circumspect. Even under the circumstances, people were going to talk if they found out.

"There are people here to see you," Keller said. "You need to talk to them."

"What's going on?" Adam asked from the couch.

"I don't know. Keller's here with a couple of people."

Adam frowned. "First he's keeping people away? Now he's bringing them around? That doesn't make sense."

Marion silently agreed, but she opened the door.

"Morning, Miss Hart." Keller touched his hat. "I'd like to present Captain Edward Brubaker and Lieutenant Christine Evans. They're with the United States Army. They insisted on seeing you."

"I'd like to see some identification." Marion didn't step out of the way of the door.

"Yes, ma'am." Brubaker reached under his jacket. Marion caught a brief glimpse of the pistol nestled in a shoulder holster. Then Brubaker handed over his identification and that of his associate.

Marion read through them quickly. "Criminal Investigation Division?" She handed them back.

"It means just what it says, ma'am." Brubaker handed Christine Evans her identification back and put away his own. "We investigate criminals for the United States Army. We thought you could help us. Might be we could help you."

Marion stepped back and asked them in.

Chapter 25

"Do you recognize this man?" Christine Evans took a series of pictures out of a slim valise and laid them across the table at the back of the hotel room.

Marion looked at the pictures. She felt horrible sitting there knowing that she hadn't showered or changed out of yesterday's clothes. Under the circumstances, she forgave herself, but it still chipped away at her confidence.

The man in the pictures was immediately recognizable. They'd all been taken from different angles and in different places, usually from a distance. But there was no mistaking who he was. The fear that had haunted her over the last two days returned with a vengeance.

"This is the man who broke into my apartment," Marion whispered. "Who is he?"

"His name is Evaristo Melendez," Christine said.

Marion figured that Brubaker had chosen Christine to act as point on their interview either because she was better at it, was less threatening, was a woman, or all of the above. The big army captain sat in a chair nearby and watched intently.

"The name doesn't mean anything to me," Marion said.

"Evaristo Melendez is a Cuban national," Christine said. Her voice was well-modulated and she spoke with an authority that belied her years. "When Fidel Castro came to power in Cuba, Melendez helped organize the resistance movement. He was a key player in the Bay of Pigs."

Marion recalled that event in 1961. The Central Intelligence Agency had funded the resistance movement by the Cuban people who wanted out from under Castro's rule. The effort had ended badly for the resistance fighters.

"Needless to say, Melendez wasn't a big fan of the United States government when he finished that," Christine said. "Outcast from his own country, he turned to what he knew best—killing. He became a mercenary, and his first client was the CIA."

Marion decided she liked the no-nonsense approach Christine took to the interview.

"For three or four years, Melendez stayed true to the CIA and only worked for them," Christine said. "But they eventually had a falling-out at some point. Melendez began working for whoever paid the most. Including the Russians and Chinese. He's a deadly man. He's even taken out American targets during the last few years."

"We already had an idea that he was a dangerous man," Adam said. "Where are you going with this?"

Unperturbed, Christine opened another folder and spread out more pictures. "U.S. Army CID learned that Melendez picked up a protégé." She placed the pictures on the table. "We haven't been able to identify her."

Her.

Knowing what she was going to find, Marion leaned closer to the photographs and studied them. The photographers hadn't been able to get as close to the woman as they had Melendez. Sometimes she'd even had to be circled in red ink to single her out in a crowd.

In fact, Marion wasn't sure that it was even the same woman. Her hair was different in nearly every photograph. Sometimes it was long, sometimes short. The hue varied from platinum blond to red to black, and every color in between.

"Are you sure these pictures are of the same woman?" Marion asked.

"We believe so," Christine said. "Every time one of those pictures was taken, someone in them died. She either killed them herself or acted as bait for Melendez."

"You think this is the woman we're holding in the jail," Marion said.

"That's correct," Christine said. "Unfortunately we haven't had any solid evidence. We didn't have any fingerprints from her that we've been able to match up. Until you sent a set in and directed them to military services. We only just made the identification because the fingerprint cards have to be individually reviewed."

"So this is her?"

"Her fingerprints implicate her in two assassinations of military officers in Vietnam."

Marion leaned back in her chair. Her thoughts spun. "Who is she?"

Christine shook her head. "The woman remains a cipher. We haven't been able to tie anything to her."

"Did she leave the playing card with the two men she assassinated?" The word sounded ugly and brutal when Marion voiced it.

Christine's brow furrowed. "I don't know what you're talking about."

"She left a signature behind," Brubaker said. "The Queen of Hearts. And no, no playing card was found with these men."

"You were informed about the one left on Colonel Tom Marker's body?" Marion asked.

Christine and Brubaker nodded. "We thought you weren't sure whether Marker had it or the woman did."

"We're thinking the woman left it." Marion quickly brought them up-to-date on the Mafia connection Turnbull had discovered through the dead arsonist. "I have to admit I'm confused as to why you're here."

"To see you," Brubaker said.

"Why?"

"Because you've built a rapport with Amanda Weaver and Evaristo Melendez."

"One hates me and the other has threatened to kill me," Marion said. "I wouldn't call that a rapport."

Brubaker grinned bleakly. "Perhaps it's not a peaceful accord, but it does count as communication for our purposes. We want to use that to bring in Evaristo."

Marion sat quietly. She knew she wasn't going to like what the CID people had to say.

"We want to exploit that relationship," Brubaker went on.

"How?"

"We want you to bring Melendez out into the open."

"How am I going to do that? I'm off the case."

Brubaker grinned. "I think Mr. Turnbull will be amenable to reassigning you. If the United States government asks him to." He reached into his jacket and produced a letter with a presidential seal.

"An awful lot of these are floating around right now," Marion said.

"These are confusing times, Miss Hart. A lot of distrust and suspicion exists out in the world. We're going through growing pains." Brubaker tapped the paper. "But this will get Mr. Turnbull on our side. I guarantee it." Brubaker looked at her speculatively. "The question is, do you feel up to helping us?"

"You shouldn't do this, Marion."

Marion stood near the hotel room window. She made certain she didn't stand in front of it. Keller on the day of her arrival, and Brubaker before he'd left, had cautioned her about that.

"Then what should I do, Adam?" Marion felt torn and confused. Mostly, though, she felt scared.

"Tell them to take Weaver, or whatever the hell her name is, back to Washington with them. Wash your hands of this."

"And what if Melendez still decides to kill me anyway to vent his frustration? Or my parents? He could kill us so the next person he threatens know what's coming."

Adam cursed and paced the hotel room floor.

Thirty-seven minutes had passed since the CID team had left with Keller. None of those minutes had been restful.

"Brubaker says he has a team on hand that can do this." Marion made herself talk calmly. "Lieutenant Evans is going to be with me every step of the way."

They'd planned to pass Christine off as an associate. Brubaker's comment, sexist as it was, was true when he said no one would expect a woman to carry a pistol, much less know how to use one. Christine, they assured her, was certified as a pistol and rifle marksman. That had surprised Marion.

"I don't like it," Adam said.

"Neither do I." Marion wrapped her arms around herself. "The only choice I've got is to let Brubaker and his team take Melendez. That's the only way I'm going to be free of this." She walked over to him and looked him in the eye. "That's the only way *we're* going to be free of this."

"I know." Adam put his arms around her. "Dammit, I know. I just don't like it."

"Neither do I. Weaver's pregnant. I don't like the idea of risking the baby's life."

Adam held her tightly. "I know. But I can't even imagine what a child raised by that woman would be like." He turned Marion's head toward his and kissed her.

Marion returned to work on Monday. She worked through her caseload but didn't go outside the building. It still made her nervous to think that Melendez was out there. The partial history Brubaker and Christine had briefed her on had mentioned his facility for demolitions.

At 6:27, she left the office and went to the jail. Christine stayed with her every step of the way. Marion didn't know how the younger woman could have remained so calm and quiet.

"Do you do this a lot?" Marion asked while they waited in the observation area outside the interview room. Inside the room, deputies secured Amanda Weaver to a chair that was bolted to the floor.

"Do I do what, ma'am?" Christine asked politely.

"Don't call me ma'am."

"It's respect," Christine said quietly. "I'm supposed to show respect at all times."

"If you call me 'ma'am' in front of Weaver, she's going to

know something is up. A coworker in the DA's office wouldn't call me that."

Christine appeared to think about that for a moment. "Yes, ma'am. I won't make that mistake in front of her."

Marion sincerely hoped not. Then she went to speak with Amanda Weaver.

Inside the room with the woman, Marion didn't have to act scared. She was. Her legs quivered and her stomach threatened to flip-flop as she pulled out the chair and sat down.

"We have court tomorrow," Marion said.

Amanda Weaver toyed with the cigarette pack on the table in front of her. "Is there a reason my attorney isn't here?" She didn't sound threatened, just curious.

"A man came by my apartment Thursday night," Marion said.

"My attorney?"

"No."

"That's too bad. That would have been amusing. He does find you attractive, muffin."

Marion ignored the jibe. "The man that came to my apartment knows you. He's threatened my life, and the lives of my parents, if I don't drop the charges against you."

A smile spread across Weaver's face. "Ah, muffin, that man can be very intimidating, can't he?"

"Yes."

"Another thing you should remember is that he never threatens lightly. If he said he'll kill you, he will."

"I believe him."

"Good. Then when am I getting out of here?"

"I can't drop the charges."

Weaver showed mock sadness. "Then it's *ciao* to you, muffin. Try to die quickly. There's less pain that way."

Marion forced herself to breathe. "I don't want to die."

"I didn't want to go to prison, but it was the price I was willing to pay when I killed Tom Marker."

"Why did you kill him?"

Weaver turned the cigarette pack over a few times. "He betrayed me, muffin. Left me out to die in Vietnam. All for something he was running on the outside of his mission." She laughed. "Everybody thinks Marker is such a hero. He's not, you know. He's a killer. Like me. The CIA trained us both."

"The CIA hasn't claimed you."

"The CIA will see me dead before they do. Who do you think told the arsonist's boss I was here?"

"You mean Fanelli? The guy who tried to torch you? Even if you got out of here, do you think a guy like Salvatore Giambi will forgive and forget?"

Weaver smiled. "No. A man like him never forgives. Neither do I. Marker found that out in the motel room that night." She paused. "So what kind of dog-and-pony show are you going to put on with me in court, muffin?"

Marion paused, just long enough to let Weaver think she was hesitating. "You're not going to court," she whispered.

"Why not?"

"Because I'm going to set you free tomorrow morning and you're going to tell that man that came to see me that it's over. I help you and you help me."

Interest flickered in Weaver's eyes. "How are you going to free me?"

"I've figured out a way to do it at the courthouse. You've been sick the last few days, haven't you?"

"You've been spying on me."

"The sheriff told me. He was concerned that you weren't going to be able to stand trial."

"It's nothing," Weaver said. "Just bad food." She shook out a cigarette and pointed to the book of matches on Marion's side of the table.

"You're not sick from bad food," Marion said. "You're pregnant." Despite her fear, she took some sadistic pleasure in the surprise that showed on Weaver's face. No matter how conniving the woman could be, she hadn't expected that.

Weaver opened her mouth to say something, then closed it.

"You're pregnant," Marion repeated. "The doctor's report confirmed it. He doesn't think you're any further along than a few weeks. So while we're doing this tomorrow, you need to be careful. You don't want to lose the baby."

Weaver didn't say anything.

"Do you understand?"

Slowly Weaver nodded.

"You shouldn't be smoking," Marion said. "It's bad for the baby." She stood up from the chair and left. It was hard to resist looking back over her shoulder to see how Weaver was dealing with everything.

The phone call came at Marion's apartment shortly after ten.

"I'm told you'll be able to free your prisoner tomorrow morning," the accented voice said without preamble.

Marion picked up the phone and paced with it. She'd intentionally ordered an extra-long cord so she could walk and think at the same time.

From a chair in the corner of the room, with a Colt .45 naked on her thigh, Christine watched her.

"Yes. How did you know?"

She didn't really care because the plan she'd set up with Brubaker and Christine had been kept from everyone. Not even Adam knew the particulars. What she was doing was dangerous, but it was all she knew to do.

"It doesn't matter," Evaristo said.

Either he'd bought off a jailer or he was networking through the jail population. Marion knew it had to be one of those. Perhaps it was just his own ego talking.

"But I was not told how you would do it," Evaristo said. "That I need to know."

Marion took him through the planned escape.

When she was finished, he said, "If there is any trickery, or any mistakes, rest assured that you will die."

Marion believed him. But she also believed Brubaker when he'd told her the men he had working the trap were all crack shots. In the end, if she was going to be free of the threats, she had to believe in Brubaker.

"I understand," she said.

"Your friends in the sheriff's office aren't going to care for your decision," Evaristo said.

"I want to live more than I want to be a prosecuting attorney," Marion said. "They identified the man who tried to kill Weaver. They knew Giambi would send someone else. I guess he wants to do the job himself."

Evaristo chuckled. "I will see you tomorrow."

Marion listened to the sharp disconnect in her ear. She let out a long, tense breath, then cradled the phone. She felt like she was going to be sick.

"That was good," Christine said. "There at the end."

Marion looked at her.

"The part about making him think you believe Giambi sent him," Christine explained.

"Let's just hope he buys it," Marion said.

"In the meantime, we should get some sleep."

Marion looked at the younger woman.

"Probably too much to hope for, I suppose," Christine said.

It was. Even knowing that Christine was armed and trained and inside the house, even knowing that Brubaker's men were in place around her apartment building, Marion knew there was no way she was going to sleep.

"I've got a half gallon of peach ice cream in the freezer," Marion said, "a six-pack of root beer and a deck of cards."

To her surprise, Christine grinned. "Floats and gin rummy? So it's sort of like a sleepover."

Marion smiled. "It can be."

"Penny a point?" Christine asked. "Just to make it interesting?"

Despite the tension that was so heavy Marion thought it was going to drive her to her knees, she laughed. "As if coming face-to-face with an international assassin in the morning isn't going to be interesting enough."

"If you owe me a lot of money," Christine offered, "maybe I'll feel more protective of you. I mean, it is a strategy."

Marion shook her head, envying the other woman her sense of humor and pluckiness. This was exactly the kind of woman she wanted her school to turn out. Then she headed to the kitchen to make the floats.

Chapter 26

Maricopa County Courthouse
Phoenix, Arizona
Tuesday, June 4, 1968
The Past

The escape went like clockwork. Marion decided that if she ever had to take up a life of crime, she might have a future.

A few minutes before nine, Weaver had an attack of morning sickness that drenched the shoes of two deputies and three newspaper reporters. All the men were appalled and curses filled the hallway outside the courtroom.

Anxiety filled Marion as she and Christine grabbed Weaver under the arms and headed for the women's restroom. Weaver stumbled along with them. Her leg chains clanked against the floor.

"Are you going to be all right in there?" a big deputy asked.

Marion had asked Keller to keep only male personnel on hand for the escape to cut down on the number of women involved.

"Yes," Marion responded.

"I'm not really supposed to let the prisoner leave my sight," the deputy said.

Weaver heaved dramatically and the deputy quick-stepped back.

"Do you want to come in and watch?" Christine asked.

"Nope." The deputy shook his head vehemently. "If you need anything, I'll be right out here."

Marion guided Weaver into the restroom. Two women were inside, but as soon as they saw Weaver in chains and listened to her retching, they fled.

Taking the handcuff key from her pocket, Marion started opening the cuffs. Weaver tried to stand still, but ended up being sick in the sink. The stench almost gagged Marion.

"You're overdoing it," Marion said.

"I ate a big breakfast," Weaver said. "I wanted to be as sick as I could."

When she had the last of the chains off, Marion knew she was walking a thin line. There was nothing to keep Weaver from killing her if she wanted to. Christine wore her service weapon in a shoulder holster under her jacket, but it would take a moment to get the weapon into play.

"What about her?" Weaver nodded toward Christine.

"I told her that I'd been threatened. She's helping me. Us." Marion knew the likelihood of an argument was slim.

Weaver wiped her mouth with the back of her hand. "Well, muffin, how does it feel to take part in your first jailbreak?"

"We need to go," Marion said. She pointed toward the window high on the wall. She felt certain they could get through.

Prisoners in the past had escaped that way when they weren't guarded. Usually, with handcuffs on, flight was impossible.

Weaver wiped her face with wet paper towels, then headed for the last stall. She wedged herself up and through the window. When she was through, she looked back at Marion.

"Let's go, muffin. I don't want to leave you behind. I may need a hostage."

Reluctantly Marion climbed up and crawled through the window. Christine followed. They stood in the alley behind the courthouse. Traffic was sparse.

"Why's she coming?" Weaver snapped, staring at Christine.

"Do you want her to stay behind to be questioned by the deputies when they come looking for us?" Marion demanded.

Weaver growled a curse. "Where are the clothes?"

Marion pointed at the paper bag tucked into a cardboard box beside the trash bin. One of Brubaker's men had stashed it there during the night.

Without hesitation or modesty, Weaver stripped and put on the gray slacks and white blouse contained in the paper bag. She stepped into a pair of flats that Marion had deliberately chosen as a size too large so they would provide awkward footing.

Then they were off, walking quickly. Marion felt the morning heat baking down into her, but an icy ball had formed in the pit of her stomach.

Adam Gracelyn sat in the pilot's seat of the Augusta Bell 47G two-seater helicopter. Sheriff Keller sat in the co-pilot's seat.

The Maricopa County sheriff's office didn't yet have a helicopter, and it would have been too easy for Evaristo Melendez to track if it had. They still weren't sure how many men the assassin had bankrolled on his attempt to get Amanda Weaver out of custody.

The helicopter belonged to Big Jim Gracelyn and was used to oversee his herds of cattle and horses. Truth to tell, it was also something of a toy that he could afford. He'd piloted Bell helicopters in World War II and the Korean War. Adam had learned to fly as a boy, though neither one of them had talked about it around his mother.

Adam wanted to be airborne, but Brubaker hadn't cleared him for takeoff. Anything could tip Evaristo off. Adam thought about Marion, the way she'd looked in jeans that day he'd taken her up into the White Tank mountain range and how her hair smelled fresh from the shower. His heart ached when he thought he might not see her again.

Keller's big paw smacked into his shoulder.

Turning to the man, Adam listened hard to hear the sheriff over the radio commentary between Brubaker and his men.

"You holding up okay?" Keller asked.

Adam nodded. It was harder to tell if someone was lying if they only responded in a nod, right?

"It's gonna be okay," Keller said. "Brubaker and his boys know what they're doing."

Adam hoped to God that they did, because he couldn't imagine a world without Marion Hart in it. He looked back at the helicopter. The tail section was a long skeleton. The nose was a Plexiglas bubble. For all intents and purposes, it looked like a giant insect.

"Okay," Brubaker said over the radio, "we're in motion. Gracelyn, get up there."

None of Brubaker's men were qualified on helicopters, otherwise Adam felt certain the military would have confiscated the aircraft.

Adam worked the yoke. The helicopter sprang from the ground and clawed into the air.

Keller shifted in the seat and brought out the bolt-action .30-30 rifle equipped with a sniper scope. He cradled the weapon in his arms.

In the air, Adam kicked the rear rotor around, dipped the nose to allow the blades to bite into the wind, and roared toward downtown Phoenix.

Weaver's big breakfast was working against her. She fought nausea. Marion watched the woman occasionally stagger and felt sorry for her. She didn't know that her freedom was going to be short-lived.

Christine followed them, staying slightly back and to the right. As she'd explained to Marion last night over gin rummy and root beer floats, the position allowed her a constant field of fire.

Marion wished they had one of the military walkie-talkies with them, but Christine had pointed out the units were too big and were noisy to use.

Anxiety threaded through Marion. Had the deputy discovered that they'd escaped? Surely by now that had happened. The streets would flood with the local police. Keller hadn't dared bring them into the loop.

She glanced skyward and wondered where Adam was and if he was all right.

Adam flew high over the city. Everything looked different from the helicopter, but he'd flown over Phoenix enough to recognize the streets.

He listened to the constant radio communication between the

Army soldiers. They sounded competent and confident, exactly the kind of guys he'd want looking over his shoulder in a situation like this.

But they weren't looking over his shoulder. They were looking over Marion's.

A few minutes later, the calm and collected trap Brubaker and his people had set became a snarling death machine. Whatever luck they'd had in closing in on their quarry had run out.

Gasping for breath, Marion stood beside the phone booth in front of the convenience store as Weaver pulled open the door.

Christine was right behind her, looking as though she'd been out for a walk in the park. Not a hair was out of place and she wasn't winded at all.

"Change," Weaver demanded.

Marion searched her pockets and came up empty. She pulled a few bills from her pocket and pressed them into Weaver's hand.

Weaver entered the store and got change from the cashier. She was back in seconds. Marion and Christine stayed with her the whole way.

Leaning into the phone, Weaver dropped coins into the slot. She waited a moment, then started talking in rapid Spanish.

Marion wondered how the number had been set up. Or perhaps it was one Weaver and Evaristo had already put into play in the event something went wrong. Or maybe Evaristo had bribed a jailer or another prisoner to get a message to Weaver. Either way, they were obviously in contact.

Without warning, Christine freed her pistol from the shoulder holster under her arm and stepped into the booth after Weaver.

"It's over," Christine said. "She knows we're setting up Evaristo."

She grabbed Weaver by the hair and yanked her out of the booth. Weaver stumbled back, then she dropped and uncoiled in a martial arts kick so fast that Marion almost didn't see it.

The kick connected with Christine's right hand and sent the pistol loose. Christine recovered quickly and dropped back into a crouch with her hands held high and in close to her face.

In disbelief, Marion watched as the two women battled. The movements were short, choppy and explosive, but it was more like a dance than a fight. Marion had never seen anything like it on episodes of *The Green Hornet*. Kato's foes generally didn't know the same fighting style.

Making herself move, Marion ran for Christine's pistol. She knew how to use it from lessons she'd taken. She pulled the pistol up from the ground. It felt hard and heavy in her hand.

"Stop!" she shouted as she leveled the pistol. "Stop or I'll shoot!" She didn't know if she could, though. She kept thinking about the baby Weaver carried. Could she kill an innocent, too? Because there was no way to kill Weaver without doing that.

A sedan pulled across the street and gunned through the convenience store parking lot. Four men with guns got out.

For a minute Marion thought they were Brubaker's people. Then she saw that three of them had swarthy Indian or Latino complexions. They leveled their weapons at once.

A jeep roared in from the street and the men inside wore O.D. Army fatigues and battle helmets. The cavalry had arrived.

Evaristo's people didn't hesitate about swinging their weapons toward the jeep. They opened fire at once. Bullets scored the jeep and drove the men inside to cover. The military people opened fire as well. Their bullets cleared the sedan and stretched dead and wounded men across the parking area.

Traffic shrilled to a stop out in the street. Pedestrians turned tail and ran.

A fist came out of nowhere and slammed into Marion's jaw. Dazed by the impact, her knees came apart beneath her and she fell. She dropped the pistol she'd been holding but it never hit the ground.

In the next moment, Weaver grabbed it out of midair and swung it toward the soldiers. She fired even as she reached down and caught Marion by the hair.

One of the two surviving soldiers pitched back and lay still. Weaver fired twice more and the second soldier joined the first.

Weaver screwed the hot barrel into the base of Marion's neck. "Get on your feet! Get on your feet now or so help me I'm going to pull this trigger!"

Marion stood with effort. Weaver kept a tight grip on her hair and walked her out toward the street as a dark blue Chevelle roared to a stop at the curb.

Evaristo and two other men were inside. Evaristo reached across and pushed the passenger door open.

"Get in," he ordered. Since he was speaking English, Marion assumed he was speaking to her.

Before she could move, Weaver shoved her inside, then pushed her over again with her hips till Marion was sandwiched between Evaristo and Weaver.

"So, you think you're clever, eh?" Evaristo growled.

Looking back at the convenience store, Marion didn't answer. She saw Christine Evans lying on the ground. Blood stained her jacket. Evidently someone had shot her.

"She's not too clever," Weaver said.

"She brought the Army into this." Evaristo drove the Chevelle with the nerve-racking skill of a stock car racer. "I didn't expect that. The sheriff, I expected that. But not the Army." He looked at Marion as he steered between two stopped cars and slid sideways through a red light so he could make the illegal turn. "Who are those people? The state militia?"

Marion wasn't going to reply. Then Weaver shoved the heated gun muzzle up under her chin.

"You'll answer our questions now, muffin. I don't play by the same rules you do in your interviews."

"They belong to a man named Brubaker," Marion said. "He identified Evaristo from his fingerprints."

"What about me?" Weaver asked.

"They don't know who you are." Marion hated the smug smile that dawned on the woman's face.

"There," Keller said. He pointed down through the Plexiglas bubble at the Chevelle tearing through the heart of the city.

Adam saw the car. Brubaker's men had identified the car as they'd set out in pursuit. A military jeep had followed the Chevelle for a short distance, but the jeep was clearly outmatched. The sports car easily pulled away.

"They're not running stock in that car," Keller observed.

Adam grew frustrated. Reports from soldiers on the ground confirmed that Marion had been taken hostage by Weaver and Evaristo. With all the buildings around, he couldn't drop the helicopter any lower to see what was going on in the car.

"Just stay with them," Keller advised. "They're running southwest, probably headed for I-10 toward Tucson."

"Once they get out in the desert," Brubaker said over the radio, "they're going to be harder than hell to root out of there. Evaristo and his men can vanish out there. And it's less than two hundred miles to Mexico. You can bet the farm that he's got papers for that country."

"He's got Marion," Adam grated. "If they haven't already killed her, there's no reason to keep her alive after they make their escape." He angled the helicopter in pursuit.

"We can call ahead to Tucson and alert the police there," Keller said. "They should be able to meet us halfway. But that's a hundred and ten miles. It'll take thirty or forty minutes at least to get them there."

"Evaristo knows that," Brubaker said. "He'll get off somewhere along the way, lose the car, and fade into the countryside."

"What went wrong back there?" Adam demanded. "I thought you said everything was under control."

"Everything was under control," Brubaker retorted. "Till Weaver got wise. I don't know what busted us out."

"We'll worry about that after we get Marion back," Keller said. "Can you get us close enough to that car for me to shoot out the tires once we get out of town?"

"I can fly faster than they can drive, if that's what you're asking. But you can't shoot the tires out. Marion's in that car."

Keller looked at Adam. "What we can't do is let them get off with her. If we do, I promise you the likelihood of ever seeing her again is slim to none."

Adam knew that, but it was hard to accept that. He kept the Chevelle in sight as they saw the city limits ahead.

"There's a helicopter following us."

Marion turned to look through the back windshield. The helicopter looked like a dragonfly high up in the blue sky.

"Is it the police?" Evaristo asked.

"They don't have a helicopter," one of the men said. "It's somebody else."

"They use them up here to check on the cattle sometimes," the second man in the back seat said. "Maybe it's some farmer who was listening in on the police radio."

As Marion watched, Evaristo tapped the accelerator, then the brake and the accelerator again to slide around an eighteen-wheeler just barely under control. The man was an expert driver. The speedometer was holding steady between a hundred and twenty and a hundred and forty now that they were out of Phoenix.

Evaristo and Weaver talked back and forth in Spanish. The woman spoke like a native, without a trace of an accent. Marion couldn't help watching her in wonder. What had happened in her life to bring her to this point? Where had she really grown up? What had the business with Colonel Thomas Marker truly been all about?

A thousand other questions danced through her head.

But she stayed focused on the most important one: How was she going to get out of her current situation alive?

"Hey," one of the men called out.

"What?" Evaristo asked.

The man spoke in Spanish then. He pointed out the back window.

The helicopter descended in a rush. It dropped down like a hawk taking a mouse. Only seconds later, the landing skids grated against the top of the car.

The extra weight of the helicopter made the Chevelle lunge out of control. Evaristo fought the wheel as the car slid off the road in a long plume of dust.

Marion braced herself as best she could. She'd never had a car wreck, but she'd seen the occasional one along the highways and interstates. They were always cataclysmic things. She'd even prosecuted one drunk driver that had been responsible for killing a woman and two children. Those pictures had been hard to look at.

In the next instant, the helicopter dropped into view on the right. It paced the car only a couple of feet above the flat desert.

Marion recognized Sheriff Keller first. Then she saw Adam in the pilot's seat.

Beside her, Weaver aimed her pistol and started squeezing off shots. Bullets scarred the Plexiglas nose. Evaristo shouted encouragement.

Unable to sit idly by while Weaver shot the helicopter, Marion turned and reached for the steering wheel with both hands. Evaristo tried to fight her off, but that only made matters worse. Marion held on to the steering wheel after she'd pulled it to the right as far as she could.

The car swerved out of control, pulling hard to the right and going off-road. Everyone inside the car screamed. Marion was pretty certain she did, too, but things turned confusing really quickly.

Out of control, slamming across the uneven ground, the car rolled over onto its side and skidded cross-country. It hit an incline and went airborne.

Adam stared in disbelief as the Chevelle spun and launched through the air. The vehicle landed on its side and cut a deep furrow through the landscape. Two yucca cactus were mown down.

Then it came to a rest against a sandy hillock covered with twisted Joshua trees and scabrous tufts of grass.

Working quickly, Adam dropped the helicopter to the ground. He unbuckled himself from the seat and ran for the car. The Colt .45 revolver strapped to his thigh banged him heavily.

"Marion! Marion!" His feet drummed against the ground. He was certain he was only going to find her broken and tangled body. Nothing could have survived that crash.

Weaver pulled herself through the passenger door and fell onto the ground.

Nothing human, Adam amended. He heard Keller shouting behind him, but he ignored the man and closed the distance.

One of the men in the back crawled through the broken back glass. He rolled to one knee and brought his rifle to his shoulder.

Adam clawed for his revolver but he knew he wasn't going to get to it in time. He was just pulling the weapon up when the flat crack of a rifle shot ripped by him.

The man at the back of the car froze for just a moment, then he toppled over onto his face. He didn't move again.

When he looked back to where he'd last seen Weaver, she was no longer there. Adam was almost to the Chevelle when Weaver stepped back around the front of the car with Marion in front of her.

Marion stood there looking dazed and helpless. The woman's gun was pressed into the side of Marion's neck.

"Not another step," Weaver warned.

Feeling like she was still asleep but that pain throbbed within her even though it felt miles away, Marion stood on the hot desert sand

and watched as Adam stopped in front of her. He held a large black pistol in one hand.

"Throw the gun down," Weaver ordered.

"Okay," Adam said. "Okay. Just don't hurt her. You don't have to hurt her." He leaned forward, dropping to one knee to place the pistol on the ground.

"Don't put your weapon down, Adam." Sheriff Keller stood behind Adam. He had a rifle raised to his shoulder. "If you put your weapon down, she's going to kill us all."

Movement to Marion's right drew her attention. Glancing in that direction, she saw Evaristo Melendez stagger through the same broken windshield Weaver had dragged her through only a moment ago.

Blood stained Evaristo's face and dripped from his chin. He carried a pistol in each hand as he stood with his back to the car. Green radiator fluid pooled at his feet.

"I'll kill her," Weaver said. "Do you want her death to be on your hands, Sheriff?"

"Her death will be on my hands even if I did put my weapon down," Keller said. "As long as I'm holding this rifle, I still get to vote on who lives and who dies."

Evaristo whispered to Weaver in Spanish. Although she didn't understand the words, Marion knew the intent. Evaristo lifted both his weapons and spun around the front of the car. He leveled the guns before him and fired as quickly as he could.

Horrified, Marion could only watch for a moment. Adam twisted away and dropped to the ground. Keller held his stance for just a moment as he pulled the rifle toward Evaristo. The rifle thundered once, then Keller was knocked backward. The rifle flew from his hands.

At the same time, though, Evaristo stopped firing and looked down at the center of his chest in shocked disbelief. A small hole right over his heart suddenly wept tears of blood.

He went down like a balloon with the air let out of it. *"Madre de Dios,"* he said hoarsely. He collapsed to his knees and stayed that way even after there was no more life left in him.

"No!" Weaver said. *"No!* Evaristo!"

Taking advantage of the woman's confused emotional state, Marion whirled and delivered a palm strike to Weaver's face. The woman's head snapped back, but she reacted instantly with a backfist that caught Marion along the side of her head and knocked her down.

Pain exploded inside Marion's head. Whatever pain she hadn't been feeling before from the wreck suddenly rushed into her like an express train. She tried to get to her feet as Weaver pointed the gun at her.

Tears streamed down the woman's face. "You took him from me! You did this! I'm going to kill you!"

A shot suddenly rang out.

Weaver stiffened and took two backward steps. Blood showed on her blouse near her abdomen. Shock tightened her face.

The baby, Marion couldn't help thinking.

Weaver brought the pistol up and fired even as Marion broke out of her temporary freeze and reached for the weapon. Weaver hadn't been aiming for Marion, though. She'd aimed for Adam.

Her shot had caught him high in the chest. From the corner of her eye, Marion watched him drop the pistol and fall back onto the sand. Then she had her hands on Weaver's weapon and fought to take it away. Even as the pistol came away in her hands, Weaver lashed out with a side kick that put Marion on the ground.

Dazed, Marion reached for the pistol. For a moment she thought Weaver was going to fight her for the gun. Then the shrill sound of sirens stained the still desert air.

Marion looked down at the sand and desperately tried to meld her double vision into a single focus so she could find the gun. Finally she did. But when she looked back up, Weaver was gone.

Evaristo remained on his knees nearby. His eyes were open in surprise, but he no longer saw anything in the world around him.

After pushing herself to her feet, Marion ran back to Adam. He was flailing as he tried to get to his feet. Blood covered his chest. There was too much blood.

Marion told him to lie down and finally he did. She tore her shirtsleeves off and made compresses to cover the wounds in his shoulder and hip.

"Stay with me," she whispered past the lump in her throat. "Adam, do you hear me? I want you to stay with me."

His eyes focused on her. Incredibly he smiled that little boy smile again. "I'm not going anywhere, Marion. I'm going to be right here." He reached up and took her hand in his. "All you ever have to do is ask."

Marion leaned down and kissed him tenderly.

Chapter 27

Winter sat quietly near the fireplace in Christine Evans's home as the last words of the tale drifted away and were swallowed by the crackling fire.

The faraway look in Christine's blue eyes revealed that she hadn't quite made it back yet.

Glancing over at David where he sat farther back from the fireplace, Winter saw that he'd been mesmerized by the story of that encounter as well.

"I didn't know about that," he said finally. "Mother and Father never mentioned anything about it."

"No," Christine agreed. "It was something we rarely talked about even among ourselves. All of us lost a big chunk of our innocence that day. Death was near to all of us. Your father and I still carry our scars."

"I'd seen them," David said, "but every time I asked about them, he just said he'd gotten them in a car accident."

"Adam didn't like talking about it afterward," Christine said. "Of course, we had to. There were so many questions from law enforcement and military investigators. Things like that rarely happen."

"It's surprising there wasn't more mention of it in the news," David said. "I've researched other things around that time period, but I don't remember any of that being in the papers."

"It's because of what happened the next day," Christine said. "On June 5."

David shook his head.

"Bobby Kennedy was assassinated," Winter said, remembering now. During the time line she'd built regarding Amanda Weaver, she'd never stopped to put the picture into the larger framework. "He was shot early June 5 in the Ambassador Hotel in Los Angeles. He'd just won the California primary."

Christine nodded. "That's right. The news that was made before and even after that time was lost. The United States had its attention fixed solely on dealing with the latest tragedy. Dr. Martin Luther King was murdered on April 4. There was a lot of talk about conspiracies. Especially with all of that coming on the heels of John F. Kennedy's assassination down in Dallas, Texas. What happened to us that day…was just lost."

"Until now," Winter said.

"There's no way Amanda Weaver survived that attack," Christine said.

"You and Adam Gracelyn did," Winter pointed out. "So did Sheriff Keller."

"We were lucky," Christine said. "We also had immediate medical care. It was still a near thing for Adam and Sheriff Keller."

Winter looked at the notes she'd taken on her iPAQ. "I checked through the records of geological surveys that have been done over this area from that time on. Although there were other bodies found, other murder victims as well as unfortunate illegal aliens that didn't survive the trip from Mexico, none were ever found that might have been Amanda Weaver."

"That's a big desert out there, Winter," Christine said. "Deserts have a way of holding their secrets."

"I don't think Weaver died out there. I think she got away."

"The Army searched for her," Christine said, "but they never found her."

"Did Marion ever talk about Weaver anymore?"

"Every now and again. I think the idea of killing the baby stayed with her the longest." Christine looked at Winter. "Are you sure this is a good investment of your time? If Weaver is still alive, she's got to be nearly seventy years old."

"Mick Jagger is in his sixties and still performing at the Super Bowl," Winter pointed out. "Gene Hackman and Morgan Freeman are in their seventies and still at the top of their game." She took a breath and assembled her thoughts. "I'm not saying she's still an assassin. She's got people that can do that for her. All she has to do is be in control."

"You think this is her?" Christine asked.

"I do. As impossible as it may sound, I think that whoever Amanda Weaver really was, she's also been Marion Gracelyn's greatest opponent all these years."

"She's been in hiding for forty years."

Winter stood and paced. "I didn't say it was going to be easy. We have some things to work with." She counted off points on her fingers. "I checked. Salvatore Giambi is still alive and still connected with the Boston Mafia. He's semiretired, but we can contact him. I think your best bet for that is someone who's a professional gambler." She smiled. "Has Athena ever graduated someone with that qualification?"

"Actually there is someone," Christine said. "Her name is Bethany James."

"We'll also need a forensic profiler. Someone who can dig into the Queen of Hearts murders that took place in Boston. Since those murders took place forty-plus years ago, it's going to have to be someone good."

"Francesca Thorne," Christine said without pause. "She's absolutely amazing at what she does."

"It's going to be a dangerous job," Winter said. "David and I already know Amanda Weaver doesn't like anyone poking around in her past."

"I know someone who can protect her," Christine said. "That's not going to be a problem. Is there anything else?"

Winter looked at Christine. The next part might prove hard.

"How well did you know Eddie Brubaker?" she asked.

Christine hesitated. "Why do you ask?"

"Because someone sold Marion out," Winter said. "You and Brubaker ran that operation. None of the other military men involved even knew who you were after. You only showed them faces. Marion's notes point out that the two of you kept everything close to the vest."

"We did." Christine's face was tight.

"Someone sold out Marion that morning," Winter repeated. "He almost got Marion and you killed." She paused. "I think you know that."

Edward Brubaker had never made it to general. He'd gotten as far as the rank of colonel in the United States Army, then quietly cashiered out in 1988 after thirty-three years of experience. He'd seen action all around the globe.

His pension was decent, but it hadn't afforded the women and the fast cars that had been a part of his lifestyle during his career or afterward.

When Winter researched him, she'd discovered that he was living in a bungalow down in Palm Springs, Florida, where he was originally from. The bungalow was neatly kept with a front yard that showed signs of professional care. The Hispanic groundskeeper working at the back of the property bore that out.

A new model Lexus SUV occupied the garage.

David had insisted on coming along for the trip, and after seeing Brubaker's gruff personality, Winter was glad that David had. Plus, it gave them more time together to sort out some of their newfound feelings.

Although postcoital bliss wasn't exactly conducive to sharpening an interviewer's instincts, Winter hadn't turned down David's advances that morning. It was scary how quickly the ardor could amp up between them now that they'd unleashed it. It was hard putting the genie back into the bottle.

According to Brubaker's service record, he was seventy-two. He looked every bit of it that morning. His hair was snow-white and his short-cropped beard was gray. He wore khakis, sandals and a loose shirt. He'd left the military behind when he'd retired.

"Is there something I can do for you folks?" Brubaker asked. It was 9:27 in the morning and he already had a beer in his hand. His eyes were red-rimmed, so it was possible he'd been up all night and it wasn't late for him at all.

David flashed his United States attorney general's identification first. Winter had to admit that it carried a devastating punch to anyone who had once worked for the federal government.

"Can we come in?" David asked as he took his identification back.

"Is this official?" Brubaker asked.

"It can be." Behind the expensive sunglasses, David's expression was inscrutable.

Brubaker smiled a little uncertainly but swung the door open. "Well, come on in and take a load off. I've been working for the government almost half my life."

Winter walked into the room. The living room was outfitted with a big-screen TV and Surround Sound system. The man certainly liked his techno-toys. There were a few pictures on the wall that showed a much younger Brubaker stationed at different bases around the world.

Brubaker waved them to seats on the couch.

"Can I get you a beer?" he asked. "Or coffee? Maybe it's early for you."

They both declined the offer.

Brubaker sat in an easy chair. "Can you tell me what this is about?" he asked with a grin. "Or are you gonna make me guess?"

"Amanda Weaver," David said. They had agreed that he would take point on the interview.

Sitting back in the easy chair, Brubaker took a pull off his beer. "That was something from a long time ago." He shook his head. "I'm getting foggy. Can't remember everything these days. Arizona, as I recall. Or maybe New Mexico."

"You'll remember Amanda Weaver," David said. "After she made her escape in Phoenix, Arizona, all those years ago, you started getting monthly payments."

Brubaker frowned. "I don't know what you're talking about."

Winter reached into the aluminum briefcase she carried and took out the bank records. Even with David's U.S. attorney general position the records had been hard to get. She pushed the papers across the coffee table toward Brubaker.

"It was June, 1968," David said. "The U.S. Army CID had gotten a call from a young assistant district attorney in Phoenix. She'd been threatened by a man who'd left his fingerprints on her bedroom clock."

Reaching into the briefcase, Winter took out more papers.

"The Army sent you and Lieutenant Second Grade Christine Evans to investigate. You were the lead on an investigation into Colonel Thomas Marker."

Brubaker nodded. "I remember Marker. The Army didn't like the way he seemed to cash in on the POWs he found and freed."

"What do you mean?" David asked.

Brubaker took a pull on his beer. "Marker took advantage of what the Army sent him in there to do. He was supposed to pull those prisoners out of Victor Charlie's guesthouses, but he wasn't supposed to profit from it."

"But he did."

"Yeah." Brubaker nodded. "Some of those guys Marker pulled out of those places belonged to wealthy families. They could show their appreciation in a lot of ways other families couldn't."

"That doesn't seem too egregious," David said.

Brubaker reached back and massaged his neck. "We looked into Marker's field reports. Got what we thought was an anomaly."

"What was the anomaly?"

"Marker worked through information he got from informants. The hill people, the Hmong, scouted the area and told him where the POWs were. Sometimes they even got names. We had reason to believe that Marker was specifically targeting people who could be *appreciative.*"

"Do you have names?"

"Sure. Bartholomew, Kent, Captain USAF. Windam, Morgan, Commander, USN. Jorgansen, Philip, USMC. Altogether there were about twenty names on the list we put together."

"That's a lot of appreciative people," David said.

Brubaker nodded. "When Marker mustered out, ahead of a potential court-martial, I might add, he had a cushy life set up for himself Stateside. He wasn't going to have to work again."

"Because of the *appreciative* people?"

"Kemo sabe, you got no idea how appreciative people can be

when you bring back their kid from the dead. Marker was making bank on that."

"Till Amanda Weaver shot him to death in the Kellogg Motel."

Brubaker frowned and nodded. "Marker had that one coming."

"Why?"

"Amanda Weaver wasn't her real name. I guess you people know that or you wouldn't be here."

David neither confirmed nor denied. Winter watched him and realized how good he was. He had a focused mind. Maybe she was better at *feeling* her way through an interview, but David was sharper about getting what he wanted by peeling away other issues.

"What was her real name?" David asked.

"I never knew."

"What did you know about her?"

After a brief hesitation and a final pull on the beer bottle, Brubaker said, "She was a mercenary. Sometimes the CIA used her. Sometimes the United States military did. There were others, but she was one of them. She was good at what she did. As long as she was, nobody asked questions."

"Did the CIA know she was working with Evaristo Melendez at the time?"

"Yeah. But it wasn't a problem at first. Then Melendez became more apolitical. He started bagging targets on both sides of the fence. One night he worked for us. One night he worked for them. It was like having a fox in a henhouse. You never knew where he was going to strike and he knew too much about how we did our business to be able to keep him out."

"Was that why Marker set up Amanda Weaver in Vietnam?"

"That was a separate issue, man. Marker got in a bind trying to get a group of prisoners out of Victor Charlie's home-away-from-home. Weaver had a history with the VC. She claimed her kills. Left a signature behind."

"A playing card," David said.

Brubaker nodded. "That's right. The Queen of Hearts. Just like she left on Marker in Phoenix."

"What happened?"

"Marker called her into the area to do a job near where the POWs were being held. Then he tipped off the VC."

"He used her as a diversion."

"That's about the size of it." Brubaker flashed a wan smile. "So you can see, I understood why she'd be ticked at him. From what I heard, she was wounded pretty badly. She ended up killing like thirty guys that came after her, but that number may have been inflated. But she made it out of the jungle. After that, the CIA and the Army couldn't reach her anymore."

"Why wasn't Marker punished?"

Brubaker laughed bitterly. "Man, the guy was a freaking hero. He went behind enemy lines and pulled our POWs out of deathtraps. People *loved* him. We loved him. The guy was like John Wayne and Clint Eastwood all rolled into one. 'Course, that was a little bit ahead of Eastwood's time. Except for those spaghetti westerns."

"Let's get back to June 4, 1968," David said. "You sold out Marion Hart by tipping off Evaristo about the trap."

Sighing expansively, Brubaker leaned back in the chair. Winter thought the man looked old and tired. She almost felt sorry for him.

"I didn't tip off Evaristo," Brubaker said. "I tipped her off. Amanda Weaver. I went to the jail and talked to her."

"You let her know you were U.S. Army CID?" Winter couldn't believe it.

"You have to remember, before she was Marker's murderer, she was a hero to us. She waded into Vietnam and did what most of us couldn't. She put the fear of divine retribution from the United States Army into Victor Charlie's head."

Winter heard the hero worship in the old soldier's words. He meant what he was saying.

Brubaker shook his head. "I just didn't know how screwed up the situation was going to become. No one should have gotten hurt. Amanda Weaver should have lost Marion Hart and Lieutenant Evans as soon as she was out of that courthouse. Instead she kept them with her. I didn't even know Lieutenant Evans could speak Spanish. That was a surprise to everybody. Then it turned bloody."

David flipped a hand over to the bank records. "Where did the money come from?"

Once she'd suspected someone had deliberately sabotaged the CID trap, Winter had looked into the money of everyone involved. Money was always the best indicator of when things were going wrong. The world was filled with payoffs when scandal, theft, and duplicity of any form were in the mix.

"From her," Brubaker said. "She said I earned it." He sighed. "I didn't want to take it at first. Some of my men were killed in that firefight. It felt too much like blood money. It just piled up in that bank down in the Caymans."

That was true. Winter had noted the discrepancy.

"Then, after I'd mustered out and realized how far retirement was gonna take me, I started taking the money out. A little at a time. Then I got to where I just used it like I did the retirement."

"You could have arrested him, you know," Winter said as they pulled away from the bungalow. "There's no statute of limitations on murder. And those soldiers did get killed in that firefight."

"I know," David said. He pulled the rental car out into traffic and accelerated up to speed. "But I think I can understand what he was trying to do."

"Because he thought Amanda Weaver was some kind of hero?"

"Yeah. He was trying to cut her a break. I think Brubaker still wanted the shot at Evaristo, but he was willing to let Amanda Weaver go. In the end, though, she showed her true colors. She kept Mother and Christine with her as hostage insurance. She deliberately didn't lose them."

"Or maybe your mom and Christine were that good," Winter pointed out. "Not much got by them. Except this woman did."

David was silent for a time. "She was behind the kidnappings. I want her found, Winter. This vendetta between her and my mother has spilled over onto the school. I want her found and stopped before things get any worse."

Tenderly Winter reached over and took his hand. "We'll find her."

"She's been hidden for forty years," David said.

"I know, but we weren't looking for her before. And with all the webs she's woven, she can't stay hidden now that we know what we're looking for."

"Webs," David said. "The problem with webs is that if you're prey and you touch them, you get trapped and eaten."

"That depends," Winter said, "on whether you're the spider or the fly. This time around, we're going to be the spider. We'll find out who she was, then where she's at. Then we'll close her down once and for all."

"You sound awfully confident." David's eyes searched hers.

"A woman like that isn't going to make many friends. All we've got to do is find her enemies."

"Or the long line of dead people she's left behind her," David said bleakly. Abruptly he changed directions and cut through traffic.

"What are you doing? The airport is in the other direction."

"I'm taking you to the beach. After everything we've been through since you started this, we deserve a walk along the ocean and maybe a couple cold beers at a cantina. We can be tourists for a few hours. Christine and Allison are already working on what you turned up. They don't need us right now. And we're not turning in Brubaker." David squeezed her hand. "Just for a little while, I want to pretend the world is a small place and that nothing we do really matters."

"All right," Winter said. She couldn't help smiling. She knew they couldn't put off the coming battle for long, but for the moment the idea of stepping down from it sounded good.

The idea of being in the sun, walking through curling ocean waves across wet sand, listening to the sounds of people who might be at the beach enjoying themselves sounded wonderful.

"You're going to have to be careful," Winter chided.

"What do you mean?"

"Word might leak out that you're not the workaholic everyone thinks you are."

"Why? Because I surrender to a small diversion every now and again?" His words were playful, but his smile was sincere.

"I refuse to consider being a small diversion," Winter said.

"You know," David said, "I used to watch my mother and father and wonder what it was like to be in love like that. I thought they were the exception to the rule. But they weren't. They were just in love." He held up her hand and kissed it. "I love you, Winter."

His words, though he hadn't spoken them outside the bedrooms they'd shared, thrilled Winter. Even though she'd felt his love for her was true, it felt good to hear him say it somewhere other than there. She was surprised to find no hesitation inside herself.

"I love you," she said. She held on to his hand and looked out toward the azure of the ocean in the distance. Maybe there was a storm ahead, but she was going to enjoy the calm before it.

* * * * *

Don't miss the next
Athena Force Adventure!
STACKED DECK
by Terry Watkins
Available December 2007

Chapter 1

Las Vegas, March

Bethany James, a twenty-eight-year-old Vegas poker phenom, stared at her quarry with a hunter's gaze as he riffled his chips, little columns neatly folding between his fingers. The tempo grew faster. It was one of his "tells."

"So you want to gamble," he said when she pushed her bet in. "Did you hit the river?"

"Jump in and find out."

She ignored the familiar buzz on her PDA for the fourth or fifth time as she studied her opponent's face, her unflinching stare boring into him like a surgeon's scalpel, cutting away the outer layer, seeing the tightened muscles beneath his expression of calm.

He was bluffing all the way and she was going to take him down.

The other three men, all under thirty years of age, had already been small-stacked and eliminated one at a time.

Truth, as her gambler father once said—quoting his hero, the great billionaire gambler Kerry Packer—is what is left when all the lies and secrets, those little "tells," have been revealed and your lie is the last lie standing. That is the moment when you take control of the game.

She waited for her opponent to play his mind games, knowing he was already looking to come over the top, maybe even go "all in" after she'd set him up by limping in with a small bet to look weak, enticing him into believing he could buy the pot with a bluff.

Through the window to the right of the dealer's head, over the empty flower box, beyond the patio of this estate on Sunrise Mountain, Beth stared for a moment to rest her tired eyes, her gaze lingering on the shimmer sea of orange that was the neon metropolis of Las Vegas.

Someone once said of her that she was just like the city she grew up in. A chameleon, a changeling, an impostor.

Yes, true. Survival demanded it.

Beth could see nearly all the casinos from where she sat and she was outlawed from just about every one of them and forced to use disguises when she did attempt entry. Now she mostly played in high-stakes private games like this one.

The city below was laced with traffic, like a vast tangle of white and red snakes, and in the darkening sky to the east the east planes stacked up like a string of bobbing Chinese lanterns as they descended on McCarren International Airport.

Her eyes rested, she returned her focus to the game.

This twenty-three-hour marathon of Texas Hold'em was nearing its denouement. She glanced to her left at the man she was heads-up with: black shaggy hair, an angled face, and whiskey-colored eyes. She could smell blood, see it in his play, the faltering steps of a confused and tiring animal.

She knew her adversary was a member of a sophisticated cheating crew, but tonight he was freelancing.

The owner of this house was a friend of hers and knew something was going on between her and the man she was now heads-up with. The man was an addicted gambler who believed that with or without cheating, he could take down anyone, especially a woman.

Beth knew a lot more about him than she had told her friend. She knew he needed a big score to service his debts.

She'd set the bait and her prey was ready to walk into the trap. Just you and me, babe.

She gave him a stone-cold stare and worked her fake tell.

The buy-in for this winner-take-all game had been fifty thousand. The quarter mil take would pay the bills for a long time, but Beth had another use for her money.

The man she was about to crush belonged to one of the largest and most sophisticated cheating crews working the international circuit, a crew that had started twenty years ago in Vegas. The one her father had once belonged to, before he was murdered and dumped in a garbage bin sixteen years ago.

The crew was directed and financed by a secret backer who either was her father's killer, or knew that killer's identity. To find out who the backer was she had to flip one of his people. She'd chosen carefully.

The one she'd chosen as the weak link was now heads-up with her. She knew he was mortgaged to the hilt, his sources tapped out, and in deep hock to loan sharks. He'd borrowed heavily for this last stand and she was going to snatch the prize away from him.

Once she had him at her mercy, she'd make him an offer he couldn't refuse.

ATHENA FORCE

*Heart-pounding romance
and thrilling adventure.*

She's their ace in the hole.

Posing as a glamorous high roller, Bethany James, a
professional gambler and sometimes government agent,
uncovers a mob boss's deadly secrets...and the ugly sins
from his past. But when a daredevil with a tantalizing
drawl calls her bluff, the stakes—and her heart rate—
become much, much higher. Beth can't help but wonder:
Have the cards been finally stacked against her?

ATHENA FORCE

Will the women of Athena unravel Arachne's
powerful web of blackmail and death...or succumb
to their enemies' deadly secrets?

Look for

STACKED DECK
by *Terry Watkins*.

Available December wherever you buy books.

Visit Silhouette Books at www.eHarlequin.com   AF38976